Theatre
&
Performing Arts
Collections

Theatre & Performing Arts Collections is volume 1, number 1 of the *Special Collections* series of thematic journal issues.

Series Editor: Lee Ash, Library Consultant, Bethany, CT

Other titles in this series:

Biochemistry Collections, edited by Bernard S. Schlessinger

Gerontology & Geriatrics Collections, edited by Prisca von Dorotka Bagnell

Science/Fiction Collections: Fantasy, Supernatural & Weird Tales, edited by Hal Hall

Theatre
&
Performing Arts
Collections

Louis A. Rachow, Guest Editor

Volume 1, Number 1, Fall 1981
Special Collections

The Haworth Press
New York

Special Collections is published quarterly in Fall, Winter, Spring, and Summer.

BUSINESS OFFICE. All subscription and advertising inquiries should be directed to The Haworth Press, 149 Fifth Avenue, New York, NY 10010. Telephone (212) 228-2800

SUBSCRIPTIONS are on an academic year, per volume basis only. Payment must be made in U.S. or Canadian funds only. $85.00. Postage and handling: U.S. orders, add $1.75; Canadian orders, add $6.00 U.S. currency or $6.50 Canadian currency. Foreign rates: add $40.00 (includes postage and handling).

CHANGE OF ADDRESS. Please notify the Subscription Department, The Haworth Press, 149 Fifth Avenue, New York, NY 10010 of address changes. Please allow six weeks for processing; include old and new addresses, including ZIP codes.

Application to mail at Second-Class postal rates pending at New York, NY and additional mailing offices.

POSTMASTER: Send address changes to The Haworth Press, 149 Fifth Avenue, New York, New York 10010.

Library of Congress Cataloging in Publication Data

Main entry under title:

Theatre & performing arts collections.

(Special collections ; v. 1, no. 1)

Bibliography p.

Contents: Historical introduction and the state of the art / Louis A. Rachow -- Theatre materials in the Library of Congress / Walter Zvonchenko -- The New York Public Library: the Billy Rose Theatre Collection / Paul Myers -- [etc.]

    1. Performing arts--Library resources--United States. I. Rachow, Louis A. II. Series.

PN1577.T43   016.7902   81-6567

ISBN 0-917724-47-X   AACR2

Theatre
&
Performing Arts
Collections

Special Collections
Volume 1, Number 1, Fall 1981

FOREWORD

I wish to welcome our readers to *Special Collections*. When I proposed this publication to The Haworth Press some months ago, I really did not know that the Editorship would fall to me (though I hoped it might), but the need for what we have planned seemed apparent in the library and book review literature. The Haworth Press, always progressive and open-minded, has given this publication considerable attention, and we all want to create wide reader interest. *Special Collections* has potentials for usefulness beyond the library field, and we expect to to attract collectors and antiquarians of all kinds, as well as publishers and scholars.

It is my hope that this first issue of *Special Collections* will demonstrate one form that successive parts will follow. The publishers and I want to remain as consistent as possible in presenting, through the four issues of every year, not necessarily in this order, one issue relating to collections in The Arts, another in The Sciences, one for The Social Sciences, and a fourth in The Humanities. These terms may be interpreted broadly, and the first year's schedule includes this one followed by Biochemistry, then Geriatrics & Gerontology, and last, Science Fiction (including Fantasy, Supernatural, Weird).

All this makes for an assorted menu that we believe will be attractive and useful to special collections librarians, collectors, antiquarian dealers, students, and scholars. Here is a foretaste of the tentative second-year plan: Ballet & The Dance; Aeronautics; Banking & Finance; Animal Husbandry, Physiology, and Veterinary Medicine. I will always be anxious for suggestions of additional subjects that readers would find helpful and for the names of possible contributors.

For the first few issues at least the character of the contents of *Special Collections* will probably vary some until we find the most useful formulas to develop. We know, for instance, that the second number, "Biochemistry," guest edited by Dean Bernard Schlessinger of the Graduate Library School of the University of Rhode Island, himself a biochemist, will be somewhat different in the character of its articles.

In general, however, it is my intention to try for the following pattern as consistently as possible. Each number will aim to describe major and unusual collections whose content or emphases are special subject fields. Each issue will have articles by authoritative contributors who will offer major surveys featuring the history, content, and unusual resources (including books, serials, files, indexes, prints, maps, memorabilia, and other holdings) in four to six of the large special collections in a single field.

Special Collections, Vol. 1(1), Fall 1981

Nearly always there will be a survey of the Library of Congress's holdings in all its departments if they are significant. In addition, there will be guides to the subject holdings in other collections in the United States and Canada, sometimes with a general piece on "the state of the art" and an article on bibliographic control of the subject. Featured will be directories of other collections of the same subject, and, frequently, there will be articles by private specialist collectors, antiquarian dealers, and specialist publishers.

In each issue there will be a book review section featuring books relating to the subject, and I will, myself, do an additional essay-type review article covering publications that will be of interest to most special collections librarians and their users. This latter section will include comments on Guides to Collections and Resources; Indexes; Directories; Dictionaries; Encyclopedias, Atlases, and Other Reference Books (including subject histories); Bibliographies and Special Booksellers' Catalogues; Books About Books—Rare Books, Collecting, Essays, Biographies, etc.; and works concerning Special Collections Administration. Complete citations, keyed to numbers in the text, with names of publishers and prices, will be given. Libraries, publishers, and scholars are urged to send review copies (and be sure to indicate availability, address, and price).

Special Collections, working with an authoritative Board of Advisors and specialist Guest Editors, will attempt to present more thorough and skillful descriptions and current analyses of library resources than are usually available through the general guides such as those by Downs and my own *Subject Collections*, for example. I hope that *Special Collections* will help serve to improve the coordination of similar subject collections as well as methods and techniques for cooperative acquisitions in library network systems.

Louis Rachow has done a fine job as Guest Editor for this first issue in our series. I congratulate him for his broad historical introduction and his other contributions. I am, of course, particularly grateful to the other contributors, among whom I would especially point to Franklyn Lenthall's piece on the theatre memorabilia at Boothbay, Maine. This article, unusual in books about library materials, suggests how artifacts and related visual pieces can supply spirited and inspiring supports for exhibition, display, and understanding of special collections.

I will be most appreciative if readers would write me about their interests, opinions, and suggestions, at any time. *Special Collections* is an open-entry series, and the publishers and I want to make it as useful as possible.

Lee Ash
Editor

66 Humiston Drive
Bethany, CT 06525

Correspondence and review copies of publications should be sent to this address.

HISTORICAL INTRODUCTION
AND THE STATE OF THE ART

From the days of Thespis to the knighthood of Henry Irving society in general censured those who trod the boards, and historians frowned upon the theatre as a discipline worthy of scholarly attention. The records of perform-ances, past and present, were neglected, ignored, and uncataloged—either tossed into cartons and relegated to attics and basements for future genera-tions to discard, or they were filed in the nearest wastebasket. Only the *drama* and the literature of the stage (commentaries and criticisms, histories and reviews) were considered to be of substantial interest. With the first quarter of this century, however, the aesthetic theories of avant-garde theatre stylists brought a fresh dramatic consciousness to both Europe and America. It was then that collections of theatrical ephemera (playbills and programs, photo-graphs and engravings, clippings, along with stage and costume designs), promptbooks and playscripts, stage memorabilia, as well as scenery and stage machinery, took on new and exciting dimensions. The "new movement" works of Appia, Craig, Antoine, Copeau, Stanislavsky, and Robert Edmond Jones lit up not only theatre marquees throughout the world, but exhibition cases in libraries, museums, and universities.

Nevertheless, before taste for the intellectual content of the theatre matured in this country, theatre treasures were bountiful and preserved in Europe in many places and forms. For example, the Drottningholm Theatre, near Stockholm, had its heyday during the reign of Gustaf III (1772-92) when the Frenchman, Louis-Jean Desprez, was commissioned to design the theatre's costumes and scenery. Now those renditions, as well as the 17th and 18th-cen-tury French stage designs collected by Baron Tessin and his son, form one of the most important deposits in the Drottningholm Museum. The German actress and dramatist, Clara Ziegler, bequeathed her home and library to the city of Munich as a theatre museum upon her death in 1909, together with a legacy for the maintenance of a theatre collection. Another example is the Raymond Mander and Joe Mitchenson Theatre Collection in Sydenham, a working-class suburb of London—one of the notable private collections in the English-speaking world. Theatres themselves came to the early realization of the worth and significance of their respective archives: La Scala in Milan, the Opéra and the Comédie Française in Paris, the Finnish National Theatre, and more recently, the Shubert Organization in New York are among good exam-ples. Nearly every important theatre in Russia has developed a museum and

Special Collections, Vol. 1(1), Fall 1981
© 1981 The Haworth Press

library with government support an integral part of the national cultural and political program.

Although American theatre libraries and collections gained recognition when the "new movement" in America took hold, it was not until the 1930s that techniques for organization, cataloging, and classification of collected materials were accelerated and encouraged by professional librarians and archivists. As early as 1932 between sixty and seventy theatre collections in libraries and museums were recorded throughout the United States. In 1933 *Theatre Arts Monthly*, under the editorship of Edith J. R. Isaacs, published a series of descriptive articles on these respective museums and collections. The Library Committee of the National Theatre Conference, chaired by Rosamond Gilder, followed suit in 1934 by sponsoring an intensive survey of theatrical holdings in public, private, and academic libraries. The Committee focused attention on the growing need for library facilities on the part of the steadily increasing numbers of directors, actors, and staff involved in a variety of theatre programs in the United States.

In 1934 the American Library Association took cognizance of this need and awarded a scholarship to George Freedley, curator of the Theatre Collection of The New York Public Library, to visit, study, and evaluate some major European collections of theatre and drama. That same year a roundtable on theatre-library relations considered the increasing demands for professional organization, and a joint committee with the National Theatre Conference was appointed to foster coordination between the two groups. The NTC, which had been organized two years earlier, had among its objectives broadening and strengthening dramatic education, recognizing the importance of the theatre both as an art form as well as a factor in the community's social and educational life. It seemed appropriate, therefore, for librarians to embrace membership in the National Theatre Conference as a practical method of cooperation between theatres and libraries. These early hopes were not fulfilled, however, and by the end of 1937 the structure of the Conference had been so altered that its membership was reduced to a council of twenty-five constituent representatives from college and university theatre departments.

Because of the disappointments encountered in this initial attempt at professional recognition and participation, and realizing the importance and need for organization, a number of theatre historians, librarians, and curators met in June 1937 under the chairmanship of Harry M. Lydenberg, director of The New York Public Library. Among those present were the curators of the Harvard Theatre Collection, the Brander Matthews Dramatic Museum of Columbia University, the William Seymour Theatre Collection at Princeton University, and the Museum of the City of New York. It was at this meeting that the group successfully founded and launched the Theatre Library Association. In the following year TLA was accepted as an affiliate of the American Library Association. Since then theatre and performing arts collections have grown to surprising proportions and are continuing to do so.

Holdings of theatricana are now more commonly called "performing arts collections," a term covering both the live and recorded aspects of theatrical and dramatic performances. This first issue of *Special Collections* is devoted to the legitimate stage, although the Wisconsin and Texas articles are more inclusive. Other disciplines and divisions of the performing arts, such as ballet and the dance, music, film, and broadcasting, will very likely be featured in future issues and will then include such collections as the American Film Institute, the Broadcast Pioneers Library, the Dance and Music Divisions of The New York Public Library, the George Foster Peabody Radio and Television Collection, the Popular Culture Library and Audio Center at Bowling Green State University, the Television Information Office, and others, some of which are reviewed in Volumes I-IV of *Performing Arts Resources* published by the Theatre Library Association, 1974-1977.

In addition to the major theatre collections described in this issue, mention must be made of some others of distinction in the various regions of the United States, collections which have not been reviewed here for a variety of reasons. The Boston-Cambridge area, for example, is blessed with two outstanding collections: the Twentieth Century Archives in the Mugar Memorial Library at Boston University and the Theatre Collection at Harvard University. Under the skillful guidance of Curator Howard B. Gottlieb, Boston University has established an enviable collection development program resulting in the acquisition of the personal papers and literary productions of numerous actors and actresses, musicians (composers and performers) in all fields. A sampling of names include David Amram, Robert Ardrey, Ilka Chase, Bette Davis, Lonne Elder, Ella Fitzgerald, Tamara Geva, Roddy McDowall, and Myrna Loy. These acquisitions, through the early part of 1975, are mostly cited (by name of person) in Ash's *Subject Collections* (5th edition, 1978), and complete lists of holdings are available by writing Mr. Gottlieb.

The Harvard Theatre Collection, under the curatorship of Jeanne Newlin, is one of the western hemisphere's most distinguished repositories of original American and English stage resources. It was founded in 1901 through the efforts of Professor George Pierce Baker with his presentation of a collection of portraits of David Garrick as a memorial to the noted librarian and historian Justin Winsor. The following year the actor John Drew purchased the library of the noted bibliographer Robert W. Lowe and donated it to Harvard. In 1915 Robert Gould Shaw became the first curator, and with the gift of his collection (and later that of Evert Jansen Wendell in 1918), Harvard's performing arts research collection was formally established.

Encompassing all aspects of the history of performance throughout the world, with emphasis on the English and American stage, history of ballet and the dance, the Harvard Theatre Collection continues to build upon its founding collections. The areas of cinema and popular entertainment, such as fairground, circus, minstrel, and vaudeville also are well represented. The collection is estimated to contain over 3,000,000 playbills and programs, some

500,000 photographs, 250,000 engraved portraits and scenes, 15,000 scenery and costume designs, and nearly 5,000 promptbooks, in addition to manuscripts, printed books, journals, and newsclippings. Special holdings include the George Pierce Baker Papers; the Percy MacKaye Papers; the H. W. L. Dana Collection on the Russian theatre; the John and Rita Russell Viennese Collections; the John Thayer Collection of Film Portraits; and the Angus McBean Collection of 30,000 glass negatives and proofs of scenes and personalities of the English stage, particularly the Old Vic and Stratford-upon-Avon from 1937 to 1964. The photographer's copyright is held by Harvard, and prints from the original negatives may be ordered from the Theatre Collection.

Found among the ballet and the dance holdings are the George Chaffee Collection of books, libretti, prints, and drawings on the history of ballet; the William Como Collection on contemporary dance; and the Sergejev Collection of primary materials documenting the Russian ballet of the late imperial period. Printed books, manuscripts, and drawings are cataloged by author, title, and subject. The vast collections of historical and modern playbills and programs are arranged by name of theatre and chronologically by season. *The Catalogue of Engraved Dramatic Portraits in the Harvard Theatre Collection*, compiled by Lillian A. Hall, was published in four volumes in 1930-1934. Rotating exhibitions of Harvard Theatre Collection materials are prepared by the staff for display in the Edward Sheldon Exhibition Rooms and elsewhere in the library. For a detailed and historical review of these theatrical holdings the reader is referred to William Van Lennep's excellent article, "The Harvard Theatre Collection," which appeared in the Autumn 1952 issue of the *Harvard Library Bulletin*.

Theatrical treasures of all ages also are to be found in Manhattan's institutions of culture and learning. These include the Theatre Collection of the Museum of the City of New York which comprises an outstanding amount of memorabilia illustrating the dramatic and musical events in New York from colonial times to the present. Of particular interest are the photographs and information on theatre buildings and architecture from the John Street Theatre to the Palace renovations and to the Uris, one of the newest of the three Broadway theatres housed in a skyscraper complex. The Museum's aim continues to be collecting and preserving material in all theatrical media, making everything available to students and professional researchers. Complementing this program is the arrangement of frequent public exhibitions.

In the field of design research the Museum has the original scene and costume drawings of the Dazian Library for Theatrical Design; the Charles W. Witham drawings (1869-1880); also, the more recent originals of Robert Edmond Jones, Donald Oenslager, Boris Aronson, and Oliver Smith. There are also a number of actual stage models representative of the 19th and 20th-century designers, one of the latest being Ming Cho Lee. The manuscript and orchestration holdings contain playscripts and promptbooks of George M. Cohan, Eugene O'Neill, Harry B. Smith, E. H. Sothern, and Julia Marlowe, in addition to those by stage managers and producers. Portraits and caricatures are represented by artists John Singer Sargent, Joseph Cummings Chase, Henry Inman, and Alex Gard. The costumes at the Museum range from the early 19th century to Edwin Booth's Hamlet to the latest Broadway creation. Highly prized are the Léon Bakst costumes for the 1916 Hippodrome production of *The Sleeping Beauty* executed by Dazian. Special attention is given to design and fabric analysis, theatrical importance, and original designers and manufacturers. Although the Museum's theatrical exhibitions may be viewed during regular hours, Curator Mary C. Henderson stresses the fact that an appointment is absolutely necessary for research purposes.

The Shubert Archive is perhaps the world's largest theatrical collection centered in a single institution, housed in the Daniel Frohman office suite on the third floor of the Lyceum Theatre. Opened by Frohman in 1903, the Lyceum has been designated a registered national historic landmark and continues to be New York's oldest playhouse still in legitimate use. It is here that the tasks of cataloging, processing, and preserving this vast treasure trove are performed. Brooks McNamara, archive director and professor of drama at New York University, tells how the Shubert Archive came into being in the first issue of the Shubert Archive newsletter, *The Passing Show* (Winter 1977).

The International Theatre Institute was chartered by Unesco, "to promote the exchange of knowledge and practice in the theatre arts." Eleven nations took part in that historic meeting in 1948. Today ITI centers exist in over seventy countries. Since 1949 when the charter was accepted by the United States, Rosamond Gilder has been the active president of ITI/US. In 1968, after twenty years as a department of the American National Theatre and Academy, ITI/US became an independent, nonprofit service organization with Martha W. Coigney as its director. The library was officially opened in 1970 with Elizabeth Burdick as director.

The ITI/US collection consists of archives and other materials documenting all aspects of modern theatre throughout the world since World War II. Its holdings cover six continents, one hundred eighteen countries, and seventy ITI centers, affiliates, and associates. Here one can find with ease and delight foreign items generally not available in this country—books, plays, newspapers, periodicals, yearbooks, pamphlets and monographs, articles, programs, brochures, production schedules, newsletters, and house organs—nearly all of which are gathered through an international exchange program. Mrs. Burdick reports that:

> nearly 5,000 foreign plays, representing seventy-one countries are cataloged, and the American play index records 1,700 titles. The Center receives and shelves one hundred eighty-five foreign and domestic peri-

odicals on the performing groups and maintains files documenting the
activities of 700 performing groups across the United States. Although
nearly 3,500 volumes are housed here, the core of the library is non-book
material and theatre ephemera.

The library provides information and offers research assistance to students, teachers, scholars, writers, theatre professionals, and others in need of
its services. The library staff edits and publishes *Theatre Notes*, a newsletter on
companies touring the United States and abroad. ITI/US distributes in this
country *International Theatre Information*, the bilingual review and information organ of the ITI Secretariat in Paris, and sends *The Drama Review* to the
major ITI Centers abroad. Researchers intending overseas travel should be in
touch with the United States office to confirm the latest information regarding
specific centers and to obtain a correct list of their addresses.

Two important collections on Black theatre are to be found in New York.
The first is the Armstead-Johnson Foundation for Theatre Research founded
in 1974 by Director-Curator Helen Johnson. Among the materials preserved
by the Foundation are rare books, posters, photographs, scripts, contracts,
letters, costumes, broadsides, playbills, instruments, and taped interviews
with performers. All periods of American theatrical history, from slavery to
the present, are represented including the little known fact that Blacks appeared on the New York stage as early as 1821. Except for small grants from the
New York Foundation for the Arts, IBM, the CBS Foundation, and a few
private donations, Ms. Johnson has supported the Foundation and acquisitions for the collection on her own. The Foundation, located in the historic
Hotel Chelsea, highlights more than ten years of research by Ms. Johnson.
Exhibitions may be seen by appointment. The Schomburg Center for Research in Black Culture of The New York Public Library collects materials in
all formats about Black peoples throughout the world including theatre, drama, and performers. The Center's holdings are described in *The Dictionary
Catalog of the Schomburg Collection* (Boston: G. K. Hall, 1962-1975) and
Bibliographic Guide to Black Studies, also published by G. K. Hall. Since 1972
the Center's holdings have been listed in the *Dictionary Catalog of the Research Libraries, New York Public Library*.

In addition, there are a number of societies and institutions in the metropol-
itan area whose cultural research facilities embrace theatre materials within a
larger framework of historical and literary resources; namely, the Cooper-
Hewitt Museum of Design, the Hispanic Society of America, the New York
Historical Society, the Pierpont Morgan Library, and the YIVO Institute for
Jewish Research. Descriptions of these and other holdings appear in Louis A.
Rachow's "Performing Arts Research Collections in New York City" (Volume I of *Performing Arts Resources*, 1974). Not to be overlooked are the
libraries of the city's acting and dramatic schools: Actor's Studio, American

Academy of Dramatic Art, Juilliard School of Acting, Neighborhood Playhouse School of the Theatre, as well as the schools of fashion and design libraries: the Fashion Institute of Technology, National Design Center, Parsons School of Design, and the Traphagen School of Fashion.

Among the theatrical resources in the District of Columbia area are the holdings in the Library of Congress, the Folger Shakespeare Library, the lately established library at the John F. Kennedy Center for the Performing Arts, and the Research Center for the Federal Theatre Project at George Mason University in Fairfax, Virginia. Walter Zvonchenko, Theatre Reference Librarian at the Library of Congress, provides an informative account of the LC collections elsewhere in this issue. Folger librarians Nati H. Krivasky and Laetitia Yeandle present an overall view of "Theatrical Holdings of the Folger Shakespeare Library" in Volume I of *Performing Arts Resources* (1974). The library's printed books and manuscripts are described in G. K. Hall's *Catalog of Printed Books of the Folger Shakespeare Library* (1970), the *Catalog of Manuscripts of the Folger Shakespeare Library* (1971), and *The Widening Circle: the Story of the Folger Library and its Collections* (Washington, D. C.: Folger Shakespeare Library, 1976).

The Performing Arts Library at the John F. Kennedy Center is a joint project of the Kennedy Center and the Library of Congress, bringing together program and archival resources of the Center with LC's extensive collections under the supervision of specialized reference librarians. The jointly sponsored library makes available a core reference collection of approximately 5,000 volumes, plus current issues of major domestic and foreign periodicals devoted to the performing arts, to researchers and performers associated with the Kennedy Center. The facility houses photograph files of the Center's productions and includes viewing rooms for film and television clips and soundproof rooms for recordings and tapes. A special feature is a video display computer link-up with LC, making it possible for the serious researcher to have access to LC cataloged materials. The founding of the Kennedy Center is a step toward paving the way for a much needed clearinghouse for bibliographical information on the performing arts, as well as a computer-readable data base.

Although a paragraph on the Federal Theatre Project appears in Zvonchenko's "Theatre Materials in the Library of Congress," it is of interest to note that the formation of the FTP marked the inauguration of the federal government into promotion and management of the arts—a footnote of artistic and historical relevance, particularly within the context of governmental support for the arts during the past decade and of increasing concern over such issues as arts management. Adding to the value of FTP's resources is George Mason University Research Center's oral history collection of interviews with former Federal Theatre personnel—administrative staff, playwrights, directors, and other artists. At this writing, *A Calendar of Federal*

Theatre Productions, 1935-39 is being prepared for publication by Greenwood Press, and a future volume of *Performing Arts Resources* will describe the holdings in detail. For those interested in keeping abreast of FTP activities a subscription to the Center's occasional newsletter, *Federal One*, is available by writing Curator Laraine Correll. Mention must also be made of the richly illustrated survey, *Free, Adult, Uncensored: the Living History of the Federal Theatre Project*, edited by John O'Connor and Lorraine Brown (New Republic, distributed by Simon and Schuster, 1978), which serves as an excellent introduction to the collection.

Though still in its infancy, the Charles MacArthur Center for American Theatre, a unit of the Florida State University School of Theatre in Tallahassee, has made its imprint on the American theatrical scene with a three-pronged program of research, production, and publication, appropriately devoted to the Center's namesake. To implement its goals, the Center is divided into three main areas: the Resource Division, the Research Division, and the Performance Division. The Resource Division houses the Center's resource materials and special collections, while the Research Division coordinates the research projects and maintains responsibility for the American Theatre Oral History Program as well as the publication projects. The Belknap Collection for the Performing Arts at Gainesville is another of Florida's contributions to the field of theatre research. Former curator Laraine Correll writes of its founding and activities in Volume I of *Performing Arts Resources* (1974).

Specific remarks must be made about some of the theatre collections on the West Coast, namely, the University of California at Davis, whose holdings include the production records of American and foreign theatres and alternative theatre groups such as The Living Theatre, Bread and Puppet Theatre, San Francisco Mime Troupe, Firehouse Theatre, Open Theatre, Le Théâtre Euh, and Theatre Laboratoire Vicinal. Descriptions of these holdings and others are found in Marion K. Whalon's "Avant-garde and Radical Theatre Holdings" (*Broadside*, Winter 1976) and Robert K. Sarlos' "The Theatre Collection at Davis" (*American Society for Theatre Research Newsletter*, Fall 1974). The defunct Pasadena Playhouse materials are now housed in the California State University Library at Long Beach. Washington State University Libraries in Pullman have acquired the Robert Cushman Butler Collection of some 1,600 theatrical illustrations comprising sheet music covers, programs and playbills; manuscripts of actors, actresses, and playwrights; and several extra-illustrated volumes of theatrical history and reminiscences concentrating on 18th-19th-century British and American drama.

One of the most impressive nonacademic collections of theatricana in the West is that of the Music Center of Los Angeles Operating Company and its facilities: the Ahmanson Theatre, the Dorothy Chandler Pavilion, and the Mark Taper Forum. Housed in the Ahmanson Theatre, the Music Center

Archives began in 1969 at the instigation of House Managers Kenn Randall and Norman Macdonald. On their own initiative, the two collected materials from the previous five years of the Center's existence, culminating in what is now called the Kenn Randall Collection of souvenir programs, promptbooks, press books, clippings, and photographs. Together, a next step was the purchase of the Raymond F. Barnes Collection containing complete files on the early years of the Biltmore Theatre and the Philharmonic Auditorium, as well as a nucleus of reference books, playbills, and photographs. A card index covering the theatre in Los Angeles from the beginnings to 1940, with information on plays, players, designers, and directors is also maintained.

The most frequent users of the Archives are the resident companies. The Center itself relied solely upon its resources of fact-sheets, proposals, clippings of early fund-raising events, and photographs of groundbreaking ceremonies for publication of *The Music Center Story: a Decade of Achievement, 1964-1974.* Graduate students, theatre buffs, documentary producers, writers, and others request information daily ranging from basic facts about the Center's productions to detailed historic research about the early days of the Los Angeles stage.

No sooner will these pages go to press than new and additional information on performing arts resources will appear on the horizon. Alert librarians and curators, however, need not be discouraged. By assiduously scanning the many publications featuring collections and collections development programs, one can be enlightened of the latest developments. Among these tools are AB *Bookman's Weekly*, ACRL's *College & Research Libraries News*, *Manuscripts* (Manuscript Society), and *Broadside*, quarterly newsletter of the Theatre Library Association. These, as well as others, feature news items relating to recent library and museum acquisitions—both by gift and by purchase. The reader is referred also to "Performing Arts Resources—A Directory" in this issue, which is a select listing of libraries and institutions—by state in the United States and by province in Canada—containing performing arts material.

Louis A. Rachow
President, Theatre Library Association; Guest Editor

THEATRE MATERIALS IN THE LIBRARY OF CONGRESS

Walter Zvonchenko, Theatre Reference Librarian

This survey of theatre materials in the Library of Congress is intended as an overall guide to the actual location of general categories of theatre materials and of some specific collections and individual items of particular importance. It has not been possible to present an exhaustive survey, but it is hoped that this outline, however brief, will serve as a reasonable indication of the great strength of the Library in the subject area, a strength which enables the Library to serve as a center with few peers for the study of theatre.

The collections are extremely varied in kind and include well over a million individual items. The materials have come to the Library through purchase, gift, exchange, and copyright deposit and cover all aspects of the theatre and its history throughout the world. In addition to books and periodicals, they include playbills, manuscripts, letters, promptbooks, and iconography.

Theatre materials are housed in several custodial divisions, most of which are responsible for maintaining and making available materials in particular formats or languages (e.g., Asian) rather than subject areas. Usually, it is format or language which will determine the choice of custodial division for particular items. Hence, most iconography, including posters, drawings, and photographs, is located in the Prints and Photographs Division, while most collections of manuscripts, including personal and business papers, will be found in the Manuscript Division. The Rare Book and Special Collections Division houses rare books, some manuscripts, and certain collections of material, which, though often heterogeneous in kind of item and content, are, for various reasons, kept together rather than dispersed. Similarly, the literature in the vernacular of certain nonwestern nations and areas will be found in the appropriate section and division of Area Studies. So it is that, with the major exception of materials on lyric theatre, which are kept in the Music Division, special collections containing theatre items will be found in the appropriate format or language division.

To indicate most clearly the actual location of kinds of theatre items in the Library of Congress, this survey will consider those items by Library division.

Walter Zvonchenko is Theatre Reference Librarian, Performing Arts Library, Library of Congress, Washington, D.C. 20540.

Special Collections, Vol. 1(1), Fall 1981

General Collections

The vast majority of theatre materials in book and serial form are in the Library's general collections and are served to readers in the Library's main reading rooms. The collection of American drama is undoubtedly the largest in the world, due primarily to deposit for copyright registration, as a result of which, since 1870, hundreds of thousands of American scripts, published and unpublished, have come to the Library. A considerable number of these are housed in the general collections. In addition, the Library's broad acquisition policies with respect to foreign materials have resulted in the development of a collection of foreign play titles, which, in overall numbers, is certainly one of the largest such collections in the world. The Library has gathered well over 100,000 titles covering the history and theory, architecture, and scenic and costume design of theatre; a large number of theatre bibliographies; and catalogs from theatre museum exhibitions from all parts of the world.

Over the years, the Library has acquired many special groups of material related to the theatre that have been added to the general collections, either wholly or in part. An example is the Raymond Toinet Collection of French literature, which contains a large number of editions of plays, primarily of the 17th and early 18th centuries. While many titles have been incorporated into the collections of the Rare Book and Special Collections Division, others are in the general collections.

The Library makes an effort to receive all current significant theatre periodicals, both domestic and foreign, and, whenever possible, attempts to acquire out-of-print titles either in original copy or in microform. Current issues may be found in the Serial and Government Publications Division, while most bound titles are kept in the general collections.

Rare Book and Special Collections Division

Among the theatre materials in the Rare Book and Special Collections Division are approximately 3,000 American plays, largely manuscript or typescript, deposited for copyright. While most of the plays date from the period 1870 through 1916, the collection also includes scripts of writers such as Eugene O'Neill, Maxwell Anderson, and Arthur Miller.

The division also holds the Francis Longe Collection of theatre works published in English between 1607 and 1812. The collection was assembled by the Longe family of Norfolk, England and was purchased by the Library of Congress in 1908. It includes original plays, theatrical adaptations, and translations credited to over six hundred playwrights and is particularly rich in the works of lesser known 17th-century figures. The collection also contains early editions of plays by such prominent authors as Christopher Marlowe and John Webster, among others. The 2,105 plays are bound as a 331-volume set and listed by author or title in a card index. Approximately 400 librettos from the Longe Collection are described in Oscar Sonneck's *Catalogue of Opera Librettos; Printed before 1800.*

Among the Shakespeare items in the Rare Book and Special Collections Division are copies of the 1599 Quarto edition of *Romeo and Juliet*, the First Folio edition (1623), both from the collection given to the Library by John Davis Batchelder, the Quarto edition (1619) of *Midsummer-Night's Dream*, and copies of the 1632, 1664, and 1685 folios.

The George Fabyan Collection includes valuable material for the study of the Shakespeare-Bacon controversy. Of the sixty-nine distinct editions of Bacon's works printed between 1597 and 1640 which are listed in Pollard and Redgrave's *Short-Title Catalogue of English Books . . .* , copies of thirty-three are in the Fabyan Collection, and twenty-five of the thirty-three in more than one copy.

The collection of incunabula in the Rare Book and Special Collections Division is the largest in the western hemisphere and includes eight editions of Terence and four of Plautus. Among the Terence items are four copies of a Strasbourg incunabulum of 1496, particularly important for the history of theatre production because it includes woodcuts of what are believed to be among the first representations of performance of Terence on the Renaissance stage. There is also a copy of a German translation of 1486 of Terence's *Eunuchus* and four copies of the Aldine Aristophanes of 1498. Also in the division is a Plautus manuscript of eighty-seven leaves dated 1487 which contains eight of his plays.

Among the rarest pieces in the Henry James Collection is a copy of the dramatization of *Daisy Miller* which was privately printed in 1882 for copyright purposes.

Other theatre materials in the division include more than 8,000 playbills from English and American theatrical productions of the 19th and 20th centuries. A card index arranged by title serves as a guide to the playbills.

Because they are of special interest or value, certain periodicals are housed in the Rare Book and Special Collections Division. Among these are Richard Steele's *The Theatre* of 1720, the oldest English theatre periodical in the Library, and John Payne's *The Thespian Mirror* of 1805, the oldest American theatre periodical.

Manuscript Division

The collections of the Manuscript Division include papers of prominent figures from virtually all professions in theatre, including actors, directors, producers, writers, and variety artists. The collections of papers range in size from a single item to hundreds of thousands of items and may include business records, scripts, promptbooks, playbills, personal and business correspondence, and scrapbooks. In addition to information on particular personalities, many collections contain material on significant productions and on critical developments in the history of the modern theatre.

Of special note among the collections are the papers of a number of renowned American actresses. The papers of Margaret Webster, numbering approximately 7,000 items, cover all aspects of her career as actress, theatrical producer, director, author, and lecturer. They include professional and family correspondence, family papers, promptbooks of plays and operas, musical scores, setting and staging diagrams, and extensive scrapbooks of photographs and clippings. Family papers pertain chiefly to Miss Webster's parents, Dame May Whitty and Benjamin Webster, and their careers on the British stage. The papers also reflect Miss Webster's career in the American theatre from 1937 to 1970, her professional association with Eva Le Gallienne and Cheryl Crawford in the American Repertory Theatre in New York, and Miss Webster's activities in experimental theatre with Marweb Productions.

The papers of Minnie Maddern Fiske cover the years 1884 to 1932 and are 18,000 in number. They include the papers of Mrs. Fiske's husband, Harrison Grey Fiske, and constitute a detailed picture of the period during which American theatre came of age. The correspondence files contain letters of some of the most distinguished figures in theatre, literature, music, and art. There are promptbooks with marginal notes made by Mrs. Fiske and theatrical financial records of several kinds. Throughout the collection are papers reflecting the continuing controversy between the Fiskes and the powerful theatrical trusts of the late 19th and early 20th centuries.

The papers of Ruth Gordon, actress and playwright, comprise nearly 6,000 items. They include general correspondence concerning Miss Gordon's career, box office statements, production material, programs, publicity material, reviews and general business papers for Thornton Wilder's *The Matchmaker* and other plays; Miss Gordon's financial papers (1937-1959); and biographical material.

The papers of Laura Keene (1826-1873), actress and theatre manager, afford invaluable insight into the business of American theatre in the East in the mid-19th century. Her papers are largely business records and include correspondence, trusts, insurance policies, contracts with players, play copyrights, and publishing ventures.

The papers of Charlotte Cushman document the career of the important American actress both in the United States and in England. The collection is rich in material relating to Shakespearean production in the 19th century on the English-speaking stage.

The papers of Garson Kanin, numbering 2,500 items, include extensive coverage of the history of Mr. Kanin's play *Born Yesterday* (1946), financial papers, and correspondence.

New York theatrical and literary agent Lucy Kroll's papers consist of almost 100,000 items and are a record of Miss Kroll's business relationships with a vast number of prominent figures in theatre as well as in radio, film, and television from the 1940s into the 1970s. The collection includes a large number of playbills from theatre productions, most of them in New York, from the same period.

An important collection for the study of the variety stage in the United States at the turn of this century are the 2,000 items of the vaudeville headliner, humorist, comic impersonator and "storyteller," Marshall Pinckney Wilder (1859-1915). The items include correspondence, diaries, humor notes, and clippings which supplied the raw material for Wilder's performances, notebooks containing lists of theatrical agents and performers across the country, scrapbooks of playbills and theatrical broadsides, and many photographs of theatre-related personalities and events of this period.

The Manuscript Division also houses the papers of Hume Cronyn and Jessica Tandy, numbering nearly 24,000 items, Richard Mansfield, Fanny Kemble, Jed Harris, May Robson, and Richard Coe, among whose 4,000 items are a very large collection of playbills. Among the playscripts in the division are works by Tennessee Williams, George S. Kaufman, Lillian Hellman, Clifford Odets, John La Touche, Maxwell Anderson, Archibald MacLeish, and Mae West and several variety theatre sketches written by W. C. Fields. There is also a playscript for the original production of *Animal Crackers* included among the Groucho Marx papers.

Federal Theatre Project*

The enormous files of the Federal Theatre Project constitute one of the most significant sources for the study of modern theatre in the United States. Established in 1935 as part of the Works Progress Administration and supporting 150 separate producing units throughout the United States, the FTP produced over 830 major stage plays, 6,000 radio programs, and innumerable marionette plays, vaudeville shows, outdoor pageants, and circuses. At the conclusion of the FTP project in 1939, its production materials were sent to the Library of Congress, which placed them on deposit at George Mason University in Fairfax, Virginia in 1974. This is the largest single gathering of FTP materials and includes 7,000 playscripts, 25,000 photographs, 1,000 posters, over 1,600 costume designs, 350 scene designs, 450 production notebooks, 1,700 programs and heralds, and eighteen cubic feet of research materials and play readers' reports. This collection is currently served by the special collections unit of the George Mason University Library.

---

* Additional information on the FTP appears in the Introduction.—Editor

Music Division

Several special collections in the Music Division are of great importance for the study of lyric theatre, the American lyric theatre in particular. The George and Ira Gershwin Collection is the largest public collection of original source materials for the study of George Gershwin. It includes all major Gershwin manuscripts, holograph sketches and scores, student notebooks, scrapbooks, financial records, contracts, telegrams, and scripts for Gershwin stage and film productions. Ira Gershwin has contributed annotations for many items and also has contributed drafts of his own lyrics and personal correspondence.

Among the manuscripts which Richard Rodgers gave to the Library are piano-vocal scores for many of the musical comedies that he wrote with Lorenz Hart and scores for all the theatre productions that he wrote with Oscar Hammerstein II. The orchestrations by Robert Russell Bennett for eight of the Rodgers and Hammerstein musicals were donated to the Library by Dorothy Hammerstein and Richard Rodgers. Dorothy Hammerstein also gave a large collection of the papers of Oscar Hammerstein II to the Library. The collection includes materials relating to his early musicals, for which he wrote both "book" and lyrics, as well as those that date from his collaboration with Richard Rodgers. The collection also contains scripts, notes, librettos, correspondence, printed music, pictorial materials, playbills, and awards. *Oklahoma* and *South Pacific* are particularly well documented.

The extensive Victor Herbert Collection in the Music Division includes holographs of Herbert operettas such as *Babes in Toyland* and *Naughty Marietta*, and many others.

The Romberg Collection includes holographs of many of the most popular works of Sigmund Romberg, including *Blossom Time*, *The Student Prince*, *The Desert Song*, and *New Moon*. Copyists' manuscripts, printed music, librettos, and film scripts of Romberg's works are also in the collection.

The Albert Schatz Collection consists of over 12,000 printed librettos, primarily of German and Italian texts of the 17th and 18th centuries. The Schatz Collection also includes research files containing a thoroughly documented chronological list of opera performance from 1541 to 1901. The collection of opera full scores in the Music Division, including many copyists' manuscripts commissioned expressly for this collection, is without parallel. Coupled with the Schatz Collection and the piano-vocal scores found elsewhere in the division, these full scores constitute an invaluable resource for the study of opera.

Prints and Photographs Division

There are few major collections in the Prints and Photographs Division which consist primarily of theatre material. But, among the many groups and types of material in this division, which houses millions of items, there are vast numbers which are theatre related.

The remarkable performing arts poster collection numbers 10,000 items— 5,000 of which are 19th-century lithographs, chromolithographs, and wood-cuts pertaining to circus, rodeo, minstrelsy, specialty acts, burlesque, magic, vaudeville, opera, operetta, and theatre. The remaining 5,000 are 20th-century foreign and domestic theatre and film posters. Ranging in size from small window cards to immense multiple-sheet posters, these lithographs and woodcuts constitute a panorama of American theatre during the later 19th century and include many brilliantly colored illustrations of Kiralfy specta-cles, *East Lynne* (1881), *Diplomacy* (1878), Thomas Keane in *Macbeth* (1884), the Joseph Hart Vaudeville Co.'s *Clever Carrie* (1899), and a large number of poster advertisements for the leading minstrel groups of the time. American theatre in the earlier 19th century is well documented through prints from engravers and lithographers of the period, of whom Currier and Ives and Thomas and Wylie were the most prominent.

The theatre-related photographs in the division constitute one of the largest groups of theatre materials in the Library of Congress. They include original daguerreotypes from the middle of the 19th century of Jenny Lind and Junius Brutus Booth, Sr. and original Mathew Brady glass plate negatives. The Library's photograph collections are especially strong in coverage of theatre personalities and history, primarily in the United States, since the beginning of the last quarter of the 19th century. The division holds an exceedingly large number of portraits of theatre personalities, which are the work of noted theatrical photographers such as Napoleon Sarony, Aimee Dupont, Joseph Byron, Otto Sarony, B. J. Falk, and Arnold Genthe.

Numbering more than 2,000 prints, the Minnie Maddern Fiske collection in the Prints and Photographs Division constitutes the largest photographic record of any single actor in the division. It includes studio portraits of Mrs. Fiske, scenes from many of her plays and the plays of contemporaries such as George Arliss and Otis Skinner, and photographs used in designing stage sets. The division holds the collection of Alfred Cheney Johnston, who created an invaluable record of earlier 20th-century American variety theatre with his photographs of a great number of Ziegfeld girls and prominent New York musical comedy and Hollywood personalities. The Library has acquired pho-tographic collections from major news service figures and organizations—the National Photo Company Collection, *New York World-Telegram and Sun* Collection, George Grantham Bain Collection, and the Washington Press Photo Bureau Collection, among whose enormous files will be found hundreds of pieces related to the world of the theatre. The division also maintains extensive biographic, subject, and geographic catalogs, which will lead the reader to other significant stores of coverage of theatre personalities and theatre buildings.

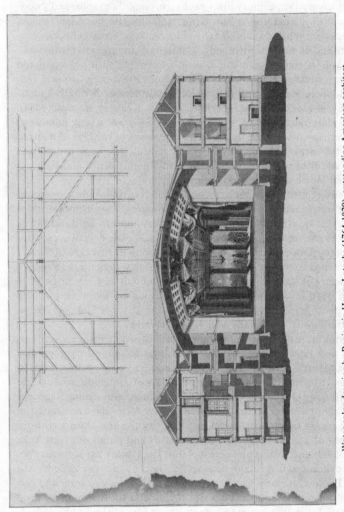

Water color drawing by Benjamin Henry Latrobe (1764-1820), outstanding American architect, of the framing of the front of the stage for a theatre which was projected for Richmond, Virginia at the close of the 18th century, but never built. This drawing is one of several for this project in the Prints and Photographs Division of the Library of Congress. (Reproduced from the Collections of the Library of Congress. Negative number LC USZ62-22888.)

Material on theatre buildings in the division includes original and measured drawings, historical prints, and various types of photographs, spanning the period from 1798 to the present. Two important collections which include material on theatre building are the Historic American Buildings Survey (HABS), begun in 1933, and the Historic American Engineering Record (HAER), begun in 1969. HABS records American buildings which are important architecturally, while HAER documents monuments of American engineering. Both collections, the work of professional staff within the Department of the Interior, are maintained and made available in the Prints and Photographs Division of the Library of Congress.

Area Studies Divisions

Collections of plays and other theatre-related materials in Middle Eastern or Asian languages will be found in the African and Middle East Division and the Asian Division respectively. Translations of such titles into European languages will be found in the Library's General Collections.

The collection of original Chinese language plays is the largest outside China and includes several anthologies from the Yuan period (1260-1368). These plays are maintained in the Chinese and Korean Section of the Asian Division. Similarly, the collection of Japanese plays is the largest outside Japan and is comprehensive in its coverage of Nō, Kabuki, and Kyōgen titles. These titles are housed in the Japanese Section of the Asian Division. The Library's Sanskrit Collection, in the Southern Asia Section of the Asian Division, includes a significant number of plays by classical writers such as Kalidasa and Bhasa. The section also has custody of representative contemporary plays in Bengali, Hindi, Tamil, and other modern Indic languages and a number of play titles from the classical theatre of Southeast Asia.

Holdings in Hebrew and Yiddish drama range from the earliest plays printed in Hebrew in the first half of the 18th-century to the modern dramatic literature published in the United States and Israel. These titles are in the Hebraic Section of the African and Middle Eastern Division. The Near East Section of the African and Middle Eastern Division holds a substantial number of plays, as well as criticism and production history in Arabic, Turkish, and Persian.

The Hispanic Division maintains custody of approximately 300 Spanish play titles of the 19th and 20th centuries, most of which derive from the period 1900 through 1930.

Microform Reading Room

The Microform Reading Room houses a large number of important items concerned wholly or in part with theatre. In 1938, the Hispanic Society of America gave a collection of 8,000 plays to the Library. These were published principally in Madrid and Barcelona after 1850 and include many works by lesser known Spanish writers and regional pieces written in the Catalan and Galician dialects. The pieces include comedy, drama, and zarzuelas and, in some cases, contain handwritten stage directions and textual changes. The microfilm of the collection will be completed this year. Catalog entries for the plays will be available both in the Microform Reading Room and the Hispanic Division.

The Microform Reading Room holds many important titles, which, while not unique to the Library of Congress, will not often be found in library collections and which are of serious interest to researchers in theatre. Among these are the film made available to date of *Variety*; *Spanish Drama of the Golden Age* (a copy of the Comedia Collection in the University of Pennsylvania Libraries); the collection of dissertations from United States universities based on *Dissertation Abstracts International*; and *Three Centuries of English and American Plays*, which consists of over 5,000 plays including English titles dating from 1515 to 1800 and American titles dating from 1714 to 1830.

The finding tools maintained by the divisions for theatre collections in their custody enable the reader to make intelligent use of what might otherwise be an overwhelming body of theatre material. In addition to the theatre source materials in the individual divisions, large theatre reference collections will be found in the Main Reading Room of the Library and especially in the newly opened Performing Arts Library in the John F. Kennedy Center for the Performing Arts, a joint project of the Kennedy Center and the Library of Congress.

So often the proper study of theatre requires serious investigation into a vast range of other subject areas, both in the humanities and in the social sciences. The enormous size and comprehensiveness of the collections of the Library of Congress allow the researcher in theatre unusual freedom to pursue almost any avenue of inquiry, however distant from theatre the avenue might seem. It is the extraordinary strength of its collections as a whole coupled with, and supporting, the theatre materials in the various divisions, which enables the Library of Congress to serve as a center, perhaps without parallel, for the study of the theatre.

THE NEW YORK PUBLIC LIBRARY:
THE BILLY ROSE THEATRE COLLECTION

Paul Myers, Curator

The Billy Rose Theatre Collection is part of the Research Library of The New York Public Library—and, more specifically—a division of the Performing Arts Research Center. It is located on the third floor of the Library and Museum of the Performing Arts, 111 Amsterdam Avenue, New York, in the northwest corner of the Lincoln Center complex.

The inception of the Collection dates back to 1929, when David Belasco offered his archives to The New York Public Library with the proviso that, if the gift was accepted, it would be the beginning of an ongoing theatre collection. The second condition was that a qualified librarian should be appointed to administer the Collection and to build on the Belasco gift. The Library accepted this offer and, with the advice of George Pierce Baker, the founder of the famed '47 Workshop at Harvard University and later at Yale University, invited George Freedley (1904-1967) to become Chief of the new Theatre Collection. Mr. Freedley was a graduate of the Yale School of Drama and was then working in New York as an actor and stage manager for the Theatre Guild.

The Theatre Collection opened to the public in 1931 in a small alcove containing two tables in the northwest corner of The New York Public Library's Central Building, at Fifth Avenue and 42nd Street. In 1965, the Collection moved to its present location at Lincoln Center along with the Music Division, the Dance Collection, and the Rodgers and Hammerstein Archives of Recorded Sound. Though called a "theatre" collection, the archive houses material also on the cinema, radio and television, magic, marionettes and puppets, circus, night clubs, vaudeville, amusement parks, minstrels, fairs, and carnivals.

Among the important collections acquired since the founding are the Robinson Locke Collection of Dramatic Scrapbooks comprising some 900 bound volumes and over 2,300 portfolios of loose clippings, photographs, programs, and holograph letters covering the careers of stage and film figures from about 1870 to 1920, amassed by the publisher of the Toledo (Ohio) *Daily Blade*; the extensive Chamberlain and Lyman Brown Theatrical Agency Col-

Paul Myers has retired as Curator of The Billy Rose Theatre Collection, The New York Public Library.

lection of business and personal papers, programs, inscribed photographs, and voluminous correspondence as described by Betty Wharton in Volume I of *Performing Arts Resources* (1974); the Hiram Stead Collection on the British theatre covering roughly the years 1672 to 1932 with 600 portfolios of letters, autographs, and written copies of leases and documents relating to litigation, supplementing a vast file of playbills and portraits; and the Henin Collection of the Parisian stage for the 18th and 19th centuries with some important material from the 1600s.

The George Becks Collection is composed mostly of promptbooks and holograph scripts of 18th and 19th-century plays produced in the United States and England. George Becks, the Shakespearean actor and stage manager, inherited the scripts of Mrs. Lander (the former Jean Davenport, first actress to play Marguerite in *Camille* and the adapter of that play into English), adding them to his own lifelong collection, which came to the Library in 1905. The acquisition of this collection of promptbooks so impressed the Dramatists' Guild of the Authors' League of America that a resolution was passed on 10 May 1932 urging the Guild members to deposit typescripts and promptcopies of their unpublished plays in the Library. Since that time the collection of scripts has grown to 22,200 plays, 2,400 screenplays, 1,000 television plays and series scripts, and 8,400 radio scripts: manuscripts, drafts, and typescripts, for example, by Edward Albee, Jerome Lawrence and Robert E. Lee, Samuel Taylor, Edward Goodman, Ferenc Molnar, Elmer Rice, S. N. Behrman, and Maxwell Anderson.

Photographs, prints, lithographs, posters, slides, and motion picture and television stills at the Library run into several millions. Programs and playbills number well over a million. Original drawings for costumes and scenery and pen and pencil portraits (including theatrical caricatures) run to several thousand—the cooperation of artists and producers is sought to increase this total as time goes on. Such designers as Robert Edmond Jones, Claude Bragdon, Donald Oenslager, Nat Karson, H. M. Crayon, Boris Aronson, Jo Mielziner, Mstislav Valerianovich Dobujinsky, Aline Bernstein, Howard Bay, and David Ffolkes are represented.

In addition to those on designers and dramatists, collections centered on performing artists, directors, or producing firms have become a significant tribute to the great of the theatre world. Such persons as Sophie Tucker, Lee Simonson, Simon Lissim, Townsend Walsh, Alice and Irene Lewisohn, Gilbert Gabriel, John Golden, Katharine Cornell and Guthrie McClintic, Augustin Daly, Helen Hayes, Burl Ives, Gertrude Lawrence, Hallie Flanagan, Cheryl Crawford, Paul Muni, Maurice Evans, Bert Lahr, and Carl Van Vechten have been so honored. Similarly, such managerial firms and organizations as Klaw and Erlanger, Gates and Morange, Jones and Green, the Living Theatre (the internationally renowned experimental group headed by Julian Beck and Judith Malina), Playwrights Company, the Provincetown

Theatrical montage. (Photograph by Bob Serating.)

Playhouse, the Vivian Beaumont Theatre (from the ANTA-Washington Square days to the administration of Jules Irving in the 1970s), Actors' Equity Association, American Theatre Wing-Stage Door Canteens, The Players, Alexander H. Cohen, and Leland Hayward are included.

Some photographers—the late Francis Bruguière is one—have presented thousands of their own photographs. White Studio key sheets, negatives, and prints cover the New York theatrical scene from about 1910 to 1936. The Vandamm Studio Collection of Theatrical Photographs contains prints and negatives of stage productions and photographs of actors from prior to 1920 to 1960. These two collections are, in effect, a photographic history of five decades of the New York stage. Alfredo Valente has donated his negatives, and Leo Friedman has given numerous prints and negatives of Broadway shows. The Collection also has many caricatures by Al Frueh, Al Hirschfeld, and Alex Gard.

In 1907 the Library laid the foundation for what is now one of the largest book and periodical collections relating to motion pictures in any public institution being among the earliest subscribers to the first periodical of the industry, the *Moving Picture World*, now the *Motion Pictures Herald*. By that time it already had the first scattered books on the still embryonic cinematic art. Choicest of these was the *History of the Kinematograph, Kinetoscope*, and *Kineto-Phonograph* (1895). From those early days to these, printed annals of the motion pictures have been collected. Of trade publications, such house organs as the *Edison Kinetogram* which began in 1909, is typical. Another early item is the first printed press sheet, in one of three voluminous scrapbooks on the Kalem Company presented by Hal Hode. Now, the Theatre Collection offers a selection of the best known fan magazines, including *Photoplay, Picture Play, Moving Picture Stories*, and *Motion Picture Classic*. Periodicals in English, French, German, Italian, Spanish, Swedish, and Russian are available in current issues, in bound volumes, and on microfilm.

The Robinson Locke Collection also contains hundreds of portfolios of film information covering the early careers of Mary Pickford, Douglas Fairbanks, Charles Chaplin, and Theda Bara, and those operatic and stage artists who had film careers such as Mary Garden, Jane Cowl, Ethel Barrymore, and Geraldine Farrar. George Kleine, pioneer with Edison, presented his account books, business papers, scrapbooks, and press sheets, which give a clear picture of business conditions in the early period of production.

In 1928, through the good offices of the late Frank J. Wilstach and the Motion Picture Producers and Distributors of America, Inc., the major film companies began to present stills (now totalling more than a million) and pressbooks of their current pictures. Paramount Pictures Corporation assembled for the Library a full set of pressbooks dating from 1919. In 1933, Universal Pictures, Inc. deposited its linen books of stills, adding to them annually. A full set of scrapbooks and stills for Inspiration Pictures Inc. contains a record of films of Richard Barthelmess and Lillian and Dorothy Gish, *The White Sister, Romola, The Bright Shawl*, and *Tol'able David* among them. In 1938, Metro-Goldwyn-Mayer donated a set of continuities for its films released since January 1, 1928 and continued to donate scripts until 1945. Also, there are scrapbooks from New York's Capitol Theatre and

Loew's Inc. Many other film companies have found the Collection a convenient repository and reliable custodian. Their generous gifts have occasionally served as insurance against difficulties with their own files. Since January 1, 1930 one or more reviews for every film released in New York has been preserved. Newspapers from New York, London, Paris, Moscow, and Los Angeles are clipped currently for a biographical file now numbering several millions of items.

Radio made its importance known nationally by the broadcast of the election returns in November 1920, and soon after the NYPL began collecting radio books and periodicals. Since 1931 news and trade papers have been clipped for reviews, biographical matter, and current trends. The radio companies as well as local stations have supplied press material, programs, and scripts.

Television, now a major area of the performing arts, is chronicled in similar depth. There are many scripts for television productions, including Hallmark Productions, soap operas, and situation comedy series. Vaudeville is represented by files on performers, including those from other areas of the performing arts who also appeared in vaudeville. There are photographs, scrapbooks, reviews, and programs, with a complete run of programs of the Palace Theatre when it was the premier American vaudeville house.

Many other aspects of entertainment, including burlesque, marionettes of all countries, nightclubs, fairs, carnivals, and amusement parks, are documented through clippings, reviews, photographs, and miscellanea. The circus collection contains rare 19th and 20th-century American, British, and European playbills, posters, and route books. There is material on special attractions such as aquacades and the Old Globe Theatre at the Chicago and New York World Fairs. At the center of the magic collection is the book, scrapbook, and periodical collection of the Society of American Magicians, much of it rare and out-of-print information on how to perform the illusions of the trade, which is available to members of the Society and, with special permission, to other serious researchers.

In 1970 a remarkable new educational and research tool was provided by the Theatre Collection with the establishment of the Theatre on Film and Tape Collection (TOFT). The filming or videotaping of live performances now preserves for posterity all the qualities of a production otherwise lost the moment the last curtain falls. The TOFT collection includes productions of Shakespeare's plays, other classics of the theatre, contemporary experimental productions, and commercial Broadway musicals and plays; informal dialogues with important theatrical personalities about their careers and techniques and other theatre-related films and videotapes are constantly being acquired.

The Billy Rose Theatre Collection, like all other units of the Performing Arts Research Center and the Research Libraries, is privately funded. In

February 1979 the Theatre Collection was named after the late Mr. Rose, theatrical producer, impresario, and songwriter, when the Billy Rose Foundation made a generous gift towards the operating costs of the Collection. In announcing the gift, Library President Richard A. Couper noted that Billy Rose, who had much success in his professional career as a songwriter, had spent a considerable amount of time at the Library analyzing the lyrics of popular songs. "He then went on," Couper said, "to make many significant contributions to entertainment and, by creating the Billy Rose Foundation, he continues to enrich the lives of all of us."* The Theatre Collection and other units of The New York Public Library depend upon the continuing support of individuals, foundations, and corporations to improve the collections and help keep them open for professional, scholarly, artistic, and commercial use.

The collection that now bears the name Billy Rose is a busy place indeed. From a university professor researching circus performances in small New England towns in the 1880s to a fan sighing over photographs of Elvis Presley or (still today) Rudolph Valentino, from a working Broadway set designer looking at sketches used forty years ago to a graduate student writing a thesis on popular films of the 1940s, the people who fill the collection's reading rooms are as diverse in their objectives and educational attainments as the great archive itself. This is also true of the donors. When Sophie Tucker gave the Library thirteen trunks full of material covering her career in vaudeville, carnivals, movies, nightclubs, musicals, and television in 1949, the presentation ceremony was held in the main lobby of the Fifth Avenue building. Curator George Freedley and Director of the Library Ralph A. Beals made formal speeches of acceptance, to which Miss Tucker replied in her inimitable voice as she handed Mr. Beals the keys to the first trunk, "Here are the keys, Baby."

---

* *Library Lines*, 9:1, March 1979.

THE PLAYERS, NEW YORK

Louis A. Rachow, Curator & Librarian

The Players was founded in 1888 by the celebrated American actor Edwin Booth as a place where actors and dramatists could mingle in good fellowship with craftsmen of the fine arts as well as those of the performing arts. The seed had been planted a decade before when Booth enjoyed the hospitality of the famed Garrick Club of London. The dream became a reality in the summer of 1887 aboard the yacht *Oneida* in Boothbay Harbor, Maine, where financier Elias C. Benedict hosted friends Edwin Booth, Lawrence Barrett, Thomas Bailey Aldrich, Laurence Hutton, William Bispham, and Parke Godwin.

Before going on tour that September, Booth made the final decision to assume the cost of housing The Players after consulting with playwright and theatre manager Augustin Daly and Union Square Theatre manager Albert M. Palmer. On January 6, 1888, Daly invited fifteen fellow companions of the actor to breakfast at Delmonico's—the fifteen who were to become the club's incorporators: actors Joseph Jefferson, John Drew, Lawrence Barrett, James Lewis, Henry Edwards, and John A. Lane (banker turned actor); Albert M. Palmer and Augustin Daly; lawyers Joseph F. Daly and Stephen H. Olin; businessman William Bispham; Professor Brander Matthews; authors Laurence Hutton and Samuel L. Clemens; and General William Tecumseh Sherman. Upon purchasing the Clarkson Potter residence at Number 16 Gramercy Park in the Spring of 1888, Booth commissioned architect Stanford White to transform the brownstone into a clubhouse complete with Greek columns and a street-level entrance. In over three-quarters of a century, The Players has toasted eight presidents: Booth, Jefferson, Drew, Walter Hampden, Howard Lindsay, Dennis King, Alfred Drake, and currently, Roland Winters. The club has since become a Registered National Historic Landmark.

From the start, The Players was charged with creating "a library relating to the history of the American stage, and the preservation of pictures, bills of the play, photographs and curiosities."* Booth's personal collection of a thousand volumes became the nucleus of the library. As it expanded from decade to decade, the library evolved into an important source for students and scholars of theatrical history and biography. Official recognition of the need to open its doors to the world of research came in 1957 with the founding of

Louis A. Rachow is Curator and Librarian of The Walter Hampden-Edwin Booth Theatre Collection and Library at The Players, 16 Gramercy Park, New York, NY 10003.

* Certificate of Incorporation of The Players, New York, 9 February 1888.

the Walter Hampden Memorial Library at The Players, named in honor of the club's fourth president, one of the most renowned of 20th-century actors. Permanently chartered under the Education Law of the State of New York as The Walter Hampden-Edwin Booth Theatre Collection and Library, it serves as a notable memorial to the American and English stage and to the percipience of the great Player who conceived it and ensured its perpetuity.

The Edwin Booth Collection

Edwin Booth was a scholar as well as an actor. One need only browse through his Shakespearean promptbooks or read his letters to Horace Howard Furness, the eminent littérateur and compiler of the *Variorum Shakespeare*, to appreciate the degree of his scholarship. The tragedian was quick to realize that his art, the art of acting, demanded documentation and testimonials if it were to acquire a dignity comparable to that of literature, music, painting, or sculpture. With this thought in mind, he nourished and preserved a library of diaries, biographies, letters, encyclopedia, critical treatises on the drama, manuals of play production, works of dramatists from all over the world, and many different editions of Shakespeare—a collection that today bears eloquent evidence of Booth's reading and reflection.

Included in the Booth papers and correspondence are records dealing with his theatre experiences and theatrical business matters: ledgers, account books, and journals of Booth's Theatre as well as the Booth-Barrett and Booth-Modjeska tours, numerous playbills, photographs, and scrapbooks. The original draft of Booth's proclamation "To the People of the United States" upon the assassination of President Abraham Lincoln by John Wilkes Booth is here also. Two descriptive articles on the Booth Collection have been compiled and published by Professor L. Terry Oggel of Northwestern University: "The Edwin Booth Promptbook Collection at The Players: a Descriptive Catalog" (American Society for Theatre Research, *Theatre Survey*, May 1973) and "A Short Title Guide to the Edwin Booth Literary Materials at The Players" (Theatre Library Association, *Performing Arts Resources*, Volume 3, 1976).

The Walter Hampden Collection

Walter Hampden was at once actor, director, manager, promoter, and critic. The proof of his universal influence can be found in his personal collection of promptbooks and scripts, letters, photographs, notices, reviews, programs, ledgers, blueprints, and drawings. Among the Walter Hampden Company, Inc. holdings are theatre contracts and leases, box office statements, production cost lists, route books, stockholder records, and clipping books. The collection includes photographs and biographical sketches of leading members of the Comédie-Française when Hampden studied with Georges Berr and Eugène Sylvain, souvenir programs, and photographs of productions at London's Adelphi Theatre, and photographs and notices of Mabel Moore (Mrs. Walter Hampden). A doctoral dissertation based on this collection entitled *Walter Hampden's Career as Actor-Manager*, by Gene J. Parola, Indiana University (1970), is on deposit in the library.

The John Mulholland Magic Collection

In addition to being a talented magician, John Mulholland was a profound student of magic. "The conjurer is an actor who, to perform his feats, combines psychology with manual dexterity and, frequently, with mechanical apparatus," he wrote for the *Encyclopedia Britannica*. During the later years of his life he was primarily concerned with organizing the vast collection of books, pamphlets and brochures, photographs, posters, medallions, and relics on the history and art of magic that is now in the library.

Reginald Scot's *Discourie of Witchcraft* (1584) is the oldest book in the collection. Written in opposition to the then commonly held belief that the cause of anything not understood was the effort of devils, witches, and imps, it was also the first printed account of magicians' secret methods. Henry Dean's *Hocus Pocus* (1795) was the first magic book published in America. One of two copies located in the United States is included in the collection; the other is at the Massachusetts Historical Society. Representing magic publications during the latter half of the 18th century are several illustrated pamphlets, mainly chapbooks. The "tuppence colored" books are of particular interest. Thousands of letters, programs, playbills, and other advertising, added to periodical and newspaper articles, augment the record. At least a third of the collection is made up of magicians' privately circulated material. The periodicals, issued and edited by magicians, are the greatest source of biographical and historical data in the field for the past seventy-five years—both American and foreign.

The Union Square Theatre Collection

The Union Square Theatre was an institution of outstanding success during the years 1872-1883 under stage manager Albert M. Palmer, an incorporator and vice-president of The Players. Prior to his managing career Palmer had been a librarian and, following his bent, collected and recorded the history of that theatrical decade in meticulous detail. Included in this record is John Oxenford's *The Two Orphans*, complete with playbills of the first, 100th, and last performances, as well as legal documents pertaining to the production. The collection is illustrated with portraits, views, autograph letters, programs, biographies and autobiographies of respective actors and actresses who appeared in the Union Square Theatre. Original contracts for plays produced, accounts of the burning of the theatre, and other contemporaneous material form a portion of the collection. Comprising twenty-four large portfolios, this material was the gift of Butler Davenport, a member of The Players prior to 1916 and founder-manager of the Davenport Free Theatre. Out of these documents came the first dissertation for the degree of Doctor of Philosophy to be written based solely on holdings from the Library—Pat M. Ryan's *A. M. Palmer, Producer: a Study of Management, Dramaturgy and Stagecraft in the American Theatre, 1872-96*, for the Graduate School of Yale University (1959).

William Henderson Collection of English Playbills

The William Henderson Collection of English playbills consists of forty albums containing some 4,000 bills between the years 1747 and 1888. Many of the bills bear evidence of having belonged to strolling companies of players; the box office "takings" are sometimes given and changes in cast are indicated. Playbills illustrative of the "First Appearances of Actors, Plays acted for the First Time, London Theatres, London Benefits, Provincial Theatres and Shakespeare Plays" are a sampling of unusual items in the collection. The country bills of York, Durham, Newcastle, Leeds, and other circuits detail appearances of the Kembles, Miss Mellon, Macready, and others prior to their London debuts. Representative examples are the teenaged Miss Mellon performing in a travelling booth in the yard of a Yorkshire inn and Edmund Kean, in the season of 1806 at the Haymarket Theatre, playing minor parts, perhaps the most important being Rosencrantz in *Hamlet*.

The Max Gordon Collection

Headlining the list of playscripts in the Max Gordon Collection are Clare Boothe Luce's *The Women*, Noel Coward's *Design for Living*, Oscar Hammerstein and Jerome Kern's *Very Warm for May*, Moss Hart and George S. Kaufman's *The Man who Came to Dinner*, Ruth Gordon's *Over Twenty-One*, Garson Kanin's *Born Yesterday*, and Howard Teichmann and Kaufman's *The Solid Gold Cadillac*. These are only a few of the 130 scripts once used by directors, designers, and other practitioners of the theatre. In addition, the collection contains press books, route books, playbills, photograph albums, and sheet music of instrumental parts from such musical scores as Cole Porter's *Anything Goes*, Arthur Schwartz's *The Band Wagon*, and Jerome Kern's *The Cat and the Fiddle*. Gordon's correspondence and business records of his years as producer are housed in the William Seymour Theatre Collection at Princeton University.

The Robert B. Mantell Collection

Through the courtesy of Miss Genevieve Hamper (the former Mrs. Robert B. Mantell) and actor John Alexander, the library fell heir not only to Mantell's promptbooks of his hit plays including *By Secret Warrant, Dagger and Cross, Face in the Moonlight, Louis XI*, and *Richelieu*, but also to the costume accessories he and Miss Hamper wore in their Shakespearean productions. Of more than passing interest are Shylock's scales and weight for *The Merchant of Venice*, coral beads owned by Madame Helena Modjeska, one of Samuel Phelp's snuff boxes, and a potion vial given to Dame Ellen Terry by Sir Henry Irving and used by Miss Hamper as Juliet. Rounding out this unique collection are numerous playbills, photographs, books, diaries, scrapbooks, and the *Variorum Shakespeare*.

The Chuck Callahan Burlesque Collection

For many years burlesque in America was an extemporaneous, but natural training ground for the comedian. A large majority of those who reached the pinnacle of fame and glory in movies, radio, and television graduated *summa cum laude* from burlesque. Comedians such as Bert Lahr, Leon Erroll, Bobby Clark, George Jessel, Eddie Cantor, and W. C. Fields are but a few examples of men who followed the burlesque route to stardom. From this tradition came another dedicated performer to whom the library is indebted—Chuck Callahan. Running the gamut from a Toledo, Ohio dancing bootblack and candy butcher, through a burlesque and movie script writer, to a featured player on television with Fred Allen, Robert Montgomery, and Kate Smith, Callahan made an indelible mark in the annals of the variety stage. Talented performer that he was, he will no doubt be best remembered for his abilities as a scriptwriter and composer of popular burlesque routines. *Atta Boy Petey Old Boy* and *Two Sports from Michigan* are perhaps his two most familiar acts, while the *Andy Gump* series starring Slim Summerville is representative of his work in Hollywood.

During the decade prior to his death in 1964 Chuck and Mrs. Callahan updated and rewrote much of the material for nightclub use. Although the project did not materialize, the fruits of his labors remain intact. The collection consists of nearly 300 burlesque scripts and vaudeville skits, music in manuscript, photographs, and a typescript biography of Chuck Callahan written by his widow and inscribed to The Players. A descriptive account of the collection by Llewellyn H. Hedgbeth appears in Volume III of *Performing Arts Resources* (1976).

The Tallulah Bankhead Collection

"Darling Gentlemen of The Players." So begins a telegram, dated 16 November 1960, from Tallulah Bankhead after her guest appearance at the 127th birthday celebration of Edwin Booth. For many years this was the only Bankhead item in the archives until Edward Barry Roberts' gift of a typescript of his play *Forsaking All Others*, Miss Bankhead's first New York stage appearance after her triumphant London successes, and the Vandamm photographs and the playbill of the 1933 Broadway production. Later, through the good offices of Donald Seawell, the library acquired some of the actress's collection of scripts, letters, playbills, photographs, scrapbooks, and memorabilia. Because Miss Bankhead relied on the telegram and telephone as her primary means of long distance communication, the collection contains relatively little Bankhead correspondence. People did write to her, however, and a number of letters from such famous individuals as Presidents Franklin Delano Roosevelt and Harry S. Truman, Representative Sol Bloom, Lynn Fontanne, William Langford, Richard Maney, Noel Coward, and Alan Shulman are a part of the collection. Playscripts of her Broadway plays, movie scenarios, photographs, tapes of her radio program *The Big Show*, clippings of her London stage hits, playbills, and numerous scrapbooks round out the sizeable accumulation.

The Newman Levy Collection

Lawyer, writer, and Player of distinction, Newman Levy was noted for his humorous light verse, much of which appeared in the *Saturday Evening Post*, *Harper's Magazine*, and the "Conning Tower" of *The New York Herald-Tribune*, as well as in book form. Among his nonverse works are his autobiography *My Double Life* and *The Nan Patterson Case*. He co-authored, with Edna Ferber, the three-act comedy *$1200 a Year*. Important to the library is the collection of Levy Papers dating from 1912 to 1960 which include correspondence, research notes, typescripts of short stories, plays, and poems with holograph corrections and additions. A prize item is his original typescript of an unpublished biography of Franklin P. Adams.

British Actors Orphanage Fund

The British Actors Orphanage Fund was incorporated in Los Angeles, California, in July 1940

> to promote and effect the transfer of male and female minor orphans of deceased British actors and actresses from their present home or homes in Great Britain to America . . . and to provide and pay for their complete maintenance, housing and schooling therein, during the pendency

THE PLAYERS'
First Annual
Classic Revival
THE
RIVALS
By
RICHARD BRINSLEY
SHERIDAN, ESQ.

NEW-YORK
The EMPIRE THEATRE
June 5th to 10th
Anno Domini, 1922

The Players' First Annual Classic Revival, June 1922.

of the present war between Great Britain and Germany, to the end that these orphans may be removed from the horrors and perils of such war.

The duties and activities of the Fund came to a successful conclusion in 1946 when forty-eight of the original fifty-four orphans returned to England and the remaining six either became self-supporting or their care was assumed by others. The collection consists of copies of the charter and by-laws, minutes, journals and ledgers, children's travel arrangements, working files, and preliminary and general correspondence for the years 1940-1946 featuring such luminaries as Noel Coward, Dame May Whitty, Boris Karloff, Maurice Evans, Cole Porter, Peggy Wood, Margaret Webster, and the Fund's attorney Lloyd V. Almirall.

La Mama Experimental Theatre Club

The La Mama Experimental Theatre Club, under the guidance of Ellen Stewart, was a vital force in the 1960s' revolution of the American theatre. Several hundred items documentating these activities were collected and preserved by former La Mama Board Member Paul F. Cranefield, M.D., of Rockefeller University. The collection, as a whole, may well be the most complete in existence for the years 1965-1968 since Ellen Stewart did not begin formation of systematic archives until her move from 122 Second Avenue to East 4th Street. The holdings are divided into three sections: (1) chronological records of productions containing approximately 140 manuscript and typescript leaves as well as some additional eighty pages of source material and worksheets, (2) clippings and press coverage including 123 clippings from Scottish, English, German, and American newspapers and periodicals, and (3) playbills and programs consisting of 143 broadsides and handbills together with miscellaneous bills of productions and lectures by La Mama artists. Each section has its own calendar. An idea of the historical significance of this material may be gathered from the names of the individuals who have risen to fame: Bette Midler, Kevin Conway, Sam Shepard, Joe Chaikin, Robert Patrick, Tom Eyen, Jean-Claude van Itallie, Robert Wilson, Megan Terry, Sally Kirkland, Rochelle Ownes, and Joanna Miles. One might note also the program for the first production anywhere of J. M. Tabelak's *Godspell*.

Franklin Heller Collection

Among the 110 items presented to The Players by actor-director-writer Franklin Heller, covering the years 1936-1950, are the stage manager's original working prompt copies of George S. Kaufman and Moss Hart's *The American Way*, Joseph Fields and Jerome Chodorov's *My Sister Eileen*, Hart and Kaufman's *You Can't Take It With You*, supplemented by respective flyers, programs, and reviews. A photostat of the Harvard University manuscript of Thomas Wolfe's only known play, *Mannerhouse*, together with files of correspondence regarding a proposed New York production as well as correspondence concerning literary rights to the play and its production by the Yale University Dramatic Society in 1949 are unique items in the collection. Director Heller's prompt copies of the 1937 London production of *You Can't Take*

It With You and Edwin Justin Mayer's *Children of Darkness*, as performed at
the Bucks County Playhouse in New Hope, Pennsylvania in 1948, are also of
more than routine interest. Rounding out the collection are a number of
Shakespearean acting versions, books, and programs.

Muriel Kirkland Collection

Seven manuscript diaries comprising the personal records of actess Muriel
Kirkland's experiences in the theatre, on cross-country and USO tours, and
notes on plays and fellow actors provide information on theatre in America
during the 1930s and 1940s. The diaries are illustrated with news clippings,
reviews, and scenes and interspersed with letters from Ralph Barton, Margo
Jones, Ed Begley, John Golden, Elmer Rice, Stuart Walker, Dorothy Stick-
ney, and Robert E. Sherwood among others. Kirkland notations and comments are to be found also on manuscripts and typescripts including Zoë
Akins' *The Greeks Had a Word for It* and Arthur Hopkins' *Remember This
Day*. Among the visual resources are an original Bert Sharkey pen and ink and
wash drawing depicting the actress in a scene from *The Greeks Had a Word for
It* with Dorothy Hall and Vera Teasdale and a 1939 David L. Swasey portrait
of Miss Kirkland. Photographs, posters, and programs make up the balance
of the collection.

Maurice Evans Collection

The American career of Maurice Evans, whose first appearances on the
stage were in amateur dramatizations of Thomas Hardy's novels, is revealed
in a handsome scrapbook collection, mounted on French rag paper and
bound it twenty blue fabrikoid boxed folios for his attorney Lloyd V. Almirall. The wealth of material includes reviews, programs, photographs, clippings, letters, flyers, and memorabilia for George Bernard Shaw's *The Apple
Cart*, Terence Rattigan's *The Browning Version*, John Patrick's *Teahouse of the
August Moon*, Shaw's *Heartbreak House* and *Man and Superman*, the musical
Tenderloin, *Shakespeare Revisited*, Frederick Knott's *Dial 'M' for Murder*, his
G. I. Hamlet, and his performances at New York City Center for the 1949-1952
seasons. Prompt scripts of Shakespeare's *Twelfth Night* and Henry James' *The
Aspern Papers*, stage managers' workbooks for *G. I. Hamlet* and *Man and
Superman*, typewritten texts of lectures, and souvenir programs (bound in full
morocco) enhance this eye-filling collection.

The Players Pipe Night Tape Collection

Pipe Nights at The Players began shortly after the turn of the century as
carefree, informal midnight revelries where steins of beer and ale and church-
warden pipes were the order of the day. On these occasions talents as diverse

as Mark Twain's resistless humor, Charlie Chaplin's harlequinesque antics, Harry Houdini's mind boggling feats, and Errol Garner's cool piano played to standing room only. The first tape-recorded session was the Lunt-Fontanne Pipe Night in 1963. Since then programs in honor of Maurice Chevalier, Victor Borge, James Cagney, Danny Kaye, Fredric March and Florence Eldridge, Jack Benny, Marlene Dietrich, Joseph Papp, Brooks Atkinson, Milton Berle, Schuyler Chapin, Edward R. Murrow, Rex Harrison, Bob Fosse, and Irwin Shaw have been taped for posterity—as well as the opera and the circus and the musical entertainments of *South Pacific*, *My Fair Lady*, and *Very Good Eddie*.

Paintings and Memorabilia

A unique collection of theatre art virtually obscures the walls of The Players. Edwin Booth himself presented a number of portraits including fifteen John Neagle works of American and English actors and actresses. Among these paintings are canvases of Edmund Kean as Richard III, William B. Wood, Joseph Cowell, and Mrs. Darley as Juliet. There are the masterly John Singer Sargent portraits of Edwin Booth, Lawrence Barrett, and Joseph Jefferson; a Gilbert Stuart painting of the actor-manager Thomas Abthorpe Cooper; Johann Zoffany's David Garrick; a Gainsborough likeness of the comedian Robert Palmer; John W. Alexander's rendering of Joseph Jefferson as Bob Acres in Sheridan's *The Rivals*; Eastman Johnson's John McCullough as Virginius; John Collier's life-size portrait of Edwin Booth as Cardinal Richelieu; Thomas Sully's George Frederick Cooke; caricaturist Thomas Nast's oil of William E. Burton, and a painting of Charles Kemble attributed to the school of Sir Thomas Laurence. Many other canvases by artists Henry Inman, J. Alden Weir, Childe Hassam, Robert Reid, William Merritt Chase, John Henry Twachtman, Abbott Thayer, and others may be found in various nooks and crannies throughout the clubhouse.

More recent acquisitions include Everett Raymond Kinstlers's official club portraits of Dennis King and Alfred Drake; Gordon Stevenson's likeness of Howard Lindsay and Mark Twain; Sergei Bongart's James Cagney as Admiral Halsey in the movie *The Gallant Hours*; James Montgomery Flagg's oil of John Drew; Truman Fassett's lifesize painting of Walter Hampden as Cyrano de Bergerac; Paul Swann's life-size work of Nance O'Neil as Lady Macbeth; Florence Upton's painting of Mrs. Patrick Campbell, and John Dekker's oil of John Barrymore. There are bas-reliefs and portrait busts in bronze and marble; rare miniatures and daguerreotypes; a series of life and death masks; drawings, lithographs, mezzotints, aquatints, etchings and woodcuts—an impressive array of the vivid personalities who have made stage history.

Stage memorabilia on display include personal mementoes of such famous actors and actresses as Edwin Booth (including the John Rogers life mask),

Edwin Forrest, Lester Wallack, Adelaide Neilson, Fanny Kemble, Adelaide Ristori, Charles Albert Fechter, David Garrick, E. H. Sothern, Charlotte Cushman, Sarah Bernhardt, and Charles Macready. Edwin Forrest's tomahawk from *Metamora* and the staff Miss Cushman used as Meg Merrilies are among the plethora of properties, jewelry, and curios. The John Mulholland Magic Collection contains rare sets of magicians' cups and balls from Egypt, China, Japan, Turkey, East India, and the United Kingdom; playing cards and card cases; medallions; magicians' wands and fans; toy banks; a magical watch; an assortment of vanishing vases, as well as an unusual pair of Houdini's handcuffs.

Testimonies from researchers the world over substantiate the claim that The Walter Hampden-Edwin Booth Theatre Collection and Library is one of the most vital collections of drama the theatrical world possesses. Professors, instructors, and doctoral candidates from as far as the University of Wales, the University of Australia, and from colleges and universities in this country represent one type of library user making application for research studies. Their projects have included research on the staging of Edwin Booth's Shakespearean and non-Shakespearean productions, 19th-century English actors in America, the history of the Union Square Theatre, Winthrop Ames and the New Theatre, American burlesque, the stage career of John Wilkes Booth, John Barrymore's production of *Hamlet*, Walter Hampden's career as actor-manager, American actors as political activists, *The Black Crook*, The Players, conjuring, and superstitions in the theatre. Playwrights, authors, composers, and critics comprise another group who do extensive exploration on the theatre and the drama. Actors, directors, and publishers are all represented among today's researchers. Because of the extraordinary nature of its holdings, no material is available on interlibrary loan. Photocopying is permitted in most instances. The library is open to the qualified student of the theatre—scholar, writer, historian, and layperson upon application to the librarian.

THE WILLIAM SEYMOUR
THEATRE COLLECTION,
PRINCETON UNIVERSITY LIBRARY

Mary Ann Jensen, Curator

The presentation of the William Seymour Theatre Collection to Princeton University Library took place at a dinner held at the Graduate College of the University on Sunday evening, November 29, 1936. The speakers included E. L. D. Seymour, William Seymour's eldest son; President Harold Dodds of the University; the actor Charles Coburn; and Professor George C. D. Odell of Columbia University. On the tables, at the place of each guest, was a souvenir program to which was affixed a bookplate designed and lithographed by Kyra Markham at the request of the Seymour family. Each of the 800 plus books in the Seymour Collection held one of these plates depicting a proscenium stage lit by a pilot light and surrounded by a border containing the names of some of the theatres which Seymour had served: Union Square, Baldwin, Boston Museum, Palmer's, Tremont, Metropolitan Opera, Empire, Varieties, Booth's, and Old Globe. Indeed, the original Seymour library may still be identified by these bookplates. The citation on the second page of the booklet states that:

> the William Seymour Theatre Collection commemorates the late William Seymour, who served the stage for seventy years and whose library forms the nucleus of the collection. The curator invites you to make use of its facilities, and to contribute to its value as a repository for material relating to the history of the theatre and to the lives of those who have loved it.

Steadfast in this commitment, the heads of the collection have never departed from it. During its forty-four-year history, each of its three curators has perpetuated the invitation, expanding it to include not only theatrical materials but also holdings in dance, circus, motion pictures, television—all of the popular entertainments. The first curator, Robert H. Ball, was a member of the faculty in the Department of English. Although he officially held the title of curator from 1936 to 1939, he began his appointment as Honorary Curator when the gift arrived at Princeton in July 1934. Professor Ball was succeeded

Mary Ann Jensen is Curator of the William Seymour Theatre Collection, Princeton University Library, Princeton, NJ 08544.

Special Collections, Vol. 1(1), Fall 1981
© 1981 The Haworth Press

by Marguerite Loud McAneny, who served until her retirement in 1966. The present curator has held the position since July of that year. Until 1964 the post was only a part-time appointment. Now the staff of the collection consists of a full-time curator plus one full-time assistant and a somewhat flexible number of part-time assistants.

The technicalities of staffing the Collection are probably of far less general interest, however, than is the history of its establishment and growth, but this cannot be documented without some background discussion of the life of William Seymour.[1]

Seymour was born on December 19, 1855, the son of James Seymour and Lydia Griffiths Seymour. James Seymour was a famous Irish comedian and Mrs. Seymour was a well-known actress of the day. In 1858 the Seymours were playing the Varieties Theatre in New Orleans. That theatre was then under the management of, among others, Lawrence Barrett, who was to be influential in young Willie Seymour's professional development a few years later. But now, at the age of three, Master Seymour made his first stage appearance when he was carried on by his mother who was portraying Dame Beanstalk in the popular drama, *The Rent Day*; not long thereafter he made his second appearance, sliding across the stage in *The Sea of Ice*.

In 1862, on his seventh birthday, he played his first speaking part, the role of Skutler in *To Parents and Guardians*. While a boy he gained experience playing both male and female roles and had the opportunity to play the Duke of York to Barrett's Richard III. During those years in New Orleans he met Edwin Forrest, E. L. Davenport, Edwin and John Wilkes Booth, Joseph Jefferson, Charlotte Cushman, and many others who became important in his career.

William Seymour left New Orleans in April 1865, a few days after the assassination of President Lincoln. This tragedy, and the fact that the assassin had been a friend of his mother's, continued to interest Seymour profoundly throughout his life. The Seymour Papers contain reminiscences, clippings, and correspondence relating to the event. Earlier in that year of 1865, before leaving New Orleans, he had played Hendrick in *Rip Van Winkle* with Joseph Jefferson. In 1867 he made his New York debut, appearing in the same role with Jefferson at the old Olympic Theatre. He played with Jefferson in this part for more than five hundred nights.

Seymour's professional association with Edwin Booth began at Booth's Theatre in New York in 1869, as call boy and juvenile actor. A close friend of the Seymour family, Booth had visited the Seymour home a few days after William's birth. Booth engaged him in New Orleans in 1868 after the lad, on a few minutes' notice, had replaced a sick actor as the second grave digger in *Hamlet*. Impressed, Booth brought "Master Willie Seymour," as the young

---

[1] Much of the biographical information which follows is taken from a press release prepared by the Department of Public Information, Princeton University, in 1936.

apprentice was billed, into his company, thus offering him the opportunity to appear as the Player Queen to Edwin Booth's Hamlet. Seymour's season with Booth's Theatre ended in 1871, when he went to Boston to become a member of the Globe Theatre company, which had engaged Edwin Forrest for several weeks during that season. Forrest performed, although very ill, and last appeared on the stage as Richelieu on April 2, 1872 with William Seymour playing Francois in the final production.

Later that year Seymour returned to New Orleans, becoming stage manager at the Varieties Theatre on January 1, 1873. He remained there, under Barrett, until 1875. Then he went to work for A.M. Palmer as assistant stage manager at the old Union Square Theatre in New York City where he remained for two years, learning to stage productions as well as acting in them. In 1877 he was engaged by John McCullough for the latter's stock company in San Francisco. His contract was for two years; his salary, to be paid in gold, was set at $100 per week. Although his actual stipend may have been less than that figure, the San Francisco years were not insignificant. They included an appearance in *The Passion Play*, which featured James O'Neill as the Christus. In 1879 Lawrence Barrett was bringing a touring company east from Portland, Oregon, and Seymour was engaged to manage the extensive tour.

In the winter of that year Seymour became stage manager of the Boston Museum, which was under the general management of R. M. Field. His association with the Boston Museum lasted for the next decade, as he cast and directed plays, saw to the construction of scenery, wrote program copy—in short, carried out the responsibilities of an artistic director. Additionally, he occasionally acted in a variety of small parts. Another member of the company was May Davenport, the youngest daughter of tragedian E. L. Davenport and sister to the popular actress, Fanny Davenport. Early in 1882 William Seymour married May Davenport. The marriage, lasting until Mrs. Seymour's death in 1927, produced five children.

It has been important to detail the activities of William Seymour's career because the theatre collection at Princeton is built largely upon his many associates. Fortunately for theatre historians, Seymour was more than an actor-manager and director. He had an archivist's instinct for collecting and saving, not only his own files but the papers of members of the Davenport family as well.

From 1889 to 1897 Seymour was attached to the enterprises of Abbey, Schoeffel and Grau as acting manager. Although based primarily at the Tremont Theatre in Boston, his services and abilities occasionally took him elsewhere. The last few years of the century he was associated with Sol Smith Russell, with E. H. Sothern and Julia Marlowe, and with Maude Adams. In 1900-1901 he was resident manager at the Metropolitan Opera House, but his longest association was as general stage director for Charles Frohman and the Empire Theatre from 1901 to 1919.

The Twenties were active years for Seymour as actor as well as director until the death of Mrs. Seymour in 1927, after which he retired to his long-time home in South Duxbury, Massachusetts. During the next few years he continued to direct and advise theatrical organizations in local schools, and he sat for a portrait by Mary Evangeline Walker. This charming likeness, although only the face and head were completed, hangs in the reading area of the William Seymour Theatre Collection at Princeton today. After a short illness, Seymour died on October 2, 1933, at the age of seventy-seven.

A tale, possibly apocryphal, but nonetheless a good story, has been passed along the curatorial generations of Princeton's theatre collection. It was said that William Seymour had thought that his papers would go to Harvard University's theatrical archives, but his youngest daughter, Fanny, was married to Richard M. Field, a member of the faculty of Princeton University and grandson of R. M. Field of the Boston Museum. The Fields, it is said, persuaded her sister and brothers, all direct heirs to the material, to give William Seymour's memorabilia to Princeton, thus establishing a new theatre collection in his memory.

Records of the period indicate that it was originally intended that the Laurence Hutton Collection, which had been in the possession of the University Library for some years, should be housed with the Seymour Collection. This plan never materialized, however, and the Hutton Collection continues to be shelved in other divisions of the Department of Rare Books and Special Collections, of which the Theatre Collection is also a part.

It did not take long, however, before the William Seymour Theatre Collection began to grow with the additions of other significant performing arts archives. Originally housed under a gable on the top floor of Princeton's old Pyne Library, even the Seymour Papers barely fit into the allocated space. The *Report of the Princeton University Library* for the year ending June 30, 1935 summarizes the nuclear collection as follows: ". . . thousands of plays and play bills, photographs, clippings, books on the drama and on the stage, biographies of famous actors, books on stage management and on costume, together with large numbers of letters from the celebrated actors and managers with whom he was associated."

Want of space, even in the earliest years of the collection's development, has never been a deterrent to its growth. In its infancy, the collection was augmented by gifts of books of both rare and general interest. Within five years of its dedication, the collection had not only doubled in size but had incorporated a second large archive which rendered the term "theatre collection" a misnomer because of its limitations.

This later acquisition was the gift of the Joseph T. McCaddon Collection of circus materials. Joseph McCaddon was the brother-in-law of James A. Bailey of Barnum & Bailey and was also the business manager of the Barnum & Bailey enterprises at the turn of the century. The McCaddon Collection, as it is

Unfinished portrait of William Seymour painted by Mary Evangeline Walker about 1932-33.

generally called, consists of the working papers of the company up to its merger with Ringling Bros. in 1907. It contains manuscripts, business records, photographs, couriers, posters, scrapbooks of clippings, route books, and designs for parade floats and costumes. While it is not one of our largest collections, it is a sizeable one. The circus documents have themselves doubled over the past forty years by our adding like material on a regular basis. We continue to consider circus a strong area of collecting and have very recently purchased some P. T. Barnum letters as well as an album containing photographs of the 1922 Ringling Bros. and Barnum & Bailey Combined Shows coast-to-coast tour.

Although the Princeton University curriculum has had an official Program in Theatre and Dance only since 1971, it has had an active theatrical tradition for the past one hundred years, with Triangle Club and Theatre Intime as its two major undergraduate producing organizations. The archives of both organizations are housed in the Theatre Collection, as are the records of McCarter Theatre, originally built for Triangle Club but currently celebrating its fiftieth year as a professional theatre. There are many other performing groups which appear on campus each year, and the Collection attempts to maintain records of as many productions as possible. This is a difficult task in that it is not unusual to be able to select from as many as seven or eight productions on campus on a given weekend and that the most reliable method of obtaining a playbill for the files is for the curator to attend the performance. In part, because of these records, we have been able to document some of the earliest theatrical endeavors of such alumni as Booth Tarkington, Eugene O'Neill, F. Scott Fitzgerald, Norris Houghton, Myron McCormick, Joshua Logan, Bretaigne Windust, James Stewart, José Ferrer, Mel Ferrer, Wayne Rogers, Clinton Wilder, and Richard Barr—the list, Princeton says with pride, goes on and on and continues to grow. In recent years women are being added to the impressive roster, with no less pride.

Along the way it might appear that most of our donors are Princeton alumni—or at the very least, Princeton associates. The McCaddon Collection, after all, was donated by Joseph McCaddon's two sons, both of whom graduated from Princeton. There is a collection of film scripts from James Stewart, Class of 1932. The Bretaigne Windust Papers and the Clinton Wilder Papers are in the Theatre Collection. The Manuscript Division of Princeton University Library houses the Tarkington, the O'Neill, and the Fitzgerald collections, although the Theatre Collection also holds original source material relating to each of these three writers.

Although many of the collections, perhaps even most of them, have been donated by alumni or their heirs, this is not a criterion in terms of our collection development policy. The papers of George Crouse Tyler and of Max Gordon are among our holdings, for example, and neither of these two producers had a direct Princeton association. It should be noted, though, that the Max Gordon scripts are in The Walter Hampden-Edwin Booth Theatre Collection and Library at The Players, New York City, while his correspondence and some of his business records were given to Princeton. In the case of

George Tyler, Princeton has correspondence, scripts, business records, play-bills, and photographs.

On April 30, 1949 the Harvey S. Firestone Memorial Library was officially dedicated at Princeton, and the Theatre Collection had a new home on the second floor of that building. Much larger and more efficient than its original quarters—and no doubt easier for readers to find—the new space also filled up more quickly than had been anticipated. Over the next twenty-five years collections were shifted about and "temporarily" moved to other accommodations in order to make room for new acquisitions. By 1970, materials from the Theatre Collection were housed in six different locations in Firestone Library and in another storage facility a number of miles from the main campus. It would be several more years before they would again be brought together in a single area.

The first two decades in Firestone saw the addition of the Bretaigne Windust Papers, mentioned earlier. This collection of scripts, playbills, photographs, and miscellaneous items is interesting not only for its material relating to Windust's career on Broadway, in motion pictures, and in television but also for its wealth of information dealing with the University Players. This fascinating summer stock company, working in Falmouth, Massachusetts in the late 1920s and early 30s, included a staggering assemblage of young talent from all over the United States. In the company, at one point or another, were Windust, Joshua Logan, Henry Fonda, Margaret Sullavan, Myron McCormick, James Stewart, Mildred Dunnock, Kent Smith, Norris Houghton, and many others whose names have appeared on a marquee or two over the past fifty years.

Another era and facet of theatre history is reflected in the Albert M. Friend Collection of Eighteenth Century Theatre Drawings, acquired in the 1950s. The Friend Collection, so called in memory of the art historian who gathered it, contains stage designs and sketch books attributed to the Bibienas, Domenico Fossati, Lorenzo Sacchetti, Bernardino Galliari, and Josef Platzer. There are about three hundred drawings in all, and a published checklist of this collection is available from Princeton University Library upon request. Slightly later historically are the Mathews Family Papers, a small collection representing some of the activities of members of that family, including Madame Vestris. The Sam H. Harris Collection consists of 122 bound typescripts of plays produced by Mr. Harris, some of which are unique.

Although Princeton University is noted for its fine music library, popular sheet music and materials pertaining to the musical theatre are housed in the Theatre Collection. We have a fine collection, therefore, of piano vocal scores for musicals from the period 1920 to 1970. These were the gift of Robert Sour and are among the most frequently consulted of our holdings as far as Princeton undergraduates are concerned. Augmenting this collection is a gift from the Board of Trustees of Triangle Club, a gift made up of almost three hundred cassettes of original cast recordings of musicals. Although neither the scores nor the cassettes may circulate, they may be used in a small listening area adjacent to the Theatre Collection stacks. The equipment and other furnishings for the listening room were provided through the generosity of the Triangle Trustees and members of the Princeton Class of 1922, in memory of Russell Forgan. Forgan, a member of that class, was also a president of Triangle and a long-time member of the club's Board of Trustees.

Further source material for historians of the musical stage may be provided in the Tams-Witmark Archives.[2] Donated to the University in 1972, this is a collection of orchestrations, vocal and conductors' scores, promptbooks, and other musical material relating to operettas, comic operas, and musical comedies in the Tams-Witmark Music Library. The materials in this resource date from the early part of this century only.

From England Princeton has the L. Ashton Sly Collection, relating to historic musical comedies and their production there. This is a 137-volume collection of vocal scores and/or libretti for 123 musical comedies, comic operas, and operettas, including twenty-eight full production promptbooks. Most of the musical shows represented here date from 1890 to 1940. The twenty-eight promptbooks were made and used by L. Ashton Sly, a much-respected professional director of musical comedy revivals in southwest England and South Wales from just before World War II until the mid-1960s.

Although Otto Kahn was involved in the area of international finance, his papers reflect his activities as a patron of the arts as much as they do any of his other interests. For that reason, perhaps, they have been used most frequently by scholars in the arts and are therefore housed in the Theatre Collection at Princeton. The decision to incorporate them into this area of the Department of Rare Books and Special Collections was made in 1975, when the Theatre Collection was once again preparing to move into much larger quarters. It has proved to be a sensible decision, in that so much of the material in the Kahn Papers relates to material in our other files.

Space, or more accurately, the lack of it, has always been a problem for major performing arts repositories, and obviously Princeton's experience has not been exceptional. By the mid-1970s its collection had become so decentralized as to make retrieval of materials almost impossible on short notice. But a new location, again "temporary," was made available in 1976. At the time it was anticipated that this larger area would provide a ten-year growth potential for the collection, but by the end of 1977, the William Seymour Theatre Collection had again run out of room!

For about fourteen months all of its holdings were located in one area, but this Utopian situation came to an exciting end when the Warner Bros. Archives came to Princeton. In truth, only a part of the Warner Bros. Archives

---

[2] Similar material from Tams-Witmark Music Library, Inc. may be found at the Library of Congress and at the University of Wisconsin in Madison.

came to Princeton—the business records. The production records of the company are at the University of Southern California. A very useful catalogue for the archive was made available at each institution by Warner Communications, Inc., so that it is possible to know which materials are located in New Jersey and which are on the West Coast. Because of the size of the archive—at Princeton, files are housed in three separate buildings—it is necessary to make an appointment with the curator well in advance in order to use the material, and no photocopying is permitted. At this writing, the cut-off date for material in the files is June 30, 1967. Further information about material from this archive may be obtained by writing to the curator. Again, because of its size—the printed catalogue itself is contained in 1,648 volumes—it is not possible for the staff to answer telephone reference questions regarding the Warner Bros. Archives.

The William Seymour Theatre Collection, since its beginning, has always owned an impressive number of British and American playbills from the 18th century through the current Broadway season. There have almost always been film scripts and film stills on file, and both of these resources have multiplied over the past ten years. Among the present ongoing projects within the collection, the cataloging of such material is taking top priority. As these activities take place, we continue to add to the collection with the acquisition of new materials, the most recent being the Woody Allen Papers. One dares to guess that not much dust will accumulate on the boxes containing those manuscripts!

Although departmental policy is not to lend noncirculating material from the collections for any reason, exceptions are made. While we would not lend special materials to individuals under any circumstances, occasionally we do allow other institutions to exhibit materials we own. Materials from our collections are used regularly for shows in the exhibition gallery of Firestone Library, and in the last twelve years the Theatre Collection has sponsored a major exhibit in that gallery on the average of once every three years.

One, in 1980, dealing with the history of ballet from 1616 to 1916, was titled *Let Joy Be Unconfined* and ran from February to May. In putting this exhibition together, the staff discovered dance material scattered (and "hidden") in many other areas of our shelves, not just in our rather meager dance files. It was confirmed, in fact, that Princeton does have a dance collection, but that it is in desperate need of being cataloged as such, because much of the material is to be found among theatre or circus memorabilia. Furthermore, we were privileged to work with and borrow from the private collection of Mr. Allison Delarue, a writer and dance historian who has been one of the longtime friends of the Theatre Collection at Princeton. The exhibition proved to be one of the most colorful held in Firestone, getting much attention from the press and the public.[3] A very happy consequence was that Mr. Delarue has

---

[3] A limited number of catalogues for this exhibition are still available from the Theatre Collection, Princeton University Library, $3 each.

since given some of the books from his collection to the University, thus
enhancing our ballet materials. The Theatre Collection will continue to build
this resource in the future.

And so, crowded shelves and warehouse conditions notwithstanding, our
commitment to growth and expansion continues. A small but very active part
of our space is given over to an open stack area containing noncirculating
reference materials pertinent to the performing arts plus the library's collections of books on motion pictures and on dance. The collection subscribes to
approximately 120 current periodicals annually, the unbound issues of which
are also kept on its shelves. When bound, most of the volumes are shelved in
the building's open stacks.

At this writing holdings in the William Seymour Theatre Collection are
available to qualified scholars, unless restricted for some reason, although it
cannot be stated frequently enough that it is necessary to make an appointment
well in advance in order to have access to primary source materials. While
Firestone Library is at present an open stack library, its special collections do
have shorter hours than the building itself, however. The Theatre Collection is
open from 9 a.m. until 5 p.m., Monday through Friday during Princeton's
regular school year. In that the University does not hold summer sessions, the
collection hours differ during those months.

Plans are being drawn to close the Firestone stacks in the summer of 1981.
To ensure that researchers who do not have regular borrowing privileges from
Princeton University's library system will be allowed into the building, advance arrangements will be more necessary than ever before. Appropriate
identification will continue to be required: a college or university identification card is the best form, but in lieu of that a letter from the curator confirm-
ing an appointment may also be accepted.

The William Seymour Theatre Collection[4] has grown in all ways since its
inception almost a half-century ago. In physical size and in scope of its holdings, in size of staff, and in reputation as a valuable repository for primary and
secondary source materials in the performing arts, it has developed into one of
the major collections in the United States. The staff acknowledges this with
gratitude, for it makes our jobs more interesting. We acknowledge also the
excellent groundwork of Professor Robert Ball and later the many years of
dedicated work by Marguerite McAneny in building the collections. We appreciate the support and loyalty of numerous other friends, not the least of
whom are descendants of the Davenport-Seymour family, who continue to
remember us generously. And we value our readers—our *raison d'être*.

---

[4] In referring to the William Seymour Theatre Collection we mean the entire repository of
performing arts materials at Princeton University. This should not be confused with the William
Seymour Papers, the name given the theatrical memorabilia amassed by Mr. Seymour, and which
formed the original part of the William Seymour Theatre Collection at Princeton.

Thus, in addressing the readers of this article, we wish to reiterate the original invitation from Professor Ball regarding the collection in 1936: "The curator invites you to make use of its facilities, and to contribute to its value as a repository for material relating to the history of the theatre and to the lives of those who have loved it."

THE HOBLITZELLE THEATRE ARTS LIBRARY,[1] UNIVERSITY OF TEXAS AT AUSTIN

William H. Crain, Curator

In February 1956 The Hoblitzelle Foundation presented on permanent loan to the University of Texas at Austin the Albert Davis Collection of theatrical artifacts—posters, programs, clippings, photographs, and other ephemera—collected by Mr. Davis from 1874 until 1942. The collection, aside from a few items concerning the European Theatre in the 18th and 19th centuries, is restricted to the American stage and such related areas as moving pictures, circus, magic and magicians, and pugilism. It can be dated from about 1830 to about 1940, with the richest section in the period 1860-1920. There is little manuscript material, and the greatest strength of the Davis Collection is in its photographs. Mr. Davis started asking performers for photographs during his boyhood and continued the habit into his old age. He also collected from dealers. He was fortunate in getting the cabinet photograph file of a theatrical agent and the eleven by fourteen inch sepia prints of production photographs made by the Byron, the White, and the Hall Studios between 1890 and 1925. All the best known stars are represented along with many of the lesser lights.

In June 1958 the Hoblitzelle Foundation generously presented the Messmore Kendall Collection to the University of Texas at Austin on permanent loan. This collection is especially rich in English playbills from 1754 to the 1830s, bound and unbound (about 200,000), in 18th- and 19th-century engraved theatrical portraits, in extra-illustrated books, in pamphlets, in material on the Shakespeare-Bacon controversy, and in holograph materials, as well as a watercolor portrait attributed to J. M. W. Turner. The Kendall Collection also contains many opera and concert programs and many 19th- and early 20th-century pieces of sheet music and music covers.

An interesting part of the Messmore Kendall Collection is the material concerning magic gathered by Harry Houdini, which consists of books, periodicals, photographs, clippings, posters, playbills, flyers, correspondence, and holograph descriptions of illusions and oddities. It constitutes almost a history of stage magic from the 16th century to Houdini's own day. Also, there is a great deal of William Winter material—his books, various mementoes, some of his poems and letters.

William H. Crain is Curator of The Hoblitzelle Theatre Arts Library, Humanities Research Center, The University of Texas, Austin, TX 78712.

The Davis and Kendall Collections, later given outright to the Hoblitzelle Theatre Arts Library, were joined by two earlier collections possessed by the University of Texas. As early as 1942, King Vidor presented the University with all the material he had used in making the moving picture, *H. M. Pulham, Esq.* through Interstate Circuit Incorporated, Karl Hoblitzelle's moving picture theatre chain. Manuscripts, stills, designs, publicity portraits, and many artifacts were contained in the King Vidor collection. The most interesting were a series of small model sets with a viewer which, on the principle of the periscope, gave one a camera's-eye view of the set. These small sets and the viewer were used in planning camera shots and are unusual because such equipment has been replaced by the sketchbook.

In June 1954, the Hoblitzelle Foundation had deposited on loan at the University (later given outright) the James Orchard Halliwell-Phillipps edition of Shakespeare. This imposing edition consists of sixteen large folio volumes of plays and sixteen portfolio volumes containing illustrative material for the plays.

At the same time as the Davis and Kendall Collections were made available to the Hoblitzelle Theatre Arts Library, the Foundation also gave the library a magnificent collection of sheet music used in vaudeville programs, legitimate theatre performances, silent and sound moving pictures, and concerts by the theatrical orchestra alone. Some items were original complete orchestrations for films such as *The Hunchback of Notre Dame*. Though a great deal of this music was destroyed by fire in 1965, enough remains to make an impressive research tool. Since Karl Hoblitzelle and the Foundation were responsible for the first five important collections in the library, it was natural that the theatre arts library should be named Hoblitzelle.

The Norman Bel Geddes Collection came to the Theatre Arts Library in December 1958, the gift of the Tobin Foundation of San Antonio, Texas. This collection contains Bel Geddes' theatrical, industrial, and military materials. Only the theatrical part of the collection has been cataloged; the industrial and military part remains much as Bel Geddes organized it. At least 2,500 technical drawings, eight stage models, 800 renderings, 3,000 letters and specification lists, 5,000 sketches, 5,000 photographs, and numerous industrial and military models are represented in the collection. The spectacular set and costume renderings for *The Miracle*, *The Divine Comedy*, and *King Lear* are among our favorite items for display. Visitors are also impressed by the ultra-realistic *Dead End* stage model and the gigantic *The Eternal Road* model.

Among the industrial models are cars, buses, trains, and boats, most of which were used in Futurama in the New York World's Fair of 1939. The Theatre Arts Library also has some of the tiny military models used to create the World War II battle pictures with which *Life* kept an enthralled public up to date on the progress of the war. The battleship models were all made of silver, and jewelers were employed on this project to hand-work the fine details of these models. I had always thought the silver was used because the jewelers could work it more easily than lead, but Mrs. Bel Geddes told me that wartime priorities made silver less expensive than lead. One dissertation, part of another, and two or three theses have already been written or are in progress from the Bel Geddes Collection.

In 1961, through the efforts of Chancellor Harry Ransom, the Robert Downing Theatre Collection was added to the expanding Hoblitzelle Theatre Arts Library to give support to its research potential. This collection consists of about 10,000 books on the history and theory of theatre,[2] numerous stage and screen photographs, blueprints, costume designs, theatrical correspondence, prompt scripts, autograph materials, prints, posters, typescripts of plays, Lacy acting editions, American plays inscribed by their authors, and first editions of Tennessee Williams' plays up to 1962.

Since Downing had been a stage manager in New York, there are comprehensive files on all his shows such as *A Streetcar Named Desire*, *Cat on a Hot Tin Roof*, and *Camelot*. Adding to the value of his collection are the letters and autographs of the subjects tipped into their respective biographies and memoirs, as well as Downing's own notes on matters of which he had personal knowledge or experience. Downing's interest in the Hoblitzelle Theatre Arts Library did not end with the sale of his collection. He continued to send us clippings, photographs, and books until his death in 1974, at which time he bequeathed to us all the theatrical material still in his possession.

The John Gassner Collection was purchased and added to the library in 1965 and 1966. The most important parts of this collection are the holograph and typescript versions of Dr. Gassner's many articles, lectures, reviews, and books (the proofs of some of his published materials are present as well as the final printed versions), and his voluminous correspondence. The articles, lectures, and books show Dr. Gassner's erudition; the correspondence shows his kindness. Included are pamphlets, clippings, playscripts, photographs, periodicals, personal memorabilia, and about 3,000 books used by Gassner as source material in his work. One of the pamphlets is the first edition of the first pamphlet written by Sean O'Casey. Two dissertations have already been written from the John Gassner Collection.

The G. C. Howard Collection contains manuscripts, playbills, lithographs, tintypes, posters, sheet music, and scrapbooks used to document the Howard and Fox productions of *Uncle Tom's Cabin* as adapted for the stage. There are also over 200 editions of other 19th-century plays produced by Howard and Fox. One dissertation has been drawn from the *Uncle Tom's Cabin* materials in the G. C. Howard Collection. The Leo Perper Collection is strong in dance materials and contains playbills and programs from 1930 through 1969 together with photographs and reviews of performances. It is the basis of our truly remarkable collection of dance materials. The Robert Joffrey Collection includes production photographs, posters, playbills, souvenir programs, and reviews of the Robert Joffrey Ballet Company.

The Stanley Marcus Collection of Sicilian Marionettes is a gift of Stanley Marcus of Dallas. The marionettes, some sixty-five in number, form a full company for the *Orlando Furioso* which was dramatized as a serial and played repeatedly by the marionette theatre managers. The figures were used as part of the decor in Nieman-Marcus' Fortnight in Italy and then given to the Hoblitzelle Theatre Arts Library. The marionettes, which are a little over a hundred years old, are rod puppets, operated by a rod running through the body, and cords for operation of the limbs. Some are made of cloth and wood, some entirely of wood. Some have china doll-heads with the glass eyes still intact; some have heads carved from wood and have painted eyes. All the human characters are elaborately costumed. Though the marionettes have been restored, their original armor remains.

The Marie Tempest Collection came to the Hoblitzelle Theatre Arts Library in 1968 and contains items relating to Dame Marie Tempest, one of the foremost British comediennes from the turn of the century to the early 1940s. It contains photographs, manuscript material, scrapbooks, and personal memorabilia. There are 116 separate photographs of Dame Marie (personal or in character, alone or with fellow performers). There are also two photograph albums, one of youthful pictures with autograph captions, the other of pictures taken later in her life while on an automobile trip in France. Among the manuscript materials are letters about Dame Marie from Hector Bolitho, Charles B. Cochran, Leslie Henson, W. J. Macqueen-Pope to Major Thomas Loring, her son, as well as letters from Sir Henry Irving to Mrs. Gordon Lennox (Marie Tempest) and from Marie Tempest to a Mr. Berman. There are two diaries in the collection. One is Dame Marie's travel diary of her third husband, William Graham Browne, describing a journey with her from Sydney, Australia to New York. Also among the manuscript, are the typescript of a broadcast by W. J. Macqueen-Pope about Dame Marie Tempest written for a series called *Stars of Their Day*, along with the typescript of a biographical sketch by her husband, with minor corrections in the actress' handwriting.

Besides Marie Tempest's diaries, further autobiographical manuscript materials consist of two copies of the typescript of the first six chapters of an unfinished autobiography with autograph corrections and twelve autograph pages of anecdotes, a typescript of the first three chapters of *My Wander Years* (also unfinished), and an incomplete typescript of Article VII of *Fifty Years of Memories* by Marie Tempest, a part of a serial autobiography published in *Pearson's Magazine* in 1935, Dame Marie's 50th year in the theatre. There are two scrapbooks—her first and a book of clippings presented to her on the occasion of her golden jubilee in the theatre in 1935. Among her personal memorabilia are items relating to the establishment of the Marie Tempest

Ward for indigent actors and actresses at St. George's Hospital in London with the proceeds of her golden jubilee matinee in Drury Lane (a public address appointing Dame Marie a Life Governor of St. George's Hospital, the beautifully illuminated Marie Tempest Endowment Trust Deed, and the handsomely enameled key to the Marie Tempest Ward); a certificate stating that she had been elected a Fellow of the Royal Academy of Music; her address book; and her make-up box.

The Pat Rooney Collection also came to the Hoblitzelle Theatre Arts Library in 1968. Much of this material was collected with a view to using in writing an autobiography. The collection is rich in materials having to do with the business and legal side of show business. Besides 272 pictures of the three Pat Rooneys and their friends and relations (with emphasis on Pat II), there are a 61-page typescript of family history starting with Pat I and taking the story well into the career of Pat II, another typed version of a part of the Pat Rooney story, typed pages of anecdotes and observations, lists of theatres Pat II played and performers he played with, newspaper clippings, a genealogy, and family papers such as marriage licenses, insurance policies, and Pat III's baby book. Among the business papers, there is correspondence concerning the rights to *The Daughter of Rosie O'Grady*, a popular Rooney vehicle, and the litigation between Pat Rooney II and Warner Brothers over those rights. Another interesting item is a book containing the papers drawn up to create "The Pat Rooney Co., Inc.," the purpose of which was to promote, produce, and manage vaudeville plays, acts, and sketches. There are eighteen contracts from the turn of the century to 1955 as well as other legal papers. The collection also contains eleven manuscripts of plays and sketches and one poem honoring George M. Cohan. There are about thirty pieces of printed sheet music for which Pat II wrote the lyrics and/or the music or which were associated with him, as well as thirty-one manuscript orchestrations. Besides being a good source of biographical data on the Rooney family, the collection contains much valuable material on the workings of show business, especially vaudeville.

The Jule Styne Collection contains all the material Styne produced from the beginning of his career through *Funny Girl*. In the collection are the musical manuscripts representing all the day-to-day changes in the score, as well as correspondence, production notes, and company notes placed on the callboard by the director. Among the latter is an amusing note, placed on the callboard by the director of *Funny Girl*, having to do with the correct pronunciation of Barbra Streisand's last name. The director had spent a great deal of time learning it and felt that everyone in the company should make an equal effort.

The William H. Crain Collection, like Topsy in *Uncle Tom's Cabin*, has just grown over the years as need and/or opportunity dictated. The first item, or at least the first item of any importance, was a collection of Alexandre Benois material consisting of five set renderings and some sixty-five costume renderings for an operetta entitled *Don Philippe*, which was produced in Paris during the Nazi occupation. The designs were accompanied by xerox copies of the reviews. A few years after the Crain collection came, Countess Woronzoff, who had sold the original collection through the dealer Ifan Kyrle Fletcher, arrived in the United States with about sixteen more costume designs, two sketches of properties, several production stills, the libretto, and the score folded in a real Benois poster for the show. Countess Woronzoff, who, as Barbara Nikisch, had written the libretto, played the feminine lead, and, as she told it, talked Benois into designing the show, had an interesting tale to tell about the history of *Don Philippe*. The show was an immediate success, but some ill-wisher reported to the Nazi authorities that the Countess and the composer were Jewish and the show closed. By the time this untruth was laid to rest, the show had died.

Other designers whose work is represented in the Crain Collection are: Edward Gordon Craig, Alexandra Exter, Jo Mielziner, Léon Bakst, Ernest Stern, Zig, Freddy Wittop, Erte, Brunelleschi, Louis Curti, Ranson, Alex Shanks, Hugh Willoughby, Weldy, Emile Gallois, Motley, Houghton, and Luigi Bartezago. The Crain Collection also includes books, programs, posters, photographs, negatives, moving picture footage, manuscript material, costumes, and porcelain figurines. Among the costumes are ten Diaghilev costumes—five by Léon Bakst for the ballet *Narcisse*, three by Nicholas Roerich for the ballet *The Rites of Spring*, one by Natalia Gontcharova for the ballet *Le Coq d'Or*, and one by Bakst for the ballet *Sleeping Princess*.

The Crain Collection also encompasses the entire Fred Fehl Archive of theatrical photographs, from which the illustrations for the book *On Broadway* were derived, and the Joseph Abeles Collection, which comprises 80,000 prints and negatives, both portraits and publicity pictures, of stage personalities and other public figures from 1934 to 1978. Among the moving picture items is a collection of the earliest moving picture work of Tobe Hooper, the director of *Texas Chain Saw Massacre*. Among the artifacts are stills showing how certain shots and effects were achieved. Also in the Crain moving picture material is an unpublished typescript biography of Robert Flaherty by Paul Rotha and Basil Wright together with the moving picture stills and other photographs intended to illustrate it. This manuscript was too erudite for the publishers, who later brought out a more popular biography.

My friend and colleague, Edwin Neal, who had made possible the purchase of the Tobe Hooper Collection, also discovered another cache of moving picture material containing 40,000 stills from major moving pictures (1910-1979), fifteen 16-millimeter trailers for moving pictures, 2,000 television and radio stills (1940-1979), 150 signed portraits of moving picture and television stars, 500 "behind the scenes" pictures, 200 press books (1950-1979), 2,000 negatives from studio photographers' files of television, radio, and film per-

Mannequin and poster display in the Hoblitzelle Theatre Arts Library. (Reproduced with permission of the Hoblitzelle Theatre Arts Collection, Humanities Research Center, University of Texas at Austin.)

sonalities, forty motion picture and television manuscripts, three original drawings, fifty 35-millimeter slides from major motion pictures (actually frames from the films mounted in slide mounts), 250 lobby cards (1950-1959), and fifty posters of major motion pictures.

Other collections consisting entirely of moving picture material include the Edward Carrick Collection (the name Edward Carrick was assumed by Edward Anthony Craig, son of Edward Gordon Craig) with over 1,400 original designs, 476 by Carrick himself and 976 by other prominent film designers from 1930 to 1950. The Alfred Junge Collection has over 170 original designs and 5,000 stills and design photographs made for British films from 1920 to 1960. These two collections provide a good foundation for the study of British film history, especially with regard to film design.

The Hoblitzelle Interstate Circuit Collection, given to the library by the Hoblitzelle Foundation circa 1976, holds over 450,000 cinema artifacts from the turn of the century through 1973. It includes photographs and records of the Interstate movie theatres as well as lobby cards and publicity materials. The E. V. Richards Collection is rich in pictures of theatres and in material on theatre management and publicity. It also has several of the life-size portraits of movie stars that used to hang in the lobbies of theatres.

The Ernest Lehman Collection at Austin consists of all his working papers from the beginning of his career through *The Sound of Music*, including early magazine articles and projects that were turned down. We have the day-to-day script changes and shooting schedules for *Who's Afraid of Virginia Woolf?* and *The Sound of Music*, which Lehman produced, and there are designs, sketchbooks, and casting portraits, including Elizabeth Taylor's contract with all the little "perks" she demanded as well as the million dollars she made for acting in *Virginia Woolf*. One doctoral dissertation has been based on this collection.

Another special collection, that of Philip Sills, has thousands of lobby cards and posters dating from 1940 to 1970. The John Robbins Collection contains from 150,000 to 200,000 movie stills dating from 1910 to the 1970s, contained in loose-leaf notebooks and manila folders arranged by performers. Each of the stars is sure to have a notebook; the featured players are sometimes grouped on single notebooks. The stills within a notebook are arranged more or less chronologically.

The library's Maurice Zolotow Collection consists of biographical matter—most of it originally relating to Marilyn Monroe, followed by a sizable amount of John Wayne material.

Mention must be made of the collection of title cards. Both Messmore Kendall and Harry Houdini dabbled in the moving picture industry and so had access to title cards and used these once expendable, and now very scarce, items as dividers between different batches of programs, engravings, and other materials. As a result, the Theatre Arts Library has the titles of over a hundred films, in some cases almost complete sets. The artwork on some of the title cards is beautiful.

The Joe E. Ward Collection of 19th- and 20th-century circus memorabilia includes photographs, letters, programs, playbills, posters, periodicals, route books, and costumes. Other interests of Ward are also represented; for instance, the collection contains Sousa's band uniform and trombone as well as four bound volumes of letters having to do with Sousa's Marine Band. There is also a blazer that was worn by Fred Waring, and a large chunk of the battleship *Texas*, which we use as a doorstop. The main strength of the collection, however, is in the circus material. Ward was an old gentleman who graduated as an engineer in the early part of the present century from the University of Texas at Austin (then *the* University of Texas). He was a successful consulting engineer who arranged his life so that his spare time was spent in clowning with Ringling Brothers and Barnum and Bailey. When he grew too old to clown actively, he followed the tour every year until his death. Since he was a very chauvinistic alumnus of the University of Texas, all his clown suits were orange and white—the school colors. The suggestion that Ward might give his collection to the Hoblitzelle was made by Richard Fleming, who, as a volunteer, was curator of a collection of writings by Texas students, ex-students, and faculty. When the Ward Collection is combined with the 16th through 19th-century materials of the Davis and Kendall collections, the Hoblitzelle Theatre Arts Library spans much of circus history.

A great costumer's books, clippings (both personal and source), costume renderings, photographs, and personal memorabilia are held in the Lucy Barton Collection. One of the most interesting items is a nearly complete set of the original drawings for Miss Barton's book, *Historic Costume for the Stage*. The drawings are signed by David Sarvis, the artist. The E. P. Conkle Collection is made up of books, clippings, manuscripts, correspondence, and personal memorabilia such as grade books, containing names of famous personalities. The scripts for nearly all of Dr. Conkle's plays are in this collection, as well as some short stories and a novel.

The B. Iden Payne Collection includes the manuscript of Dr. Payne's autobiography, *A Life in a Wooden O*, plus correspondence, tapes, clippings, programs, and souvenir programs. Only half of Dr. Payne's manuscript has been published. When his memoirs had brought him to Carnegie Tech, he dropped his own life and wrote almost exclusively about his method of Shakespearean production, known as Modified Elizabethan Staging. The materials include a wealth of material, on paper and in memories, on his life from 1946 to 1976 at the University of Texas at Austin.

Among other collections here at Texas, the Frances Starr Collection contains photographs, programs, souvenir programs, clippings, correspondence, and personal memorabilia of this turn-of-the-century Belasco star. There are many photographs of Miss Starr, both personal and in character, at all stages of her career and production stills from all her early Belasco plays as well as many of her later performances. There is a file of her fan mail and opening night telegrams. Her correspondence ranges from fan letters written by James

Huneker to the birth announcement of Efrem Zimbalist, Jr. The Lester Sweyd Collection contains photographs, many of them autographed, but the main part of the collection is made up of clippings about theatre, dance, opera, popular music, movies, television, circus—anything connected with show business—taken from New York and New Jersey newspapers. The Yale Puppeteers Collection includes five string marionettes, several scripts, and some pictorial material. Two of the marionettes are so-called portrait puppets of Alfred Lunt and Lynne Fontanne in *Amphytryon 38*. The Stanley Young and Nancy Ross Collection contains play and novel manuscripts, articles, art works, correspondence, playbills, and souvenir programs. The Edward G. Fletcher Collection consists of books, clippings, advertisements, catalogues, and programs.

Some additional named collections in the Hoblitzelle Theatre Arts Library are the George Greenberg Collection of books and manuscripts, the Elsie Leslie Milliken Collection of memorabilia and autographed pictures, the Burl Ives Collection of folk music and performance records, the Simon Lissom Collection of theatrical designs, the manuscript plays from the New York Poet's Theatre, the Harry Sandler Collection of theatre programs, the University microfilm series of dissertations in theatre and drama (incomplete), the J. Scott Smart Collection of costumes and art works, a Hirschfeld Collection of some sixteen drawings by the famous theatre caricaturist, the Orswell Opera Collection of programs and librettos, the Overton Puppets (once used on the Chautauqua Circuit), a complete set of the Boydell Shakespeare engravings, the Sherman Brothers Collection of music and other material relating to the movie *Mary Poppins*, and the J. C. Trewin Collection of British programs from the 1930s to the recent past.

It must be remembered that the Hoblitzelle Theatre Arts Library is only one part of the Humanities Research Center and that there are more treasures in drama and theatre in other branches of the center. In the Photography Collections, for instance, among other theatre materials, can be found a pictorial record of Christopher Morley's revival of *The Black Crook*. In the Iconography Collection are George Frederick Watts' painting *Watchman, What of the Night?* for which Ellen Terry was the model, Pasternak's portrait of Sarah Bernhardt, and a portrait of David Garrick attributed to Reynolds.

The Library and the Manuscript Collection of the Humanities Research Center, however, hold the lion's share of the drama and theatre treasures not in the Hoblitzelle Theatre Arts Library. First and foremost are the Shakespeare Folios—two of the first and varying numbers of the rest. The Aitken, Parsons, Stark, and Wrenn libraries contain at least 1,000 first editions and many more second and third editions of 17th and 18th-century English dramatic works. The Parsons Collection also contains many early editions of classical drama from Aeschylus to Seneca and twenty-nine folio volumes of Giovanni Piranesi, the 18th-century architect and spectacle designer.

The C. Hartley Grattan Collection contains more than 22,000 books, pamphlets, and periodicals. The general subject matter is relevant to all the Western Pacific islands, including studies of primitive peoples and their arts. Especially important to us are those works which describe efforts made in Australia to produce a native theatrical and dramatic art in the face of an overwhelming interest in touring groups from England and America.

The T. E. Hanley Library contains important dramatic materials relating to Dylan Thomas, Samuel Beckett, and George Bernard Shaw. The Dylan Thomas Collection contains 156 holograph pages of *Under Milkwood*, 296 pages of corrected typescript, and 213 pages of related documents, while the Samuel Beckett Collection has a 163-page manuscript in English of *Waiting for Godot* as well as a 150-page French version in Beckett's handwriting.[3]

The George Bernard Shaw Collection from the Hanley Library consists of more than 2,000 manuscript and printed items, among them original shorthand versions of his plays, early typescripts, first rough proofs, and second and third proofs with corrections in longhand. It includes French translations of some of his plays and some film scenarios. There are also production memoranda, cast lists, financial agreements, licenses for productions, and correspondence concerning the various types of productions. The printed materials include more than 300 contributions by Shaw to books and periodicals written by others and approximately 300 articles dealing with Shaw's life and works. With this collection and materials added to it, the Humanities Research Center now has a Shaw Collection with about 10,000 pieces of correspondence relating to Shaw.[4] The Humanities Research Center also holds three manuscripts of plays by Oscar Wilde; Edward Gordon Craig is also represented by a large manuscript collection.

The Humanities Research Center is open from 8 a.m. to 5 p.m. Monday through Friday. The Reading Room, with student page service, is open from 9 a.m. to 12 p.m. Saturdays. Mail order research is available within reason. If a person has a great deal of research to do, it would be advisable to visit Austin or to arrange with the research librarian of the Humanities Research Center to hire a graduate student. The staffs of most branches of the Humanities Research Center are small but helpful.

A scholar wishing to copy or quote from manuscripts or reproduce original art work must get permission from the Faculty Committee on the Use of Historic and Literary manuscripts. The permission of the Committee will usually depend upon one's having the permission of the author/artist, his/her heirs or estate representative, or evidence of a conscientious search for same. This condition *may* be waived by the Committee if the author/artist has been dead for a long time.

Should a visit to the Humanities Research Center be planned, I would advise the researcher to allow plenty of time. This article has revealed only a small portion of the treasure trove at The Humanities Research Center, and it is sometimes easier to shorten a visit than it is to lengthen it—but Texas welcomes all of you.

NOTES

1. Most of the information in this article comes from Frederick J. Hunter's *A Guide to the Theatre and Drama Collections at the University of Texas*, The Humanities Research Center, The University of Texas at Austin, 1967, pp. 3-5, and from various handlists of collections.

2. Walter Rigdon, ed. *The Biographical Encyclopaedia & Who's Who of the American Theatre*, James H. Heineman, Inc., New York, p. 420, col. 3.

3. Warren Roberts, *Twentieth Century Research Materials*, The Humanities Research Center, The University of Texas at Austin, 1972, p. 13.

4. Ibid.

WISCONSIN CENTER FOR FILM
AND THEATER RESEARCH

Tino Balio, Director

On October 22, 1971, the Wisconsin Center for Theater Research formally opened the United Artists Collection. The occasion was something of a milestone in the history of film studies, for it marked the first time that a motion picture company made available for research purposes the records of its business operation and a significant portion of its film library. Included in the gift were the corporate records of United Artists from 1919 to 1951, when the company was owned by Charlie Chaplin, Mary Pickford, Douglas Fairbanks, and D. W. Griffith; more than 1,700 feature films acquired by United Artists from Warner Brothers, RKO, and Monogram; and the Ziv Television Library of 2,000 filmed episodes from thirty-eight television series.

Research in the American motion picture industry has been severely hampered by a lack of primary source documentation. Film histories are for the most part neither definitive nor entirely accurate because writers have had to rely on secondary source materials, interviews, and trade magazines for information. Seldom have film historians written with the authoritativeness that historians in other disciplines have commanded. With the availability of the United Artists Collection, however, the qualitative level of film scholarship can be advanced. The 5,000 cubic feet of business records contain no less than the entire body of that company's surviving business records to 1950. Detailing every aspect of motion picture sales and distribution, it includes the company's corporate minutes and major financial records as well as information on production and distribution costs, film financing, and earnings. Exchange records document distribution and exploitation techniques; foreign department files give insight into the film as an international commodity; producers' records contain information on contracts and rights, plus correspondence with many of the country's leading film makers; and the files of the company's legal counsel detail a range of activities from stockholder disputes to plagiarism suits, from antitrust cases to income tax matters, exploitation techniques, regional cultural tastes, and the effects of the national economy and politics on the film industry. The heart of the business records is the legal file of the firm O'Brien, Driscoll & Raftery, the counsel for the company. All matters requir-

Tino Balio is Director of the Wisconsin Center for Film and Theater Research, 6039 Vilas Communication Hall, University of Wisconsin, Madison, WI 53706.

ing a legal opinion were referred to the firm. Contractual arrangements with producers and exhibitors, antitrust cases, and business arrangements with other studios are fully detailed. (There are no films of Chaplin, Pickford, and other producers for the company in the Collection. Until the 1950s, UA's films reverted to producers after the release periods.)

The several hundred films from RKO constitute nearly all the features produced by this major company in the 1930s and 1940s. The 200 Monogram titles are typical of small, low-budget productions during the same period.

The Warner Library, with more than 800 features, is unique in that it contains a virtually complete record of the studio's output between 1931 and 1947, from the low-budget pictures to the more prestigious releases. Its comprehensiveness allows the scholar to examine individual films in relation to the studio's overall style and to trace the careers of Warner's contract personnel. The Warner Library is also rich in manuscript documentation. Film scripts, ranging from original treatments to final shooting scripts, are available on almost every title and include works by such influential screenwriters as John Huston, William Faulkner, Robert Bruckner, the Epstein brothers, and Casey Robinson. Pressbooks, stills, and dialogues show how the films were advertised and exploited, while legal files, containing story purchase agreements and employment contracts with major stars and directors, provide important financial information. Rounding out the Warner Library are some 1,500 Vitaphone short subjects (again with scripts and dialogues) and over 300 cartoons from Warner's popular Looney Tunes and Merrie Melodies series.

Ziv Television Programs, Inc. was the most successful producer and packager of popular dramatic programs for first-run syndicated use in the early days of television. The Ziv Library contains every episode of *Boston Blackie, I Led Three Lives, Mr. District Attorney, Highway Patrol, Bat Masterson,* and thirty-three other series, a total of almost 2,000 shows produced from 1948 to 1962. Supplementing this vast film collection are scripts for these series, manuscript material, and some 40,000 still prints and negatives illustrating the production and advertising aspects of the Ziv programs.

The acquisition of the United Artists gift and its importance to film scholars led us to rename our organization to include the word "film."

The Wisconsin Center for Film and Theater Research, as we are now called, is co-sponsored by the University of Wisconsin-Madison and the State Historical Society of Wisconsin. Founded in 1960, the Center receives its operating budget from the University through the Department of Communication Arts, where the Center's director is a member of the faculty. The Historical Society provides a home for the collections, archival storage and processing facilities, a reading room and screening room, and extensive, relevant documentation in its own collections.

The Center invites the establishment of collections relating to any aspect of the performing arts by individuals as well as by corporations and private collectors. While some donors may have historic or personal ties with Wisconsin, all see the Center as a logical repository for their materials—a place where their documents are available to researchers and complemented by other collections. Although the Center cannot purchase materials, it pays for packing and shipping and can make arrangements for appraisals. The Center has nearly 200 collections from outstanding playwrights, television and motion picture writers, producers, motion picture companies, actors, and directors. In some subject areas, its source materials are preeminent.

Film

During Hollywood's golden age, when most people went to movie theaters at least once a week, motion pictures had the power to shape as well as to reflect American life styles. Today, despite being less frequently attended, they continue to do so. The Center's film collections give scholars the opportunity to investigate both the social impact of motion pictures and the development of film as an art form.

In addition to the films from the United Artists gift, the Center has more than 200 features, shorts, and documentaries from the 1890s to 1966, which further chronicle the history of cinema with films of D. W. Griffith, Erich von Stroheim, Robert Flaherty, Luis Buñuel, Ladislav Starevich, Alfred Hitchcock, Jean Renoir, Francois Truffaut, and many others. The work of contemporary film makers is exemplified in the collections of Shirley Clarke and Emilé de Antonio. De Antonio's collection includes such prints as *Point of Order* and *In the Year of the Pig*, as well as more than 500 reels of original and stock footage, out-takes, and sound tracks used in the production of his films. Clarke's collection contains several of her short films and out-takes from her features *Portrait of Jason* and *The Connection*. Features and shorts are also included in the collections of Gilbert Cates, Walter Mirisch, Lionel Rogosin, and Walter Wanger.

Dore Schary's collection provides a look at the workings of another major film company, MGM, where Schary spent several years as vice president in charge of production. Walter Wanger's contains correspondence and production and financial records of his projects as an independent producer from the 1930s into the 1950s. The Walter Mirisch collection illustrates the activities of his producing organization, and the Kirk Douglas collection details the operations of the production company founded by the actor-turned-producer.

Since the relationship between politics and the film industry has never been more clear than in the days of the hearings held by the House Committee on Un-American Activities, the Center is fortunate to have acquired particularly rich holdings in this area. It has papers not only from the Hollywood Democratic Committee and the lawyers representing the Hollywood Ten, but also from six of the Ten themselves. The collections of Alvah Bessie, Herbert

United Artists sign their corporation papers in 1919: D. W. Griffith, Mary Pickford, Albert Banzhaf, Charles Chaplin, Dennis O'Brien, and Douglas Fairbanks. (Reproduced with permission of the Wisconsin Center for Film and Theater Research.)

Biberman (and his wife, Gale Sondergaard), Ring Lardner, Jr., Albert Maltz, Samuel Ornitz, and Dalton Trumbo document motion picture careers as well as confrontations with the House Committee on Un-American Activities.

The lists of other donors who have served in the film industry reads as an honor role of accomplishment. Screenwriters (in addition to writers involved with the Hollywood Ten and Warner Brothers) include; Vera Caspary, Paddy Chayefsky, Ketti Frings, Paul Osborn, Ernest Pendrell, Howard Rodman, and James Webb. There are producers Robert Altman, Pandro S. Berman, Michael Douglas, and Norman Jewison; the designers David Ffolkes, Edith Head, and Dorothy Jeakins; composer Ernest Gold; directors Claude Binyon, John Cromwell, John Frankenheimer, and George Seaton; and actors Melvyn Douglas, Fredric March, and Agnes Moorehead.

Theatre

Theatre has undergone a tremendous change during this century due to the competition from motion pictures and television. Growing labor and production costs, along with shrinking audiences, have forced American theatre to develop beyond the traditional Broadway formula. Although Broadway is certainly not dead, theatre is finding additional strength through regional and alternative companies all over the United States. The Center's theatre collections contains the information, both economic and artistic, necessary for studying the state of the theatre today.

As with other media, today's theatre must be studied in light of its financing. The records of production companies offer concrete documentation in this area: contracts, budgets, box-office receipts, and profit-and-loss statements can reveal economic trends and provide insights into the entire process of theatrical production. Such records from producers Kermit Bloomgarden, Edward Choate, Renee Harris, Herman Levin, David Merrick, Gilbert Miller, Richard Myers, Arnold Perl, Herman Shumlin, and Dwight Deere Wiman lend particular strength to the Center's documentation of theatre in the 1940s and 1950s.

No examination of theatre would be complete without consideration of the director, the ultimate artistic voice in the shaping of each production. Collections such as those of Gerald Freedman, Moss Hart, Alan Schneider, and Michael Stewart record a wealth of directorial activity.

The art of the composer and lyricist finds a prominent place here. In addition to production records from numerous successful musical shows, collections document the individual work of Marc Blitzstein, Irving Caesar, Sheldon Harnick, Jerry Ross, Arthur Schwartz, and Stephen Sondheim. In the area of design are the costume renderings of Dorothy Jeakins; the sets of Watson Barratt, Albert Johnson, and Wolfgang Roth; and the lighting plots of Gilbert Hemsley and Jean Rosenthal. Criticism, although often damned, is vital to the excellence of the art. The Center has materials from director-critic Harold Clurman, *Theatre Arts* editor Edith J. R. Isaacs, and critics Walter Kerr (along with author and playwright Jean Kerr) and Louis Kronenberger.

New life has been infused into the theatre by the growth of regional professional theatre and experimental companies. Ronald Davis has donated papers relating to the founding of the politically oriented San Francisco Mime Troupe. Fannie Taylor's papers document the regional professional theatre movement and the role of the National Endowment for the Arts in its resurgence. Typical of the regional companies is the Milwaukee Repertory Theatre, well into its third decade, which periodically donates materials relating to its entire range of operations. Among the distinguished writers associated with the theatre who have established collections at Wisconsin are S. N. Behrman, Paddy Chayefsky, Edna Ferber, Ruth Goodman Goetz, Frances Goodrich and Albert Hackett, Moss Hart (with Kitty Carlisle), Langston Hughes, George S. Kaufman, Howard Lindsay and Russell Crouse, Terrence McNally, N. Richard Nash, and John Patrick. The collection of the Playwrights' Company includes works of its founders Maxwell Anderson, Sidney Howard, Elmer Rice, Robert E. Sherwood, and Behrman. Many other donors, although known primarily for their achievements in other fields, are also accomplished playwrights.

The unique personal and professional impact of actors such as Melvyn Douglas, Hal Holbrook, Fredric March, and Agnes Moorehead is chronicled in their respective collections. Particularly exciting are the 400 tape recordings from the Actors Studio, with Lee Strasberg's critiques of readings, improvisations, and exercises by numerous young actors who studied there in the 1950s and 1960s.

Television

The impact of television on our daily lives has, in the last thirty years, surpassed that of the Hollywood film. It has become the main source of entertainment and information in the American home, and we are just beginning to assess the relationship between this newest mass medium and American life. The Center, a pioneer collector in the television field, provides source material necessary for this assessment.

Viewing-access to the programs themselves is essential to serious research on television, and the Center holds filmed copies of a broad range of programs. The Center is particularly strong on materials relating to milestones in television documentary production. In 1952 at the NBC network, a team including Richard Hanser, Donald Hyatt, Isaac Kleinerman, and Henry Salomon produced an historic series that was the prototype of compilation documentary: *Victory at Sea*. The individual collections of these men combine to chronicle the production of this award-winning series and include the renowned musical scores by Richard Rodgers and prints of thirteen episodes. The team's second effort for NBC, *Project XX*, is also documented with research material, scripts, publicity, and prints of thirty-four episodes. The Kleinerman and Burton Benjamin collections illustrate their work at CBS on *The 20th Century* and *The 21st Century*. Included are over 100 prints from these series.

The Center also holds the collections of two other important producers of television documentaries, Ernest Pendrell and Perry Wolff. Their work, at ABC and CBS respectively, is exemplified by scripts and prints of many of their major productions. A number of other collections round out the Center's holdings of television prints. Reginald Rose has presented a complete series of films and scripts for the 260 episodes of *The Defenders*. The Nat Hiken collection contains more than 140 films from his successful comedies *You'll Never Get Rich* and *Car 54, Where Are You?* NBC has contributed episodes from each year of the long-running western series *Bonanza* (produced by David Dortort), while the Walter Mirisch collection contains all twenty-six episodes of *Wichita Town*. The Center has also received excerpts and prints of many of the Ed Sullivan variety programs and, from MTM Enterprises, a sampling of episodes from *The Mary Tyler Moore Show*. Films and kinescopes of television programs appear in other Center collections and include examples from such series as *Studio One, Electric Showcase, Person to Person, Camera Three, Omnibus, Climax, The Martha Raye Show*, and many more.

The Center's massive manuscripts holdings show aspects of television from its origins to the present day. The Paddy Chayefsky collection contains documentation of his landmark drama *Marty*, as well as teleplays for *Goodyear Theatre* and *Philco Television Playhouse*. Reginald Rose has donated scripts from *Studio One, Playhouse 90*, and *Alcoa Theatre* and extensive material on *The Defenders*. Rod Serling's papers include scripts for his work on *The Kraft Television Theatre* and *The U.S. Steel Hour*, in addition to comprehensive documentation of work on his *Twilight Zone* series. David Davidson wrote for many of these anthology series, as did Alvin Boretz, Robert Crean, Max Ehrlich, Ernest Kinoy, Loring Mandel, Jerome Ross, and Adrian Spies, all of whom have collections at the Center. Gore Vidal, whose *Visit to a Small Planet* firmly established him in early television, has donated a collection covering his entire career as a novelist, essayist, and screenwriter.

Other collections offer insights into the progression of the television series through the sixties and early seventies. The craft of the comedy writer is shown by Nat Hiken, Hal Kanter, Sidney Sheldon, and MTM Enterprises. Comedy series as diverse as *The George Gobel Show, Car 54, Where Are You?* and *The Mary Tyler Moore Show* are represented. Dramatic series such as *Doctor Kildare, Ironside, Mr. Novak, Owen Marshall*, and *Hawaii Five-O* are represented in the donations of David Harmon, Winston Miller, E. Jack Newman, Jerry McNeely, and Sy Salkowitz. Writer-producer Bruce Geller has provided almost complete records for the long-running series *Mission: Impossible*. Additional prime-time series are highlighted, and daytime television is represented by such collections as that of Irna Phillips, writer for *The Guiding Light* and *The Brighter Day*.

Directors for television include Tom Donovan, who worked on such series as *The DuPont Show of the Month*, *The U.S. Steel Hour*, and *Studio One*; John Frankenheimer, one of the best known directors to get a start during this period; and Clark Jones, who directed for *The Bell Telephone Hour*, *The Perry Como Show*, *The Carol Burnett Show*, and various specials. David Susskind's collection offers extensive information on his activities as producer for *The Armstrong Circle Theatre*, *The DuPont Show of the Month*, *East Side/West Side*, and his discussion show *Open End*. Hundreds of drawings for *The Bell Telephone Hour* have come from set designer Peter Dohanos. Promotional activities for *The Armstrong Circle Theatre* and several Alcoa-sponsored series are thoroughly documented by theatrical producer and press representative Arthur Kantor. Production schedules and financial materials so vital to understanding television are also contained in many of the collections.

Graphics and Promotional Materials

Complementing the Center's film and manuscript holdings is a file of stills, negatives, posters, pressbooks, playbills, clippings, scrapbooks, graphics, and ephemera—several million items in all. These materials have been gathered from all of the Center's collections to provide researchers with easy access to pictorial materials in various areas of the performing arts. The stills and graphics holdings are organized into several sections and indexed by title, name, place, and subject.

The Title File includes stills, negatives, pressbooks and publicity, one sheets, lobby cards, and posters on approximately 25,000 motion picture titles from the 1890s to the present. The type and amount of material on each title vary greatly. While virtually all studios are represented, there is particular emphasis on the releases of United Artists, MGM, Warner Brothers, Universal, and Republic. There are also many photographs relating to television.

The Name File consists of publicity and personal photographs on more than 8,000 individuals. Included are performers in motion pictures, TV, radio, opera, ballet, and theatre as well as producers, directors, studio executives, writers, and many others. In addition to the photographs, there are clipping files and scrapbooks that document the personal and professional lives of many of the individuals. The Name File also contains a wealth of material on the American theatre from the 1860s to the present, from Broadway productions to local repertory. The theatre material is accessible via names of performers in particular productions. Augmenting the many photographs are hundreds of scrapbooks, organized by theatrical season, containing clippings, playbills, and comments.

The Place File contains photographs and clippings depicting theatres, studios, and other related locations, while the Subject File is organized around activities and events pertaining to theatre, motion pictures, and television. Included are such headings as "Academy Awards," "Premieres," "Family Life," "World War I," and so on. Photographs in this file are cross-indexed by name or production title.

In order to provide access to the vast array of ephemera generated by the performing arts, the staff created a separate section termed the Item File. It contains such materials as movie star stamps, pennants, paper dolls, gum cards, souvenir books, original caricatures and sketches, press kits, heralds, and other publicity. Again, this material is cross-indexed by name or title.

Researchers may examine the Center's manuscript holdings at the Archives-Manuscripts Reading Room on the fourth floor of the State Historical Society between the hours of 8 a.m. and 5 p.m., Monday through Saturday. Catalogs, finding aids, reference assistance, copying machines, and microfilm viewers are available there. The Center can provide researchers with 3M continuous tone copies of photographs or photographic reproductions for a fee. Permission to publish or further reproduce such materials must be sought from the appropriate companies or individuals.

Researchers, especially those from outside Madison, are urged to write or telephone in advance. Some materials may be temporarily unavailable because of cataloging and processing; some donors have placed restrictions on the use of portions of their materials; and Saturday hours are curtailed when the University is not in session.

The Center's Film Archive, also located on the fourth floor of the Historical Society, has Steenbeck viewing machines for individual screening of films in the collections. Access to sound and graphic materials is also provided. Viewing equipment must be reserved, and researchers are encouraged to make reservations as far in advance as possible. The Film Advance is open from 8:30 a.m. to 4:30 p.m., Monday through Friday.

The Wisconsin Center for Film and Theater Research

Administrative Offices:
  6039 Vilas Communication Hall
  University of Wisconsin-Madison
  Madison, Wisconsin 53706
  (608) 262-9706

Film Archive:
  State Historical Society of Wisconsin
  816 State Street
  Madison, Wisconsin 53706
  (608) 262-0585

Archives-Manuscripts Reading Room:
  State Historical Society of Wisconsin
  816 State Street
  Madison, Wisconsin 53706
  (608) 262-3338

BIBLIOGRAPHY

Balio, Tino. *United Artists: The Company Built by the Stars*. Madison: Univ. of Wisconsin Press, 1976.

Harper, Josephine L. *Guide to the Manuscripts of the State Historical Society of Wisconsin*. Madison: State Historical Society of Wisconsin, 1966.

Johnson, Kay. "The Wisconsin Center for Theatre Research," in Ted Perry, ed. *Performing Arts Resources*. Vol. I. New York: Drama Book Specialists, Theatre Library Association, 1974.

Kaiser, Barbara J. "Resources in the Wisconsin Center for Theatre Research." *The American Archivist*, 30 (July 1967): 483-92.

Young, William C. *American Theatrical Arts: A Guide to Manuscripts and Special Collections in the United States and Canada*. Chicago: American Library Association, 1971.

THE THEATRE DEPARTMENT OF THE
METROPOLITAN TORONTO LIBRARY

Heather McCallum, Head

Canada has a long and interesting theatrical history. Apparently it began in 1606 with a marine masque, *The Theatre of Neptune*, written by Marc Lescarbot, a young lawyer from Paris. It was performed by sailors and voyageurs at Port Royal, Acadia, now Lower Granville, Nova Scotia. Three years after the entertainment, the first edition of the masque was printed in Paris; the verses are included in a volume entitled *Les Muses de la Nouvelle France*. In the 18th century, army officers put on plays and concerts to relieve the tedium of garrison life. By the beginning of the 19th century, British and American touring companies had begun to bring professional acting to Canada. Interestingly enough, the plays they performed were often only weeks behind the original London productions. Not only important plays, but important personalities appeared on the Canadian stage. Henry Irving and Sarah Bernhardt, among many others, made frequent trips to the two Canadas. These touring troupes flourished until the Second World War. The modern history of the Canadian theatre begins in the early 1950s with the arrival of television, the establishment of the Stratford Festival, and the emergence in Montreal and Toronto of professional companies with high standards. The details and the complexity of the history outlined here need not only to be written but indeed to be discovered. It is not too much to say that the study of Canadian theatre history is in its initial "heroic" or exploratory stage. For this reason a theatre collection such as the one at the Metropolitan Toronto Library takes on an importance that is perhaps greater than that of collections in countries with a longer tradition of historical investigation.

The Theatre Department is one of eleven subject departments of the Metropolitan Toronto Library, which is generally acknowledged to be the most comprehensive of Canadian public library collections. In 1977, after seventy-one years in a cramped and outdated Carnegie building, a spectacular new space designed by Raymond Moriyama was provided to serve the growing needs of a large metropolitan area. Despite its limitations, the old Carnegie building had one feature of special interest. In 1961 the renovation of its library auditorium into a 209-seat theatre permitted an important collabora-

Heather McCallum is Head of the Theatre Department of the Metropolitan Toronto Library, 789 Yonge Street, Toronto, Ontario M4W 2G8.

Special Collections, Vol. 1(1), Fall 1981
© 1981 The Haworth Press

tion with the then newly opened Theatre Department. Known as the Central Library Theatre, the space was regularly used by both professional and amateur companies for the next sixteen years, notably by the Red Barn Theatre and the Canadian Players under the professional direction of Jean Roberts and Marigold Charlesworth.

As a result of public interest in Canada's quickening theatrical activity, the Theatre Department was started in 1961. Based on an established collection, it has grown steadily since that time and is now the major library collection of theatre resources in the country. Even though good theatrical material is increasingly hard to find and although the collection was established quite late when compared to most major collections, it was not begun so late as to miss many items that cannot easily be acquired today. Supplementing its own materials are the rich resources of all the other departments of the Library, which provide the interrelationships so important to research.

The Theatre Department acquires materials on most areas of the performing arts: theatre and drama, moving pictures, dance, television and radio programming, and varieties of popular entertainment such as circus, music hall, puppetry, and pantomime. Music and opera are the responsibility of the Music Department. Knowledgeable visitors to the collection will find among the 25,000 book titles a high proportion of basic works, particularly on the English-speaking theatre. The special emphasis is on theatrical production; hence, the numerous works on theatre architecture and staging, and the attention to illustrated books. In addition, the collection emphasizes biography and English drama of all periods, in particular the drama of the 20th century. It should be stressed, however, that the collection does not neglect works on the non-English-speaking theatre and provides a more than adequate research collection. As a result of concentrated effort in the last ten years, the department is particularly strong in materials relating to Canadian theatre history. Canadian plays have been published in increasing numbers in recent years, and a comprehensive collection is available including typescripts of many unpublished plays. There has been, however, no corresponding effort towards the publication of works on Canadian theatre history; only a few dozen titles exist, supplemented by a number of excellent theses by Canadian and American scholars. Another of the department's strengths is a large assemblage of materials devoted to film. The in-depth collection of books, including many foreign-language titles, and the full runs of many of the standard film periodicals, supplemented where necessary by microforms and reprints, are heavily used. A film stills collection with the emphasis on American films of the 1950s is complemented by many autographed portraits of earlier film personalities. A collection of over 1,100 phonograph records features original casts and outstanding performances of major classical and contemporary plays, as well as radio and television shows and comedy performers.

Because of the growing interest in the performing arts as an area for research, the specialized resources of the department are used extensively by scholars and students of theatre and film, researchers, publishers, journalists, directors, stage designers, and actors, in addition to the general public. A hard-working staff of nine deal with the numerous and varied public inquiries which have reached avalanche proportions since the opening of the new, centrally located building two and a half years ago. Such inquiries originate not only in the Toronto area but in all parts of Canada and the United States. During 1979, over 123,000 items were used by over 72,000 patrons, with over 14,000 telephone requests and over 30,000 desk inquiries.

Apart from its general book and periodical collections, the department has substantial holdings in rare books. Included are over seventy-five festival books dating from the 16th to the 19th centuries. These volumes, of great importance for the history of the theatre, document royal entrances into cities as well as tournaments, wedding, and birthday celebrations. The Library's titles were published principally in France, but the Library also holds examples from the Netherlands, Belgium, Germany, Austria, Spain, and Great Britain. One of the most important festival books of the French Renaissance, *La Joyeuse et triomphante entrée de Charles IX*, contains an account of the celebrations held on the occasion of the entry into Paris of Charles IX, King of France, in 1571. A number of handsome volumes were produced in France during the reign of Louis XIV. The department's copy of *L'Entrée triomphante de Louis XIV et Marie Thérèse d'Autriche* into Paris in 1662 came from the Library of Holland House. Another work of the same period, *Courses de testes et de bague*, written by Charles Perrault, commemorates the carousel which was arranged by Louis XIV to revive the traditions of chivalry and pomp associated with medieval tournaments. The Library's copy was printed in 1670 by the Imprimerie Royale in Paris, with plates designed by Israel Silvestre. It was once in the collection of the Duchesse de Berry. Fine examples of 17th-century Italian writing and printing are included in the collection. *Il Solimano*, one of the most celebrated tragedies of 17th-century Italian literature, is decorated with etchings by Jacques Callot. The beautifully designed series of plates executed by Callot for *Combat à la barrière* represents the tournament celebrations held at the Court of Lorraine in Nancy in 1627. The rich, baroque designs of theatrical scenes done by Stefano della Bella for the opera by Giovanni Carlo Coppola, *Le Nozze degli dei*, produced in Florence in 1637, are also valuable items in the collection. The musical drama, *Il Fuoco eterno custodito dalle Vestali* by Nicolo Minatò, was commissioned in 1674 for the birth of the daughter of Emperor Leopold I of Austria. These magnificent stage decorations were engraved after designs by Ludovico Burnacini whose work influenced scenography in Germany and eastern Europe.

Twenty-four original gouache paintings of the late 18th century done by Whirsker are in the collection. They depict famous actors in roles at the Comédie Française and the Comédie Italienne. A number of these designs are reproduced in *Les Métamorphoses de Melpomene et de Thalie* which was published in Paris in 1770. Original watercolor drawings of costumes—nineteen in all—exist for the original production of *Prunella*, the play by Harley Granville-Barker and Laurence Housman. These drawings were done by the English designer Charles Wilhelm in 1904. The Library has these drawings, as well as a selection of Wilhelm's fantastic designs for pantomimes and extravaganzas at various London theatres between 1897 and 1904. The collection also includes *Die Theater Wiens*, a monumental series in seven volumes on the history and architecture of the theatres in Vienna, published between 1894 and 1909. Other treasured items are an almost complete run of the original edition of Edward Gordon Craig's journal, *The Mask*, the Nonesuch Press *Shakespeare* in seven volumes, and, among a selection of rare dance items, *The Designs of Léon Bakst for The Sleeping Princess*. A number of volumes with designs by Georges Barbier, also in the collection, represent his work for the theatre and dance and include *Designs on the Dances of Vaslav Nijinsky, Album dédié à Tamar Karsavina, Vingt-cinq costumes pour le théâtre*, and *Casanova: décors et costumes*. The comprehensive 12-volume *Monumenta scenica*, reproducing many of the original festival, scenery, and costume designs in the Theatre Collection of the National Library in Vienna, is a 20th-century rarity. Recent additions to the collection include volumes on the English stage in special bindings which have been enlarged by the insertion of engravings, letters, and other documents. Two of the most important sets of these extra-illustrated books are Percy Fitzgerald's *The Life of David Garrick*, extended by 700 illustrations, and John Doran's *Their Majesties' Servants*, extended from two to five volumes and formerly in the library of Sir John Gielgud.

Since the theatre is a transitory art, no stage design, no engraving of a theatrical scene, no photograph can faithfully portray the fleeting impression created by a performance on an audience. Such fugitive materials are all that remain, however, and so, like Autolycus in *The Winter's Tale*, the Theatre Department has become "a snapper-up of unconsidered trifles" and has gathered the resources to supply the researcher with the bases for as accurate a reconstruction as possible. In what is inevitably the department's particular area of interest, Canadian theatre history, research is seriously handicapped by a severe shortage of primary source materials and by the fragmentation of existing resources. Since the Library is situated in Toronto, the major center for English-language theatre in the country, the department is in an advantageous position to acquire and supply information on theatre activity. Accordingly, it is building up the history of all professional theatres, past and present. It relies on theatre and dance companies across the country to supply the printed record of their work (programs, posters, photographs, press releases) and receives excellent cooperation.

Playbills and theatre programs are among the most important items documenting a theatrical performance. The department's collection of 19th-century Canadian playbills is not large. Indeed, very few examples have appeared on the market since the collection was begun (while over 800 Canadian bills are in the much longer established Harvard Theatre Collection). The Toronto collection includes a selection of playbills from eastern Canada, principally from Halifax, Saint John, Quebec City, Montreal, and Toronto. Two 1852 playbills record the entertainments provided by the crews of ships wintering in the Arctic during the search for the lost Franklin expedition. One of the bills notes a production of parts of *Hamlet* in which Hamlet and Ophelia were played by the same (versatile) seaman. Several hundred British playbills, principally from Drury Lane and Covent Garden, dating from 1775 to the First World War, provide a useful record of the period. They are of particular interest when comparing the plays popular in England and in Canada in the last century. Over 18,000 house programs record professional theatre activity in centers across Canada from late in the last century to the present day. Regional theatres were established as late as the 1950s, and the collection has complete sets of programs for their productions. It has, in addition, runs of programs for most Toronto theatres including the Royal Alexandra which opened in 1907 and the Empire Theatre in the 1920s.

Another of the department's strengths is its newspaper clipping files for Canadian theatre and dance companies, for performing arts personalities (both Canadian and international), and for feature films and stage productions. Almost 900 files are heavily used to support secondary school, graduate, and undergraduate courses in Canadian theatre and drama and to supplement the few books available. These files provide a record that will form a sound basis for some of the studies that must eventually be written on Canada's theatre history. In 1979 a provincial grant funded the filming of these files; they are now available for consultation on microfiche. Many of the posters in the department's collection provide a record of Canadian stage productions, films, and ballets. These posters include fine examples of the inventive art of Vittorio Fiorucci, the Montreal-based poster artist, in addition to the work of Theo Dimson in Toronto. There is also a good selection of well designed theatre, circus, and film posters, principally from Poland, Hungary, and Denmark. British and American theatre posters from the late 19th century feature the designs of Charles Buchel and John Hassall. Two especially treasured posters designed by Alphonse Mucha depict Sarah Bernhardt in the roles of *Medée* and *Gismonde*.

The department's collection of original stage designs concentrates on designs done for Canadian productions. It includes a large selection from the Stratford Festival, Shaw Festival, regional theatres such as Vancouver Playhouse, Manitoba Theatre Centre in Winnipeg, Theatre London, Neptune Theatre in Halifax, and the National Arts Centre, Ottawa, as well as for Toronto theatres such as the Crest, Central Library Theatre, Toronto Arts Productions, and Tarragon Theatre, the National Ballet of Canada, and the

Exterior view of the Metropolitan Toronto Library. (Reproduced with permission of Applied Photography, Ltd., Toronto; Negative number 77-155-1.)

Canadian Opera Company. The complete set of designs prepared by Murray Laufer and Marie Day for the 1967 Canadian Opera Company production, *Louis Riel*, consists of preliminary sketches for the stage design and photo collages for the back projections, in addition to forty-seven costume sketches. All were the gift of the Floyd S. Chalmers Foundation. Marie Day's thirty-three costume designs for the Charlottetown Festival musical, *Anne of Green Gables*, are for a production which has toured successfully across Canada since its first appearance in 1965. Important ballet designs in the collection include work by Mstislav Dobujinsky for the Canadian ballet *Red Ear of Corn*, which was produced by Boris Volkoff in 1949; Maurice Strike's work for the National Ballet of Canada's production of *Coppelia*; and Desmond Heeley's designs for that company's *Swan Lake*. The noted painter and designer Leslie Hurry is represented by more than ninety sketches done for the Stratford and Shaw Festivals between 1956 and 1975. Over the years, designers such as Tanya Moiseiwitsch, Desmond Heeley, Brian Jackson, Hilary Corbett, and Suzanne Mess have given generously of their work. The collection now contains almost 2,000 Canadian designs. In cases where the original sketches are not available for the collection, the originals are borrowed and slides made in order to document an artist's work.

In addition to the more direct documentation of theatrical activity, the department maintains an especially interesting and growing collection of theatre iconography and of the theatrical scene as presented through the eyes of contemporary artists. The print collection of over 1,500 consists principally of theatrical portrait engravings of the 18th and 19th centuries. It includes an engraving of Edmund Kean when elected a chief and prince of the Huron tribe at Quebec in 1826. Among other notable portraits are many for Sarah Siddons, Frances Abington, Joseph Grimaldi, Charles Mathews, the Kemble family, David Garrick, Edwin Booth, George Frederick Cooke, and Helen Faucit. There is a portfolio of engravings by Alessandro Sanquirico that documents various Italian operas and ballets between 1826 and 1832. Among the rarest and most important items are the etchings done between 1738 and 1794 which depict the stage scenes in the Amsterdam Schouwburg; they provide one of the best practical records in existence for 18th century stage scenery. A representative selection of 19th century Japanese woodblock prints depicts scenes and actors from the Kabuki and Noh theatres in Edo and Osaka. A fund recently made available by Kenneth and Jean Laundy to the department for special items has permitted the purchase of 20th-century prints which portray theatre and circus scenes. The collection includes a number of original etchings by the American artist Reginald Marsh which document the art of burlesque, as well as aquatints by Dame Laura Knight illustrating her fascination with the world of theatre, ballet, and the circus—a world which she treated without sentimentality.

A gift from Miss Cara Hartwell of over 5,000 film stills began the collection of photographs which now totals over 46,000 items. It includes publicity stills and studio portraits of performing arts personalities (mainly Canadian, American, and British) and a steadily increasing collection of production photographs for professional theatre and dance companies across Canada. The Stratford and Shaw Festivals in particular have generously supplied photographs for each season's plays, many of them by Toronto photographer Robert C. Ragsdale, a long-time specialist in theatrical photography. A large collection of photographs once on display in the Walker Theatre, Winnipeg, one of the country's most important touring houses early in this century, records productions which were presented at the theatre when it first opened in 1907. The collection includes studio portraits of such stars as Mrs. Fiske, Viola Allen, and Olga Nethersole, as well as production photographs of *The Squaw Man*, starring William Faversham, and *The Inferior Sex*, with Maxine Elliott. A recent addition to the collection is an album of photographs of the E. A. McDowell Company which toured extensively in Canada between 1875 and 1890. During this period American actor/manager Eugene McDowell presented such popular plays as *The Shaughraun* and *The Colleen Bawn*. A collection of twenty-four production photographs done by London photographer Anthony Buckley for *The Glass Cage*, a play by J. B. Priestley written in 1957 for the Toronto acting family, Donald and Murray Davis and Barbara Chilcott, is available. Donald Davis presented these photographs to the collection a few years ago along with other important items related to the Crest Theatre. In addition, there is a selection of large studio portraits done by Buckley which includes photographs of Pamela Brown, Ivor Novello, Alec Guinness, Ralph Richardson, and Irene Worth. A special collection of material on Canadian-born film actor Ned Sparks includes both personal photographs and stills of his films.

The department is actively engaged in acquiring special collections relating to the history of the performing arts in Canada, and over the years gifts of scrapbooks, photographs, account books, and correspondence for theatre and dance companies and personalities have contributed significantly to the collection. In cases where important original materials are still held by theatre companies and individuals, the items are microfilmed for the collection, thus allowing access to researchers and at the same time safeguarding the original documents. One of the first gifts was an extensive collection of scrapbooks, account books, photographs, correspondence, and promptbooks belonging to the Tavernier Company whose stars Albert Tavernier and his wife Ida Van Cortland toured eastern Canada and the United States in the 1880s and 1890s. The Thomas Scott collection of scrapbooks followed; these were compiled by the gas engineer at Toronto's Grand Opera House between 1876 and 1900. A collection of charming watercolors, done by Sir John Martin Harvey while he was with Sir Henry Irving's Canadian tour in 1884, was presented to the department by Miss Agnes Barclay of Victoria, British Columbia, whose parents had entertained Sir John and Lady Martin Harvey on their subsequent tours of Canada. In recent years, the department has built up substantial collections of photographs and programs documenting the productions of such actors as Henry Irving, John Martin Harvey, and Johnston Forbes-Robertson, all of whom toured Canada extensively before the Second World War. The department received recently from Miss Pauline Home a collection of photographs and letters from Edward Gordon Craig and Ellen Terry to their lawyer, Paul Hildesheim Home, early in this century. This collection also contains a self-portrait sketch of Ellen Terry done in 1868. The department has on permanent loan from the Estate of Jack Ayre a large collection of material relating to The Dumbells, the Canadian all-soldier concert party which originated in France in 1917. The troupe played for twelve weeks on Broadway in 1921 and toured Canada with a variety of successful revues until 1929. The collection includes programs, press clippings, photographs, sheet music, correspondence, scripts, and route books, and it provides an interesting record of a type of entertainment popular in both world wars. Scrapbooks compiled by the Canadian-born actress Judith Evelyn were presented to the Library by her executor Mel Dinelli after her death in 1967. Twelve books cover her acting days which began in Canada, but they are principally a record of her Broadway career in such plays as *Angel Street* and *A Streetcar Named Desire*. Before his death in 1974, the dancer and teacher Boris Volkoff gave his extensive collection of scrapbooks, photographs, choreographic notebooks, and correspondence to the department. This especially significant material documents his 45-year career in Canada and his important contribution to the development of Canadian ballet.

Unfortunately, these treasures are less accessible than they ought to be—not because of unusual constraints but simply because of the difficulties of mounting the sort of exhibitions the materials deserve. The old Carnegie building contained excellent display space, but the present library structure allows for few exhibits. One hopes that this situation will be changed within the next few years, since a policy of regular displays of materials from the collections is an important aspect of the work of large research libraries. Meanwhile, the department continues to lend material to other institutions, notably to the Art Gallery of Ontario and to other galleries in Canada, to the National Library of Canada and the National Arts Centre in Ottawa, to the Stratford Festival, and, this year, to the Quadrennial of Theatre Design and Technology in Prague. A computer-produced acquisitions list which notes all books, periodicals, and special collections added to the collection is produced monthly. It is available in the department and by mail to interested institutions and individuals. The performing arts field lacks comprehensive indexes, so that a certain amount of indexing is done by the department staff. These publicly available indexes have been built up steadily since the department began and now constitute a valuable research resource. They include a comprehensive index to plays in collections and in periodicals, a biographical/critical index to personalities in the field, and a unique title-index to plays produced professionally in Canada. A detailed index to the newspaper files newly available on microfiche is in the process of being developed. A centralized Cataloguing Department catalogs books, periodicals, recordings, and microforms. All special collections are cataloged by department staff—stage designs, engravings, playbills, posters, photographs, and manuscript collections.

It is almost a cliché of cultural commentary that Canadians have been slow to appreciate and to collect records of their cultural past. With much primary material still unlocated, let alone examined, a great deal of the country's theatre history is still undocumented. The study of Canadian theatre and drama as an academic discipline has not kept pace with the expansion of graduate studies in the other fields of the humanities and is still in its infancy. Academic research and the publication of scholarly studies have been slow to develop. The increasing establishment of Canadian theatre history and drama courses in universities and colleges across the country only reinforces the need to remedy the situation. The Theatre Department has, since its inception, felt a responsibility to acquire archival materials to support this study and research. Over the years a great deal of encouragement and assistance has been received from established theatre collections in the United States, Great Britain, and Europe. Gifts of programs, photographs, and other materials continue to be received, and graduate students using the department's resources are generous with suggestions and information. Knowledge of and cooperation with other institutions holding theatre-related materials is an important aspect of the department's work. Extensive resources are held by national and provincial archives, universities, public and special libraries, theatre organizations, theatre companies, and private collections. The study *Theatre Resources in Canadian Collections*** appeared in 1973 after a year of research. It located and assessed theatre materials in 114 institutions across the country, with the object of encouraging the collection and preservation of such materials. In 1976, the Association for Canadian Theatre History/L'Association d'Histoire du Théâtre au Canada, an association of individuals and institutions formed to encourage and develop research in the field, was established. Members work to promote research and publication and to maintain a network for the exchange of information and work in progress. The Association's journal, *Theatre History in Canada/Histoire du théâtre au Canada*, first appeared in the spring of 1980.

The reader will conclude from much of this brief description of the theatre collection that primary source materials for the study of Canadian theatre history can be elusive, haphazardly acquired, and often fragmentary in form.

---

* National Library of Canada, Ottawa. Research Collections in Canadian Libraries: II, Special Studies; I, Theatre Resources in Canadian Collections, by Heather McCallum. Ottawa, 1973.

Items of all kinds—programs, posters, photographs, promptbooks, scrapbooks, diaries, correspondence, etc.—are eagerly sought by the Theatre Department. As historical documents of first importance, they deserve to be preserved and made available to scholars and researchers working in the field.

BIBLIOGRAPHIC CONTROL

Louis A. Rachow

Until recent years the location and accessibility of performing arts research resources were little publicized, or even encouraged, but with the proliferation of performing arts programs in the 1970s, it behooved the theatre library profession to appraise the situation in order to develop, improve, and advance the cause for more efficient and sophisticated methods of bibliographic control. *Theatre Arts Monthly*, under the editorship of Edith J. R. Isaacs, directed attention to this matter as far back as 1933, when it published a series of articles on the major theatre collections in Europe and America. In 1936, Theatre Arts, Inc., under the auspices of The New York Public Library and the National Theatre Conference (in cooperation with the American Library Association), climbed aboard the bandwagon by publishing the first handbook on the subject, *Theatre Collections in Libraries and Museums* by Rosamond Gilder and George Freedley. With the exception of Freedley's chapter on "Fugitive Material: its Care and Preservation," this modest 182-page guide is primarily of historical interest today, having gone out-of-print shortly after publication. (A revision and adaptation of the Freedley article by Louis A. Rachow was published in the January 1972 issue of *Special Libraries*.)

Almost a quarter of a century passed before a successor to the Gilder-Freedley handbook appeared. In 1952, Paul Myers, Chairman of the Library Project of the American Educational Theatre Association, began work on a revision of the American section of the 1936 guide, while André Veinstein of the Bibliothèque de l'Arsenal in Paris launched an exhaustive, worldwide inquiry on theatre libraries and collections abroad, using the Gilder-Freedley volume as a springboard. The results of this extensive project were published in 1960 by the Section for Performing Arts Libraries and Museums of the International Federation of Library Associations (IFLA) in the French-English *Bibliothèques et musées des arts du spectacle dans le monde/Performing Arts Libraries and Museums of the World*. A second edition appeared in 1967. Dr. Veinstein is currently compiling a third revision and adaptation, scheduled for publication in the early 1980s, with the continued support of the Theatre Library Association (TLA).

In the intervening years between the Veinstein editions, TLA introduced several new archives and collections in *Theatre Documentation*, published biannually from 1968 to 1972, with the cooperation of the Theatre Section of IFLA and the International Theatre Studies Program of the University of

Kansas. It has since been replaced by the annual *Performing Arts Resources* (briefly reviewed in the Guides to Collections and Resources section, following in the chapter on "Recent Materials for Theatre Collections").

The scope of *Theatre Documentation* is three-fold: (1) Bibliography, Classification and Collections; (2) Theatre Practice and Education; and (3) News of International Theatre Scholarship. In addition to bibliographical articles, the various issues provide indexes to books heretofore not indexed; accounts of film, picture, record, and general collections specializing in theatre; and studies concerning cataloging and classification systems. The "Theatre Practice and Education" section includes discussions on systems of notation in dance and stage direction; documentation and practical aspects of scene design, costuming, makeup, direction, management, and architecture; documentary materials for instructional use; and documentation of audiovisual theatre arts education. Included in the "News of International Theatre Scholarship" are reports of proceedings of congresses and colloquia devoted to documentation; news of the activities of national associations and learned societies and of the International Society of Libraries and Museums of the Performing Arts (SIBMAS); notes on exhibitions of theatrical materials; and notices of new publications related to theatre documentation.

Although *Performing Arts Resources* continues to provide the necessary guides to archives and analyses of collections, descriptions of regional holdings, and surveys of research materials, there is still a continuing absence of critical studies establishing professional standards and guidelines in theatre collections. To help fill this vacuum, TLA is presently sponsoring a study to develop data which can be used in decision-making at both the national and the individual collection levels by promoting the effectiveness of all such collections in the United States and Canada. A "Performing Arts Collection Profile," conceived by Laraine Correll, Head of Special Collections at George Mason University, has been sent to libraries, museums, and private collectors requesting information about the materials, services, and capabilities of their respective collections, as well as their attitudes concerning future policies. Breakdowns of statistical, procedural, and attitudinal data from the questionnaire will be used by TLA committees currently evaluating cataloging practices and automation-terminology standardization. The Association's Board of Directors will be able to make use of the "needs assessment" content in planning national services, while library schools will be in a more creditable position to plan relevant programs for performing arts librarians in addition to counseling students on employment opportunities.

Two major steps toward achieving bibliographic control over the vast manuscript resources of American repositories were set in motion in the late 1950s with the publication of the Library of Congress *National Union Catalog of Manuscripts, 1959-1961* and the first edition of *Subject Collections* (Bowker, 1958), compiled by Lee Ash. The collections described in the NUCM, from the initial volume to the present, are those listed in academic and public or quasi-public repositories which regularly admit researchers; those in *Subject Collections* (now in its 5th edition of 1978) consist of both primary and secondary sources and materials as reported by university, college, public, special and private libraries, museums, and historical societies. Complementing these two bibliographic landmarks is Bowker's new two-volume *Women's History Sources* (1979), edited by Andrea Hinding and reviewed in this issue's "Recent Materials for Theatre Collections." As is the case with all published and printed guides and handbooks, the inclusiveness of these volumes is dependent upon questionnaire response and the cooperation of the respective institutions surveyed. All three are indispensable to the theatre specialist as well as the generalist.

Of the specialized individual guides, published either by and/or for performing arts collections, Heather McCallum's *Theatre Resources in Canadian Collections* (Ottawa: National Library of Canada, 1973) is a fine model. The "survey-guide" provides, first, "an inventory of theatre library materials in 114 institutions across Canada: federal and provincial government collections, university and public libraries, regional theatres and theatre schools, museums and galleries, special and private collections." Her study stresses special collections and strengths, emphasizes the nonbook materials in the field which present widely varying problems of acquisition, processing, care and handling, and points out the fact that the serious shortage of material and the fragmentation of resources in certain categories emphasize the need for a greater recognition of the problems involved and the amount of work yet to be done in bibliographic control. Secondly, the report contains an assessment of the resources surveyed with recommendations for institutional and regional cooperation.

Despite glaring omissions in William C. Young's *American Theatrical Arts: a Guide to Manuscripts and Special Collections in the United States and Canada* (American Library Association, 1971), the work is an essential part of bibliographic reference. Part I includes a description of the manuscripts and special collections in numerous institutions, which are arranged by states and then in the order of the institution symbols used in the National Union Catalog of the Library of Congress or, in the case of Canada, by provinces. Part II is an index of persons and subjects.

The Humanities Research Center at the University of Texas in Austin has published a variety of guides of exceptional interest and research value. In addition to the general *Guide to the Theatre and Drama Collections at the University of Texas*, compiled by Frederick J. Hunter in 1967, descriptions of Laurence G. Avery's *Catalogue of the Maxwell Anderson Collection* (1968) and Manfred Triesch's *The Lillian Hellman Collection* (1966) are in order. Avery's guide includes listings of manuscripts of Anderson's plays, poems, and essays, both published and unpublished works, as well as letters and diaries. For each published play the chronology of the various drafts is established, and every manuscript or typescript is described. The growth of the work itself is discussed in terms of the more salient structural and thematic changes it underwent from original to final form. Descriptions of the several manuscripts located elsewhere are included. These manuscripts are cited at the appropriate places in the chronology of the drafts, with notes indicating the library where the material can be consulted. Triesch's Hellman catalog is unique in its extensive runs of various drafts of Miss Hellman's dramas (averaging from ten to eighteen versions) "arranged in chronological sequence according to internal evidence so that the reader can follow the development of each play." Entries for each play are preceded by a short comment on the drama and followed by reviews of the opening night performance. Frederick J. Hunter has also compiled a *Catalog of the Norman Bel Geddes Collection* (G. K. Hall, 1973) showing the progress of the designer's work from 1914 to 1958 and comprising all his correspondence, business files, and artistic designs.

Brief mention is made of three additional specialized sources: (1) *The Beinecke Rare Book and Manuscripts Library: a Guide to its Collections* (Yale University Library, 1975), an attractive reprint, with alterations, of the April 1974 issue of *The Yale University Library Gazette*, the addition of nearly fifty full pages of plates and an "Introduction to the Collections" by Louis L. Martz; (2) Special Collections Librarian Robert Sokan's *A Descriptive and Bibliographic Catalog of the Circus & Related Arts Collections at Illinois State University, Normal, Illinois* (Bloomington: Scarlet Ibis Press, 1976), has approximately 5,000 cataloged titles with Library of Congress classification and some 100,000 ephemeral items arranged mainly by subject; and (3) Northern Illinois University Libraries Nisbet-Snyder Drama Collection of *English and American Stage Productions: an Annotated Checklist of Prompt Books, 1800-1900* (G. K. Hall, 1973), compiled by William R. DuBois, whose emphasis is upon source material in the form of promptbooks and prompter's editions of plays, used and annotated by directors and players—a listing of over 2,000 items of which almost 700 contain handwritten annotations of stage directions, changes, cuts, casting, and scenery.

The complexion of Shakespearean production research was changed appreciably by Charles H. Shattuck with publication of his *The Shakespeare Promptbooks: a Descriptive Catalogue* (Urbana: University of Illinois Press, 1965). Here, for the first time, is a compendious listing, complete with respective library locations, of more than 2,200 promptbooks, manuscripts, and working copies devised and designed by actors, directors, and stage managers from the 1600s to the year 1961. The author's supplementary list (with corrections) appears in the Autumn 1969 issue of *Theatre Notebook* (London: Society for Theatre Research). The Folger Shakespeare Library's two-volume *Catalog of the Shakespeare Collection* (G. K. Hall, 1972) characterizes:

a collection in depth in which most of the important editions of four centuries are represented as well as the significant translations in some fifty languages. Holdings in each of the centuries are nearly complete, but most important is the area of the sixteeneth and seventeenth centuries where about ninety per cent of the known editions are represented.

The Theatre Communications Group, the national service organization for nonprofit professional theatre, has provided a directory to its extensive collection of programs from America's resident theatres, collected from the respective theatres and the Ford Foundation. The guide is, perhaps, the most comprehensive single source regarding the history of theatre funding means, including names of public and private agencies, corporations, and individuals who support the profession. Compiled and edited by Laura J. Kaminsky, *Nonprofit Repertory Theatre in North America, 1958-1975* (Greenwood Press, 1977), may be used as a reference source in itself, or in conjunction with the Greenwood Press microfiche collection, the arrangement and organization of which parallels that of the published bibliography.

Bibliographic guides to visual sources and iconographic materials are essential to performing arts research and study. Over the years the Picture Division of Special Libraries Association has made an extended effort, through questionnaires, to represent all areas of the United States and Canada in its periodic published listings of Print and Photograph Collections. Several private collections have been added to the latest edition, *Picture Sources 3* (1975). The editors categorize pictures as visual documents rather than works of art—sources of information available for reference or publication. Excluded are collections that prohibit or restrict access by outside users. The Library of Congress has published a directory "designed to provide information on the availability of visual materials in the Washington area, not only to specialists working in the media, but also to a wide variety of other potential users of pictorial materials." Compiled by Shirley L. Green, *Pictorial Resources in the Washington, D.C. Area* (1976) is especially useful in locating illustrative material relating to the Arena Stage, Ford's Theatre, the Folger Shakespeare Library, and the Theatre Department of Catholic University, and even though Paul Vanderbilt's *Guide to the Special Collections of Prints & Photographs in the Library of Congress* (1955) was published a quarter of a century ago, it remains useful.

As oral history collections continue to grow and make their mark in the bibliographic sector, their respective guides are becoming works of high quality and considerable usefulness. An excellent example is the recent *Oral History Collection of Columbia University* (1979), edited by Elizabeth B. Mason and Louis M. Starr. Stage interviews cover the theatre of Victor Herbert, Jerome Kern and George Gershwin, the stock company as training ground, the road, the Group Theatre, the Stanislavsky method, new methods of acting and directing, Actors' Studio, changes in business methods, the role of the legitimate theatre in contemporary life, artistic freedom, comparisons of stage with screen techniques, and concentration of theatre in New York City. There are numerous individual entries, some of which are also available in microform. Alan M. Meckler and Ruth McMullin's *Oral History Collections* (Bowker, 1975) was first to provide a basic guide to this invaluable bibliographic movement which began some thirty years ago with Professor Allan Nevins and his oral history interview program. The movement gained impetus when the Oral History Association was organized in 1967 at Columbia University's Conference Center at Arden House. The Library of Congress also includes listings of oral history manuscripts in its *National Union Catalog of Manuscript Collections*. An invaluable source of oral history tapes pertaining to Black American theatre and its artists can be found in the Oral History Library of the Hatch-Billops Archives as described in James V. Hatch and OMANii Abdullah's *Black Playwrights, 1823–1977* (Bowker, 1977).

Although computer-readable data bases are accepted as a normal part of library reference work in many institutions, theatre research libraries have yet to develop successfully a sophisticated automation program to meet their specific needs. As early as 1968, the Florida State University School of Theatre in Tallahassee announced plans for the coordination of a national theatre data base to contain descriptive cataloging and location information on all cataloged theatre materials in the United States. Current data from various research projects, bibliographies, and surveys were to be included. In the spring of 1972, Florida State announced the establishment of an affiliated, but independent research center—the Charles MacArthur Center for American Theatre. The first step taken by the MacArthur Center in this undertaking was a direct inquiry to seventy libraries in the United States and Canada identified as holding theatrical materials. Information was requested on basic cataloging and classification methods. The result of these contacts and the enthusiastic response from TLA and the American Theatre Association (ATA) served as a catalyst in the formation of a Steering Committee to organize a Conference on Automation and Documentation in Theatre Research Libraries. In 1975, Laraine Correll, then director of the Resource Division, and George E. Bogusch, director of the Research Division of the Charles MacArthur Center, were appointed to head the Steering Committee with the assistance of the ATA Board of Research's Theatre History Panel.

Proposals, along with grant applications, were submitted to both the Council on Library Resources (CLR) and the National Endowment for the Humanities (NEH). Five objectives were delineated: (1) a standard terminology for the documentation and automation of theatre research materials; (2) initial framework and commitment for the development of a modern classification scheme capable of serving the needs of existing libraries and future centers of research, and machine readable compatibility with the Library of Congress MARC communication format and existing library systems; (3) compilation of an informal directory of holding locations for theatrical research materials to be used as a working tool and the formulation of plans for a national inventory of research materials; (4) formulation of plans for a national theatre information system of which this conference was to be Phase I; and (5) organizational planning for a consortium of theatre research libraries. During the time the proposal was in review, reports emanating from CLR and NEH were encouraging. It was obvious, however, that a refinement of the objectives and a more thorough study pertaining to the current needs and potentials for measures of cooperation among theatre research libraries and collections were in order before such a conference could be successfully staged.

At the instigation of Alfred S. Golding, director of the Ohio State University Theatre Research Institute, a consortium of theatre departments within the "Big Ten Universities" in the midwest (Illinois, Indiana, Iowa, Michigan, Michigan State, Minnesota, Northwestern, Ohio State, Purdue, and Wisconsin) was formed in 1974 for the purpose of coordinating activities and sharing resources. A survey of theatre documents in the possession of the "Big Ten" libraries revealed that the performing arts materials were only partly cataloged with minimal cross-references in most libraries. Of those participating, Minnesota was the only library to have released a printed catalog of holdings: *Theatre Arts Library Resources: a Guide to Basic Materials in the University of Minnesota Libraries* (1973), by George Bogusch and Richard Kelly.

Under the auspices of the Committee on Institutional Cooperation, an agency created to promote collaborative effort among the ten universities, the consortium began to study the problem of how to make use of electronic data processing equipment. As a result of these initial deliberations, it was decided to identify only cataloged documents in each institution and send this body of coded data to a computer center at one of the universities. There a data base would be built which could utimately provide a catalog by a computer-output-microfiche (COM) process. The catalog, in microform, would then be available for distribution at cost to libraries in and out of the "Big Ten." It was also hoped that a means would be found to make the cataloging system compatible with others in general use, so that the data base could also be approached by "on-line" searches.

A proposal for funding was sent to the National Endowment for the Humanities in 1975. The plan mandated the application of a MARC II format for bibliographic entry, with descriptors originally intended for book materials modified for identifying performing arts documentation of a nonbook nature. Graduate students within the respective theatre departments were to be used to keypunch data on IBM cards which would be translated onto magnetic tape at each member institution. All tapes were to be then sent to Columbus, Ohio, where a computer center would meld the tape information, then sort it on five desired parameters, producing a master list and five subordinate references keyed to the master, as microfiche. The microfiche would then be reproduced for distribution by an outside commercial firm. The NEH found the methodology admirable, but saw no need to supply an out-of-house catalog of the performing arts collections, since the material was already either cataloged or available.

A review of the scale of the project was immediately set into motion with the decision to retain the MARC format. In 1977 and 1978, two events occurred which further influenced the shape of the project. One was the initiation of a pilot study to test, in a preliminary way, the adaptability of MARC to a variety of performing arts documents. The second was an invitation for the consortium to input its theatre document data into the data banks of the Ohio College Library Center (OCLC), one of the largest networks of its kind in the country. According to recent word from Professor Golding, the reshaping of this pioneering data base network project is momentarily at a standstill because of budgetary restrictions. As a result of these labors, however, Golding's proposal entitled, "A Thesaurus for the Big Ten Performing Arts Document Inventory Project" (August 1978), serves as a model to fill the still existing void in nonbook theatrical document taxonomy.

The potential of computer-readable text and programming systems has also been recognized and realized by scholars in the area of historical research. Were it not for the computer, the 11-volume *The London Stage*, 1660-1800: *a Documentary Record and Calendar of Performance* and its recently published *Index* would not have seen the light of day—certainly not within a period of eight years. Compilation of the *Index* alone would have required one handwritten card for each reference. Ultimately there would have been a file of 500,000 cards to be sorted and alphabetized, and by adding references to master cards for each item, the compiler would have had to have searched an average of 25,000 cards an infinite number of times.

The *London Stage* Information Bank (LSIB) is maintained at Laurence University in Appleton, Wisconsin as a service to scholars in the wide range of subjects covered by this comprehensive record, and researchers are encouraged to take advantage of its facilities and resources. Information about any theatre, title, performance, performer, name or title in commentary, or any combination of these can be extracted and the result rearranged by sorting, as to show trends in such matters as theatre offerings or ticket prices, stage careers of actors, royal patronage, or role histories. About eighty percent of the casts in the *London Stage* volumes do not produce references in the *Index*, because the source simply refers the reader to a previous date on which the cast was the same, noting only changes. The programs fill in and revise the missing casts to complete the record for all performers. There is also a virtual concordance to the corpus, enabling the user to extract the context of any word, word-segment, or phrase in parenthetical remarks or commentary.

The system for extracting cast lists, known to the computer as GWSJR1, is available for export to scholars engaged in similar projects. This system is suited to the creation, search, and indexing of any regularly structured reference work, be it bibliography, catalog, or inventory. Comprising more than a year's programming and seven years of testing and improving, it is written in the PL/1 language and operates on a small IBM-360 computer.

In addition to all of this, another program product is SITAR which is, as the acronym declares, a System for Interactive Text-editing, Analysis, and Retrieval. With SITAR, insertion, deletion, and replacement of text are accomplished instantly and visibly on passages displayed on the screen of a video computer terminal. The system can copy, format, and print a file; replace all instances of one word with another; and accumulate a list of all "hits" satisfying a search request. It has been used for writing the same letter with variations for various people, maintaining and searching address lists, creating and keeping up-to-date the Laurence University course catalog, writing books, and analyzing literary texts. SITAR "interacts" with its user, asking for information needed to complete a task, forgiving mistakes, and prompting sound procedure.

Still in its initial stage is a computerized bibliography to consist of approximately 12,000 entries in the INFOL-2 program at the University of Massachusetts computer center, by John Howard of the Department of Theatre at Mount Holyoke College. Entitled *Theatre Architecture, Lighting, and Scenic Construction: a Computerized Bibliography of the Historian and Practitioner*, the data base is expected to be ready for distribution within the next two years. Although most entries will not be annotated, each entry will have specific subject headings for each of the main subjects. A search by subject, author, title, publisher, date, ISBN, LC number, Dewey Decimal number, location, and one word in all titles will be possible. The proposed work is expected to be the only bibliography on the subjects which will be current, complete, and capable of future updating, since dissemination will be by machine-readable tape as well as by microfiche. The English language materials to be included cover the past and present technology of the subjects. At this writing, Greenwood Press is negotiating to print about two-thirds of the data base from camera-ready, computer-generated copy.

As this issue of *Special Collections* goes to press, the Theatre Arts Communications Group, has released *Computers and the Performing Arts*. The report focuses on current and future computer usage among theatre, symphony, dance, and opera companies in the United States and responds to the needs of arts organizations for current information on the rapidly developing field of computer technology. It also contains a comprehensive glossary of terms related to computer technology programming, which librarians and researchers should find useful as an introduction to this somewhat complex (and sometimes misunderstood) form of bibliographic control.

In summation, a word about the Theatre Library Association. The original purpose of TLA, founded in 1937, was "to bring together librarians and individuals interested in the collection and preservation of materials relating to the theatre, and to stimulate interest in the making and use of theatre collections." Upon its incorporation as a not-for-profit corporation, under the Board of Regents of the University of the State of New York in 1975, its purposes were broadened as follows:

. . . conduct activities which are exclusively charitable, literary and educational including, without limitation, the advancement of public knowledge of the theatre and theatre arts by (a) furthering the interest of collecting, preserving and using theatre material in libraries, museums and private collections; (b) assisting in the preparation of programs for library schools about the preservation of theatre materials; (c) encouraging discussion about the particular problems of librarianship in theatre and other performing arts collections; (d) answering questions about theatre library problems; (e) sponsoring courses and seminars in librarianship in the theatre and theatre arts; and (f) publishing occasional newsletters and other publications on the above subject.

A member of the steering committee from the time TLA was organized, George Freedley was elected its first president in 1941 and served in that capacity until 1962 when he retired to become chairman of the Board of Directors. Succeeding presidents were Marguerite Loud McAneny, curator emeritus of the Princeton University Library Theatre Collection (1962-1967); Louis A. Rachow, curator-librarian of The Walter Hampden-Edwin Booth Theatre Collection and Library at The Players (1967-1972); and Robert M. Henderson, chief of the Library and Museum of the Performing Arts, The New York Public Library (1972-1976). Brooks McNamara of the Graduate Drama Department of the School of the Arts at New York University was elected for a two-year term in 1976 and re-elected for another two years in 1978. The current president is Louis A. Rachow.

During its formative years, the association sponsored two publications: *Broadside*, an occasional newsletter launched in 1940 under the editorship of Sarah Chokla Gross of the McCord Theatre Museum in Dallas, Texas and *Theatre Annual*, a volume of research information, essays, and articles on the dramatic arts and theatre history, inaugurated in 1942. Sponsorship of *Theatre Annual* was relinquished in the 1950s, and publication of *Theatre Documentation* was begun in 1968 and succeeded by *Performing Arts Resources* in 1972. *Broadside* become a quarterly newsletter in 1973 when Louis A. Rachow assumed editorship upon the retirement of Mrs. Gross.

Past projects which TLA has supported and sponsored include the compilation of the two editions of *Performing Arts Libraries and Museums of the World*. In collaboration with the Readex Microprint Corporation and with the enthusiastic endorsement of theatre historians and scholars, a microprint reproduction of a collection of some 5,000 plays—extant English and American drama from 1500 to 1830—was initiated and completed during the 1940s. A checklist to the collection, entitled *Three Centuries of English and American Plays*, was subsequently published by Stechert-Hafner, Inc.

Another major contribution to theatre librarianship and research was the co-sponsorship, with the American Society for Theatre Research (ASTR), of the 1969 Sixth Congress of the International Federation for Theatre Research—the first of its kind to be held in the western hemisphere. With "Innovations in Stage and Theatre Design" as its theme, the congress attracted some two hundred members and delegates from twenty-five countries. In 1977, the two associations again joined forces to present the first Conference on the History of American Popular Entertainment, which focused on the various aspects of popular entertainment including vaudeville, burlesque, the minstrel show, the "wild west" show, and the circus through a combination of papers, demonstrations, films, and exhibits. Both conferences were held in New York at the Lincoln Center for the Performing Arts.

TLA also sponsors and administers two annual awards. The George Freedley Memorial Award, established in 1968 in memory of the late founder and first president, honors a publication in the field of theatre published in the United States. The Theatre Library Association Award, established in 1973, honors a book published in the United States in the field of recorded performance, including motion pictures and television. All entries are judged on the basis of scholarship, readability, and general contribution to the broadening of knowledge.

Membership in the Theatre Library Association is available to all individuals and institutions interested in the performing arts. The first roster recorded ninety members from America and Europe. As of 1980 membership has reached the 500 mark and includes librarians, curators, historians, playwrights, costume and scene designers, private collectors, publishers, book dealers, and laymen. Program meetings are held in conjunction with the annual American Library Association Conference, with occasional regional meetings throughout the year. The annual business meeting is held each fall in New York as dictated by the Certificate of Incorporation. The association's headquarters are in New York City, at the Library and Museum of the Performing Arts, Lincoln Center.

As I have said, the theatre library profession is always seeking and exploring avenues for improved methods of bibliographic control. The most promising study, at the moment, is the TLA sponsored "Performing Arts Collection Profile," described in this chapter. When the results of the survey and study are collected and tabulated, TLA will surely be in a better position to initiate, develop, and promulgate an automated program designed to meet the specific bibliographic needs of performing arts libraries and collections.

THE THEATRE MUSEUM, BOOTHBAY, MAINE

Franklyn Lenthall, Curator

The Nicholas Knight-Corey House in Boothbay, Maine was entered in the National Register of Historic Places by the Heritage Conservation and Recreation Service of the Department of the Interior, Washington, D.C. on March 13, 1980. More importantly, America's only theatre museum, as such, is located in an historic house, built in 1784. The Boothbay Theatre Museum moved here in 1974, having been for eighteen years at the former Boothbay Playhouse, where it was founded in 1957, and where I, the founder, served as co-owner, producer, and director of this prestigious summer theatre.

Since the age of twelve I have always had a passion for theatre, and I have always been a scavenger. After reading Eleanor Ruggles' *Prince of Players*,[1] my acquisitive instinct zeroed in on the collecting of theatre memorabilia and more especially memorabilia relating to the Booth family. When the Boothbay Playhouse was purchased in 1957 (it had been in operation since 1937), it was decided that the pseudo-rustic-nautical decor was too much in evidence in all the restaurants in the area, so the wagon wheels, hay cutters, birds' nests, harnesses, lobster traps, buoys, and fishing nets were replaced by my relatively small theatre collection. At first, a very intimate lobby, auditorium walls, and a small basement Green Room provided limited exhibition space. In 1964 a large addition in keeping with the original barnlike structure was added, and additional wall space and many exhibition cases offered feasts for the eyes of the theatre lovers who attended the plays and used this lounge area in the entre-acte and before and after the performances. During the day the new addition provided excellent rehearsal space, and the actors were consciously or unconsciously indoctrinated into the history of theatre in a way not possible at the average acting school or university. With the evident interest of theatre patrons and tourists (increased publicity prompted them to stop by for the sole purpose of viewing the material on exhibition), I instinctively broadened my collecting interests. It soon became very apparent that this would be a truly universal and inclusive collection. Particles of brick and stone from the Roman Theatre (Verulanium, A.D. 140 and 150) in St. Albans, England, and contemporary memorabilia including Noel Coward's *Present Laughter* dressing gown and Alec McCowen's "Hadrian VII" papal cap attest to the museum's claim: "Theatre memorabilia from its genesis until today."

Franklyn Lenthall is Curator of The Boothbay Theatre Museum, Corey Lane, Boothbay, ME 04537

Special Collections, Vol. 1(1), Fall 1981
© 1981 The Haworth Press

In its present location the beautiful 18th-century house and barn provide the perfect setting for this unique private collection. Gunstock beams, five working fireplaces (including the original kitchen fireplace with its twelve-foot hearth) enhance the objets d'art because all the decorative pieces relate to the theatre. After the purchase of this historic house, it was learned from two ladies, born here many years ago, that their ancestor John K. Corey, while a soldier, was present at Ford's Theatre in Washington, D.C., April 14, 1865, when actor John Wilkes Booth assassinated President Lincoln during a performance of *Our American Cousin.* This fact is of particular importance to the Theatre Museum, as is the fact that Edwin Booth, America's greatest actor and brother of the infamous John Wilkes, had sailed into Boothbay Harbor July 27, 1887, on the steam yacht *Oneida*, as guest of financier E. C. Benedict. It was on this cruise that the idea was conceived of a club for actors and The Players in Gramercy Park in New York City testifies to the fruition of Booth's dream. The letter he wrote to his daughter Edwina while becalmed in the harbor is in The New York Public Library's collection at Lincoln Center.

The museum is attractively set on five acres of verdant lawns, flowering shrubs, and a variety of old-fashioned garden flowers with ancient trees screening the enclosure from the very active surrounding village. Three formal gardens have been added to the existing ones, including a lovely Rachel garden named for the French actress who came to America in 1855 where she gave her last appearance on any stage. Another area, bordered by white lilac bushes and the clapboarded side of the barn section of the museum, features a large Victorian iron fountain surrounded by separately incised slates with the names of Garrick, Duse, Molière, Booth, Rachel, and Siddons. Now and then a guest, uninitiated in the history of theatre, queries: "Are these people buried here?" or "Is this a cemetery for pets?"

When moving the collection from the Boothbay Playhouse, the obvious choice would have been to set it up in New York City, but this was unfeasible financially, and I think that preconsciously, I chose this house as a setting for the collection because of the book *The House of Life*[2] by Mario Praz. I was very impressed by this book at the time of its publication. The author gives a most unusual and fascinating tour through his ancient flat in the Via Giulia in Rome, describing the objets d'art he has so lovingly collected over the years. I do know that, like Mario Praz, I live in a museum. It is my home, and to quote him: "I see myself as having myself become an object and an image, a museum piece among museum pieces."

The museum is open mid-June to mid-October, Monday through Saturday, by appointment only. I, personally, conduct tours through the house, "ell," and barn twice a day, and a donation of four dollars is requested. Tours are limited to ten guests, and small children are not allowed because of the openness of the museum; there are few cases or labels and no velvet divider ropes. The greater part of the permanent collection is in the house, and recurrent visitors will observe that memorabilia are changed with frequency or exchanged with items previously located in other rooms. On exhibition in a large room connecting house with barn is one of the chief attractions of the museum, a scaled model (5' × 4' × 4') of a theatre-concert hall complete with curtain that can be raised or lowered, crystal chandelier, a sound system, and elaborate lighting with a special control panel. In this same exhibition area are displayed early 18th-century peepshows, toy theatres, three-dimensional set models including the works of Joseph Urban, Stewart Chaney, and Karl Heinz Overschelp, and original set designs. Changing exhibitions are staged in the entire 18th-century barn area. Posters and portions of historic theatres long since demolished are also in this area as well as the museum's collection of early slapsticks, jester's baubles, and early stage lighting pieces of the kerosene-fueled variety. Depending on the whim of the curator, the visitor may begin the tour in the barn, then progress to the house or vice versa.

Of the sixteen rooms in the house, three are used for office-workroom-storage area. Large filing cabinets hold thousands of playbills, the earliest, a David Garrick bill, is dated 1761. The nucleus of our clipping file is a very rare collection of the American theatre historian Herbert Jackson and includes clippings from some of the earliest newspapers and magazines of this country. Other file drawers protect an exceptionally fine small collection of early engravings and lithographs. Book-type souvenir playbills and special souvenir bills of the play of the silk and more elaborate variety have their special places. Autographs and manuscripts are filed separately. Autographed photographs, and those not autographed, are filed by size. Posters are rolled in special cardboard containers, except those that were mounted for special exhibitions or when the museum acquired them, and are stored in the smallest of the three storage rooms with all framed items not on display.

The very cheerful library is completely enclosed with books, including the spaces over the doors. Thousands of volumes make up this reference library and books are acquired frequently. Two walls of a small study and two large built-in cases in the living room house more of the library, and special collections are scattered throughout the house. Our library's many one-of-a-kind books include presentation copies, Grangerized[3] editions (my favorites), copies of plays autographed by all connected with a particular production, and very special volumes once belonging to famous artists in the theatre.

The museum's holdings reflect the curator-collector's slight preference for three dimensional and more "visual" items. This preference is influenced by the fact that the success of exhibitions I have seen or set up myself is determined by the interspersing of three-dimensional theatre items and manuscript or autograph material—success in this case being measured, as it unfortunately is, by attendance records and enthusiastic news media.

The breakfast nook in the kitchen is surrounded by Minton tiles depicting scenes from many Shakespeare plays; all of this room features posters, plaques, tinware, and pottery figurines representing the great bard himself or actors portraying roles in his plays. A not-to-be-intimidated Lillie Langtry shares the Shakespearean kitchen; she is shown on a large ironstone platter as Pauline in *Lady of Lyons* and is endorsing without qualification Watt's Glycerine Jelly of Violets.

The dining room features original works of art in oil, pastel, or watercolor and includes an excellent portrait of Edwin Booth in his later years and one of him playing Hamlet at the age of thirty. A slightly forbidding Charlotte Cushman sharply contrasts with a lovely charcoal and red crayon drawing of Julia Marlowe. An 18th-century embroidery of Sarah Siddons as the tragic muse, originating in that actress's family and acquired by this museum, balances a charming pastel of Francis Wilson as Pere Marlotte, in *The Little Father of the Wilderness*. Over the fireplace mantel in the same room, "Strolling Actresses Dressing in a Barn invented, painted, engraved and published by Hogarth March 25, 1738," is complemented by Irving R. Wiles' preliminary watercolor for his oil on canvas of Julia Marlowe, painted in 1901 and now at the National Gallery of Art in Washington, D.C. On the mantel itself, a rare 18th-century bulb pot with a medallion portrait of William Henry West Betty as Hamlet (child prodigy and known as the Young Roscius) is placed between a pair of girandoles featuring the French actress Rachel as Roxane in *Bajazet* and a pair of pottery figurines circa 1830 depicting Rebecca Paton as Mandane and Mr. Wood as Atabarnes in *Artaxerxes*. Early "blue china" plates picture three of America's famous theatres, Castle Garden Theatre and Park Theatre in New York City and Boston's Federal Street Theatre; the unusual shade of blue is emphasized because of the macramé background color in this room. A small 18th-century shelf holds the sterling silver chalice presented to David Belasco by the members and staff of the *To Night [sic] or Never Company*, March 18th, 1931, and nearby a stunning silver encrusted meerschaum pipe proves an admirer's generosity when it was presented as a gift to actor George Holland in 1875. Before leaving the dining room one has to mention the gilt-framed mirror decorated with a reverse painting on glass of actress Fanny Kemble, a large crewel work of poppies executed by actress Agnes Booth and framed as a dining room tray, and a brooding Paul Robeson as Othello, as designed by Susan Parkinson for Briglin Pottery which brings a touch of the 20th century into this 18th-century room.

Passing through the front hall with its unique enclosed circular stairway, one discovers a small cupboard that follows the contours of the stair wall; here one finds examples of a tradition dating from the middle of the 18th century, figurines of great theatrical personalities made by such notable firms as Bow, Chelsea, Wedgwood, and Worcester. One shelf is devoted to exquisite pottery figures of characters from the Commedia dell'Arte and on the shelf below is a depiction of Molière and two other actors in his play *Le Bourgeois gentilhomme*. Other choice figurines include Liston in five of his roles, Madame

Vestris as "The Broom Girl," Grimaldi as Clown in *Mother Goose*, T. D. Rice dancing Jim Crow, and a Royal Doulton figurine of W. S. Penley as "Charley's Aunt."

Deep window seats in the library provide perfect niches for the three Rogers Groups[4] showing Joseph Jefferson in acts one, two, and three of *Rip Van Winkle*. Outdoor greenery and ever-changing patterns of light create the perfect backdrop for these pieces sculpted by John Rogers in December 1871. Other Rogers groups are scattered about the museum: Edwin Booth as Lear, Shylock, and Iago to Tommaso Salvini's Othello; Dion Boucicault in his play *The Shaughraun* and Joseph Jefferson as fighting Bob Acres in *The Rivals*. Other sculpture includes busts of Edwin Booth, Sir Henry Irving, and Charles Mayne Young as Hamlet; Francis Wilson as himself; a painted plaster bust of a young Madge Evans endorsing Hats for Little Ladies; the original bronze bust of actor Arthur Byron by Doris Caesar; a polychromed, life-size, half-relief plaster cast of the head of Katharine Cornell; an 1879 bronze statue of Sarah Bernhardt as the Queen in *Ruy Blas*, and a plaster reproduction of Pietro Calvi's 1822 bust of Ira Aldridge as Othello. The magnificent original is in the Schomburg Collection in New York City.

Displayed over the library fireplace is a handsome case containing two canes: one a gift to Sir Henry Irving in 1885 from Boston actor William Warren, the other a gift of actress Laura Keene to John Wilkes Booth in 1865. On the mantel itself, a pair of girandoles portraying Edwin Forrest as Metamora provides interest for the original spear carried by Forrest in productions of that play in 1861; it stands to the left of the fireplace opening. Other theatre memorabilia in this room include a terra cotta figurine of the French actor Marais as Michael Strogof; a porcelain figurine of Coquelin as Cyrano; Bernhardt's traveling clock used on her last American tour; and a rare commemorative mug showing Van Amburgh, the lion tamer from Kentucky, with his menagerie, celebrating Queen Victoria's visit to Drury Lane Theatre to see this American perform.

The house's original "borning" room has been converted to a small study and contains a large section of the museum's reference library. Twenty-three "tinsel prints," in original form, and a tuppeny black and white print, handcolored and then decorated on the surface of the print or the reverse side with pieces of fabric, tinsel, and sequins cover two walls. These charming portraits of 18th and 19th-century actors and actresses are becoming increasingly rare. An antique pine breakfront holds some of the very special volumes for which this collection is noted: for example, Francis Wilson's biography of Joseph Jefferson bound in the fabric of his Bob Acres breeches, a rare and exquisitely bound edition of *The Thespian Dictionary*,[5] with yet another copy of the same book grangerized to nine volumes; of particular interest is Roland Young's guest book with holograph material in the form of inscriptions, poetry, and works of art by his friends. The book includes interesting drawings, interspersed with bars of music written by his artistic and musical friends. The very large sterling silver loving cup adds interest with its inscription: "Presented to Shepherd 'Ned' Holland by his flock, February 16, 1913"; E. M. Holland, actor son of the famous George Holland, is so honored by his fellow Lambs. A 1782 broadside almost escapes the eye, because one is diverted by the treasure trove of books in the breakfront; it announces the appearance of Les Comediens Français et Italiens in *le Festin de Pierre*.

From the study one enters the large living room, formerly the original keeping-kitchen. The huge fireplace with its baking oven still intact dominates the room, and the wood wainscotting and gunstock beams give one the feeling of the great hall in an 18th-century Cotswold home; it is the perfect setting for the museum's choicest memorabilia. Cerulean blue is the color that attracts the eye to a beautiful tile portrait of a young Sarah Bernhardt. This portrait is centered over the fireplace mantel and is companioned by objets d'art designed by English sculptor John Flaxman for Josiah Wedgwood, the English potter; these include oval bas-relief portraits of David Garrick and Sarah Siddons and rare chess figures of Siddons playing Lady Macbeth and her brother Charles Kemble essaying the role of Macbeth. Early busts of Shakespeare, a gilded animal carved cane head used by Edwin Booth, and two exceptionally fine Hogarth engravings, one for an "Authors Benefit" and the other "For the Benefit of Mr. Walker" are in the mantel area. Because of limited space it is not practical to mention all the varieties of memorabilia on exhibit in this room, but portraits of famous actors, figurines, and stage jewelry and properties compete for the viewer's attention. Included are Sir Henry Irving's Hamlet sword, a stunning "character doll" of Katharine Cornell as Jennifer Dubedat in Shaw's *The Doctor's Dilemma*, Julia Marlowe's Juliet dagger, two additional portraits of Edwin Booth, a genre wash drawing of Edmund Kean as Macbeth, and the gold watch Joseph Jefferson gave as a Christmas present in 1870 to actor E. M. Holland.

The Museum's inclusive collection of Actress glass is a favorite of all who visit here. This rare pattern glass was last produced in 1879 when the LaBelle Glass Factory of Bridgeport, Ohio burned. A very definite design identifies all Actress glass: a stippled shell on opposite sides of standing pieces and on opposite ends of trays and dishes. The shell is surrounded by an open loop with clear grape-like cluster pendant. Below, a flower tapers to a point. Portraits of stage favorites of the "Golden Age of Theatre" appear on each piece of this fascinating glass. Eight actresses were so honored: Kate Claxton, Maggie Mitchell, Lotta Crabtree, Adelaide Neilson, Fanny Davenport, Annie Pixley, Maud Granger, and Mary Anderson. One wonders if it was by a stroke of irony or the premeditated plan of some embittered lady that the three men appearing in this glass are all confined to the cheese dish! James S. Maffitt appears on the lid as the Lone Fisherman in E. E. Rice's *Evangeline*, an outlandish, rowdy take-off on Longfellow's poem of the same name. Stuart

Actress Glass (Cheese Dish Lid). James S. Maffit appearing as The Lone Fisherman in E. E. Rice's *Evangeline*, a rowdy outlandish take-off of Longfellow's poem of the same name. Rice's *Evangeline* burst upon the theatrical scene July 27, 1874 at Niblo's Garden in New York City.

Robson and William H. Crane, as the Two Dromios in Shakespeare's *The Comedy of Errors*, are shown on the base of this piece.

Quality rather than quantity describes our collection of miniatures of notable actors and actresses. Most have been painted on ivory. The majority portray actors in particular roles and are signed by the artists. An exquisite enameled Limoges miniature of Sarah Bernhardt as L'Aiglon is enhanced by a French paste jewelled frame and is an audience favorite, as is the portrait miniature of Edwin Booth, attributed to George Hewitt Cushman. It can be used as a brooch or pendant for hanging about the neck and supposedly is the miniature that Booth placed on the breast of his first wife at the time of her death.

At Boothbay, devotees of theatre history stand entranced before cases enclosing examples of some of the most fascinating of theatre collectibles, three-dimensional theatrical souvenirs. I am very proud of this—one of the best private collections. Anent these items, the earliest date we have seen is 1875 when Daly's Fifth Avenue Theatre in New York City presented each patron with a silver watch fob (to be used as a charm by the ladies) celebrating the 100th night of *Big Bonanza*. Interestingly enough, this play also marked the first appearance of the celebrated actor John Drew in New York City. These souvenirs, like the special souvenir paper or silk playbills, were distributed by theatre managers to celebrate a particular performance or player. Most of these mementos are dated, and a legend on the object usually details all information as to the play, theatre, date, and performance being celebrated. Frequently the names of theatrical managers and proprietors as well as leading actors and actresses appear, giving the item much more historical value. Long-run plays were not common in the annals of the theatre until the past fifty years or more; one can thus understand the significance of a 50th, 100th, or 200th performance and why the people involved created something special for that particular performance. Evidence indicates that Augustin Daly, American dramatist and manager, originated this charming custom of presenting gifts to patrons, but if the idea did not originate with him, it certainly received his unqualified endorsement. He actually presented sterling silver tickets when he started Wednesday matinees for those whom he referred to as "surburban ladies." A wondrous variety of items includes stamp boxes, ink wells, letter openers, mantel and traveling clocks, candy dishes, jewelry boxes, vases, candle holders, glass slippers, match cases, cigar cutters, sugar bowls and cream pitchers, glove buttoners, and a small pink box with two crystal tears (for the 100th performance in New York of Alexander Bisson's "supreme drama of tears," *Madame X*). De Wolf Hopper actually gave out splits of champagne for the 100th performance of *Panjandrum* in 1893. Sometimes there is not the remotest connection between the play and the object presented as a souvenir but more usually there was.

Not to be ignored is our collection of spoons, buttons, coins, medals, and stamps depicting famous theatre folk; ours is a generous sampling in all these categories of theatrical collecting. Of special interest are games, if not relating directly to theatre, at least depicting the famous stars on playing cards as well as other items of interest.

On the second floor of the Boothbay Theatre Museum a small room that served as the local prison in the late 18th century (the owner at that time was constable and frequently incarcerated delinquents in his home until they could be transferred to the nearby county jail) now serves as an exhibition area for the museum's small and choice collection of costumes. One of Romeo's costumes worn by Edwin Booth for the opening of his own theatre in 1869[6] and two of his Hamlet garments are displayed with Margaret Rutherford's Miss Marple cape, Noel Coward's dressing gown given to him when he was playing *Present Laughter* with Eva Gabor, and a dressing gown worn by Katharine Cornell. As well as other costumes, there are several elaborate crowns and half crowns including two Cleopatra headdresses: one worn by the "Divine" Sarah and the other by Agnes Booth. Fans used by Minnie Maddern Fisk, Eva LeGallienne, Lillian Gish, and Mei Lan-Fang are juxtaposed with shoes worn by great ladies of the theatre. Eye-catching is the word for Josephine Hull's red satin shoe with the rhinestone encrusted heel worn by that gifted comedienne in *Minnie and Mr. Williams*, a Broadway failure of 1948.

Throughout the museum, theatre-oriented furniture blends with other predominantly 18th-century pieces. Colorado Baby Doe Tabor's burled maple desk provides excellent exhibition space for rare Booth family autograph material; Sarah Bernhardt's extremely delicate gilt lyre-back chair from her Paris salon is mounted on a small stand to discourage all those who cannot resist the temptation to sit on this unique piece; Edwin Booth's Hamlet chair, carried throughout the United States whenever he played the role for which he was most famous, is on a large dais in an appropriate setting of "royal draperies" of antique vintage. Also in the large upstairs museum room is displayed the desk used by David Warfield in his Broadway success *The Music Master*.

Make-up boxes from about 1820 (with a beautiful Boucher-like painting of Commedia dell'Arte figures on the lid), Edwin Booth's 1866 box (without fillers), and Sidney Booth's kit complete with make-up draw attention to rare and early books dealing with make-up and costuming. Sidney Booth's kit appears as it did when he last used it and includes curling irons, shoe inserts for elevating his height, as well as the baby shoes worn by his only daughter.

Items from this museum are frequently on loan to other collections, museums, or special exhibitions. Some of the more choice items in the "America on Stage - 200 Years of Performing Arts" Bicentennial Exhibition at the John F. Kennedy Center for the Performing Arts in Washington, D.C. originated in this museum as did many of the items in the "Theatrical Evolution: 1776-1976" exhibition at the Hudson River Museum. An illustrated catalogue of the latter exhibition has many photographs of articles from the Boothbay Theatre collection. Institutions as diverse as the Museum of the City of New York and the William A. Farnsworth Library and Art Museum in Rockland, Maine have enhanced exhibitions with borrowed items. "Hamlet Through the Ages," an exhibition at the Shakespeare Festival Theatre in Stratford, Connecticut, originated with this museum.

Autographs and Manuscripts: a Collector's Manual, edited by Edmund Berkeley, Jr. with Herbert E. Klingelhofer and Kenneth W. Rendell as coeditors (Scribner, 1978), has a section on American Theatre written by this curator, and much of the material discussed concerns holdings from this museum. Articles in hundreds of newspapers (literally) and in magazines have discussed and illustrated the collection in general or particular phases of it. For example, *Down East Magazine*, July 1969; *Hobbies*, a magazine for collectors, May 1971; *The Maine History News*, July 1968; *Early American Antiques*, August 1974; *Spinning Wheel Antiques* and *Early Crafts*, April 1978, and *Americana Magazine* (published by American Heritage) July-August 1978 provide the most professional and informative material. More recently, Time-Life Books published volumes entitled *The Encyclopedia of Collectibles*, with this collection being the inspiration for the section on Theatre.

It is difficult to enumerate all the truly special items in the museum. As previously stated, we do not emphasize the Booth family, but we do have very rare autograph and holograph material relating to them, America's most famous family of actors. There are hundreds of letters written by practically every member of the family; in recent months rare and informative letters were acquired of Mary Anne Holmes Booth and Mary Devlin Booth, having in common the discussion of John Wilkes Booth. Junius Brutus Booth, the elder, wrote a long letter in French to Madame Delannoy the 30th of May, 1815, telling this woman, with whom he had boarded while acting in Brussels, that he had married her daughter on the 8th of that month. This letter is one of a group of approximately 100 that surfaced in the late 1800s and apparently disappeared or were destroyed. The elder Booth's boat ticket from New Orleans to Cincinnati on the S.S. Chenoweth, dated November 20th and found on his body when he died on that voyage, is also considered one of our rarer acquisitions. Edwin Booth's last contract signed with actor Lawrence Barrett is of special interest, as is his long, detailed contract with a playwright from whom he purchased exclusive rights to a particular play authored by the gentleman.

Mary Devlin's autograph album dated 1857 with entries limited to four original poems in the hand of Edwin Booth proves conclusively that this particular Hamlet was not always the melancholy Dane. Original glass negatives, in spite of their age, superbly well depict interior views of all the rooms in Edwin Booth's Chestnut Street home in Boston. Letters written by Edwin's nephew Junius Booth III to his brother Sydney Booth (both actors were sons of Edwin's brother Junius II and the actress Agnes Booth) indicate the state of mind that prompted him to kill his wife Florence and then commit suicide. His short-lived venture of operating an early Cinema Theatre in Brightlingsea, England, without success, brought about the cause of his demise.

About seventy-five books from the Booth family's Maryland home provide the reader with information as to what the Booths read. This small collection came to the Theatre Museum through the descendants of Joseph Booth, the youngest of the children, and many of the books are inscribed from one member of the family to another. Several of the books obviously belonged to John Wilkes. With these books, we acquired Joseph's Medical Diploma and a collection of Booth's Theatre box office cash books which make interesting reading.

Since Hamlet seems to have captured the imagination of almost every actor, probably since the first performance of the play, an excellent assemblage of material about it has been acquired, from early 18th-century playbills to today's latest Hamlet. Photographs, posters, annotated scripts, and autograph and holograph material relating in particular to its production are at Boothbay. The distaff side of those who played Hamlet (many actresses did) is strongly represented by a rare life-size lithograph poster in color of Anna E. Dickinson in the part. Anna was a close friend of Abraham Lincoln and was frequently entertained at the White House. Her reputation as a vociferous American reformer and lecturer did little to ingratiate her with the critics who, furthermore, did not like her Hamlet.

Two of the curator's favorite pictures are portraits of Edwin Booth. One, an oval oil on cardboard of Booth at age nineteen, is signed on the reverse "Sitting from life of Edwin Booth by John R. Johnston artist, Baltimore 1857." Of even greater interest, because of its impeccable provenance, is a very handsome oil by Hugo Svenson. In a letter dated April 19th, 1924, written in Minneapolis, Blanche Booth writes:

> This portrait of the world famous tragedian Edwin Booth shows him at the age of about forty when acting at his own theatre, "Booth's," New York City, during the remarkably extended "run" of Shakespeare's "Hamlet," Edwin Booth being the Hamlet, and myself Blanche De Bar Booth, his niece, in support as the character of "Ophelia". The work is that of a young artist, Hugo Svenson.

In 1976 the impecunious state of the American Shakespeare Theatre at Stratford, Connecticut prompted the sale of their Shakespearean collection of paintings, watercolors, drawings, ceramics, and tapestries. This museum was fortunate in acquiring an exquisite oil painting attributed to George Clint (British, 1770-1854). The painting, called "Petruchio and the Tailor," portrays Madame Vestris and John Philip Kemble in *The Taming of the Shrew*, Act IV, Scene III. The curator was especially interested in obtaining this painting, not just because of the beauty of its artwork and the excellent reputation of the artist, but of prime importance was the fact that Madame Vestris visited America with her actor husband, Charles Mathews, in 1838. Their stage engagement, though not very profitable, attracted much publicity.

The beautifully ornate staff used by Molière, France's greatest actor and dramatist in the 17th century, was a gift from a connoisseur-collector of all things Gallic, a generous Francophile. This particular item casts a spell upon all who see it, and well it should. Quite obviously gifts of this histrionic importance are rare indeed.

Of major importance to the theatre museum are donations in recent years of the Roland Young, the Joseph Holland, and the "Doc" Rockwell collections. Young was one of our great American actors known primarily for his work in the cinema, though he had established himself as a great actor before assuming a career in the movies. Joseph Holland, though not an actor himself, was the third generation of a famous acting family beginning with the original George Holland (1791-1870); "Doc" Rockwell was one of the "true greats" of vaudeville fame. When Young's widow presented us with his effects we were overwhelmed by the treasure trove. He was not only a very talented actor, but an artist of considerable reputation, especially known for his published caricatures "Actors and Others";[7] further, he was a poet and true bibliophile. All of his library relating to theatre, as well as his original caricatures and other art work, were included in this most generous gift. The collection of correspondence with his coterie of friends, the artistic elite of his time, provides an abundance of autograph and holograph material. Roland Young's immaculate scrapbooks mirror an exciting career beginning with his first appearance on stage in London in 1908 until his death in 1953. Young had written to Thornton Wilder urging him to write plays and in a long, choice letter written May 14, 1926 Wilder says: "Oh, sure, I mean to do plays some day. But I'm awfully dogged and slow-working about it." Wilder then continues with superlative praise for Young's acting. As one would expect there are many letters from Thorne Smith (1892-1934) whose "Topper" made a great movie vehicle for Roland Young and added still further distinction to his career.

The Holland collection contains memorabilia of all the family who trod the boards including George Sr., George Le Roy, Edmund Milton, Kate, Joseph Jefferson (named after the famous actor Joe Jefferson), and Edna Holland Taylor, who is still acting in television and movies. Playbills, hundreds of photographs, scrapbooks, and rare holograph and autograph material compose this memorabilia, but a small and very special selection of three-dimensional material adds even greater interest to this recent gift.

The "Doc" Rockwell material was more than a welcome addition because the curator is making every effort to strengthen the vaudeville segment, which has been neglected too long. Rockwell starred in vaudeville and Broadway revues in the 1920s and early 1930s. He gained his nickname "Doc" because of his "quack" doctor vaudeville routine in which he compared a banana (stem) to a human spine. When Rockwell brought the act to the Fred Allen Comedy Hour he gained a national reputation. With his droll medico-foolery he played such shows as the "Greenwich Village Follies," "Broadway Nights," "Quack, Quack Doctor," and others. Voluminous files of material with thousands of notes in "Doc's" holograph explain source material for so many of his famous routines that one sees this great mind developing an idea with the inventiveness of a master of comedy. His costumes, large lobby portrait, and illuminated lobby board with three-dimensional "comments" on the ailments that all flesh is heir to are a visual projection of a very special kind of humor. His "Glass Lady" (actually constructed from plastic) is now at home in Boothbay. The life-size nude lady is very intricately wired so that strategic areas of her body can be lighted by pressing special buttons on a control panel. "Doc's" partner pressed the buttons as he gave a very straightforward lecture on the female anatomy. The humor evoked when the assistant, dressed as a nurse, pressed the wrong buttons thus creating double-entendres combined with "Doc's" pretended annoyance made this one of the brightest and funniest routines in vaudeville. Rockwell was a clever artist, and hundreds of his original drawings used for illustrations in his magazine "Dr. Rockwell's Mustard Plaster" as well as in other publications of humor can be found in our files.

Most great actors describe as their favorite role the one they are currently playing. This curator tends to favor the Theatre Museum's latest acquisition which at this time happens to be a stunning gouache painting by Don Freeman. It very strongly evokes the stimulating excitement of "backstage" portraying Ethel Barrymore, Thelma Schnee, Richard Waring, and other members of the cast of *The Corn Is Green* waiting to make entrances. Ethel Barrymore as the play's Miss Moffat is, of course, the focal point as she stands with bicycle ready for her first entrance. This painting was presented to producer-director Herman Shumlin by the cast of *The Corn Is Green*, December 21, 1940 and was especially painted by Don Freeman. On the brass plaque under the play's title incised in Welsh is "Diolch Yn Fawr."

James Harding in his engrossing book *Sacha Guitry*,[8] the life of the French playwright-actor par excellence, reminds us that Guitry was a collector of great renown whose house was a veritable museum. He tells us that Guitry used to question the hours, days, months, and years that he spent choosing items for his collection, in waiting for them, hunting for them, pursuing and finding them! He once reflected, "I'm prepared to agree that you have to be a bit crazy to be a collector. Greed soon enters into it—insatiableness appears in its turn." Is there a collector or curator who would not agree?

While enjoying the latest acquisition, I am already frenetic in my efforts to acquire some coveted object. At the very moment of this writing I am negotiating for the upholstered armchair in which American playwright George Kelly wrote most of his plays. The fact that he is one of my favorite American playwrights has not a little to do with my determination.

I do not consider this collection finite or definitive; I do know that it is unique in America. Quite obviously I am continually collecting, collating, refining, and discovering, and, of course, I am very dependent on autograph dealers, antiquarians, and friends and lovers of theatre for filling in the too many gaps. Slowly but surely, professionals in the American theatre are recognizing the importance of collections such as this, and their cooperation is of the utmost importance. My love for and fascination with everything connected with theatre, coadunate with a long working experience as actor, director, and producer, are very much reflected in my collecting habits and in the Boothbay Theatre Museum's holdings. This is not what would be considered a great scholarly collection because a reasonable emphasis on the visual and three dimensional precludes its being so. It is a labor of love . . . love for the theatre, that bewitching lady, "'tis pity she's a whore."

FOOTNOTES

1. *Prince of Players, Edwin Booth*, by Eleanor Ruggles, W. W. Norton and Company, Inc., New York, 1952.
2. *The House of Life*, by Mario Praz, Oxford University Press, 1964.
3. Rev. James Granger, a vicar of Shiplake in the 18th century, by reputation one of the poorest theologians and preachers of his age. Remembered for his idea of illustrating a dictionary of national biography; thus the term "grangerizing" is known to bibliophiles the world over.
4. John Rogers was the first American artist to give popular appeal to sculpture. He concerned himself with illustrating the daily life of America. Between 1860 and 1893 he made a successful career by reproducing 100,000 copies of his eighty statuette groups.
5. *The Thespian Dictionary: or Dramatic Biography of the Eighteeneth Century*, printed by J. Cundee in London in 1802.
6. Booth's Theatre, Twenty-third Street, between Fifth and Sixth Avenues, New York City, opened Wednesday Evening, February 3, 1869.
7. *Actors and Others*, by Roland Young with an introduction by Ashton Stevens, Pascal Covici-Publisher, Chicago, 1925.
8. *Sacha Guitry: The Last Boulevardier*, by James Harding, Charles Scribner's Sons, New York, 1968.

BOOKSELLERS AND THE PERFORMING ARTS

James Ellis, Professor, Mount Holyoke College

This brief survey of American and British booksellers with holdings of interest to the theatre librarian or collector is undertaken from the single perspective of a private collector. With a few London exceptions, all of the booksellers listed issue catalogues or lists, my chief means of acquisition. They are all dealers with whom I have done business within the past three years, which, quite arbitrarily, leaves out a few who have been of service in the past (David Batterham, Richard Booth, Bow Windows, R. R. Guest, Guildhall Bookshop, K Books, and John Wrigley, among others). Finally, these are all booksellers whose holdings at some point coincide with my collecting interests: the performing arts and popular entertainment in Britain and America from about 1776 to about 1915. For convenience, the dealers have been grouped in five categories: (1) specialists in the performing arts; (2) booksellers issuing an occasional performing arts catalogue or routinely offering a number of theatre items; (3) antiquarian booksellers (incunabula to 19th century) who regularly have some items of interest to the theatre collector; (4) dealers specializing in modern first editions (later 19th century to the present), private presses, fine printing, and the like, who regularly have some performing arts items; (5) general out-of-print booksellers whose lists of reasonably priced books are worth perusal for the occasional theatre book.

I hope the listed booksellers will not feel wrongly categorized or misrepresented as to special holdings or relative expensiveness. Anyone who has followed the antiquarian book market in recent years will know how sharply prices have been rising. This has been true of performing arts books along with other areas of specialization, so that last year's outrageous price tag may look like this year's bargain. Auctions, in particular, which seem to affect book buyers the way blood does sharks, tend to send book prices still higher. Most of the dealers listed here keep their prices competitive with one another; a few whose prices seem consistently high or low have been singled out for comment. Finally, whatever the relative cost of books may have been fifteen, ten, or even five years ago, it seems to me that on average, prices of theatre books are slightly lower in America than in Britain, and slightly lower there than on the Continent.

James Ellis is Professor of English at Mount Holyoke College, South Hadley, MA 01075.

Special Collections, Vol. 1(1), Fall 1981
© 1981 The Haworth Press

Specialists in the Performing Arts

United States. The two most active theatre book specialists in America today, both established in 1976 by very knowledgeable theatre historians, are Richard Stoddard Performing Arts Books (90 E. 10th St., New York, NY 10003) and Theatricana (Box 4244 Campus Station, Athens, GA 30602). The former is especially strong in books on technical theatre and mise-en-scène, but ranges over all the performing arts. The latter includes plays, exhibition catalogues, and some ephemera, as well as popular, scholarly, and antiquarian works in theatre history and related fields. Both are rich in materials on the American stage, including the theatre outside New York. Not to be confused with Theatricana, despite a certain proximity on the other side of the Okefenokee, is Theatricalia (Box 12501 University Station, Gainesville, FL 32604), which has issued some eleven short lists featuring elegant books on costume and decor, European as well as English and American. On the other coast are two theatre book specialists not recently heard from: Carolyn Kaplan (P.O. Box 201, Laguna Beach, CA 92652) and John Makarewich Books (P.O. Box 7032, Van Nuys, CA 91409). The former has for many years issued large, if infrequent, catalogues on theatre and drama (mostly modern and including anthologies), as well as film, television, and radio. I am indebted to her for a number of choice 19th-century American items. Makarewich's holdings seem to be essentially 20th-century, but include some unusual titles and at very reasonable prices. Also in California is a newcomer, recently established Drama Books (511 Geary St., San Francisco, CA 94102), whose price range is somewhat higher for performing arts programs, posters, prints, and designs, as well as books. Comparable in price is M. M. Einhorn Maxwell Books, At the Sign of the Dancing Bear (80 East 11th St., New York, NY 10003), for generally ordinary out-of-print stock on dance, cinema, theatre, and puppetry. In the middle of the country, R. L. Brudvig (Box 8938, Minneapolis, MN 55408) has issued a number of short but lengthening lists of standard out-of-print British and American books on the performing arts, including plays.

Great Britain. Motley Books (Mottisfont Abbey, Romsey, Hants. S05 0LP), in some ways the heir to Ifan Kyrle Fletcher, is now the longest established catalogue-issuing theatre book specialist in Britain, with by far the most comprehensive, wide-ranging holdings. Since 1964 they have issued over fifty major catalogues (with items helpfully annotated) as well as numerous special lists. They began in London but are now in magnificent quarters at Mottisfont, with their own matchless theatre collection and reference library accessible to the serious scholar upon application. Their European holdings (from Russia and Eastern Europe to Spain and Portugal) are unrivaled, as is the range of current exhibition catalogues they stock. They are increasingly interested in supplying new theatre books, and are prepared to fill standing orders from institutions for all new and forthcoming titles in any or all areas of the performing arts. Relatively recent (1973) rivals to Motley, and perhaps now with greater emphasis on larger stocks of antiquarian books, are McKenzie & Sutherland (12 Stoneleigh Park Road, Ewell, Epsom, Surrey KT19 0QT) and Peter Wood (20 Stonehill Road, Great Shelford, Cambridge CB2 5JL). McKenzie & Sutherland have already issued forty-one catalogues, with the focus on the English stage and always including some scarce books and prints. Wood, who has issued twenty-six major catalogues, ranges more generally through out-of-print and current books in the performing arts. He also offers some playbills and other ephemera. Still more recently upon the scene (1978), but issuing catalogues at a frequent rate, is A. E. Cox, whose holdings are about equally divided between "Stage and Screen." He deals almost exclusively with British material, including periodicals and ephemera.

British theatre book specialists of more limited scope, with fewer catalogues and perhaps more routine material—but also asking more modest prices— are C. D. Paramor (25 St. Mary's Square, Newmarket, Suffolk CB8 0HZ), Arena Books (Shelsley Beauchamp, Worcs. WR6 6RH), B. Heyman (45 Royston Park Rd., Hatch End, Pinner, Middlesex), Robert F. Wilson (51 King St., Wallasey, Cheshire L44 0BY), and J. & V. Vinden (15 Velindre, Three Cocks, Powys LD3 0SY). Paramor and Arena, both established about 1976, issue rather frequent lists of out-of-print items (albeit not all of them are always in "collector's state"), including fugitive titles that seldom appear elsewhere. Heyman, Wilson, and Vinden have been silent recently, but in the past have offered an attractive array of theatre books at low prices. The most recent performing arts book specialists are Geoffrey Clifton's Theatre Bookshop (Piccadilly Plaza, York Street, Manchester M1 4AF), which describes itself as "The North's leading specialist in out of print books and ephemera on the performing arts," and, also from the North, Anne FitzSimons (The Retreat, The Green, Wetheral Carlisle, Cumbria CA4 8ET), who has offered a fine theatre book search service for several years and has now issued her first catalogue, including popular entertainment and magic as well as theatre items.

Some booksellers specializing in music also deserve inclusion, not only because of their holdings in opera and ballet, but also because they often offer some fine theatre items. Richard Macnutt Ltd. (29 Mount Sion, Tunbridge Wells, Kent TN1 1TZ) issues some of the handsomest catalogues in print and routinely includes some fascinating theatre books, playbills, and autograph material. H. Baron (136 Chatsworth Rd., London NW2) would seem to have a larger, if less elegant, stock including many periodicals. Travis & Emery (17 Cecil Court, London WC2N 4EZ) is a music bookseller who does not, as far as I know, issue catalogues but is worth a visit. While in London, one should also visit David Drummond's Pleasures of Past Times (11 Cecil Court), with his large array of ephemera, sheet music, post cards, souvenir programs, as well as books. Just around the corner is Winifred A. Myers (Autographs) Ltd. (Suite

52, 91 St. Martin's Lane, London WC2), with a good selection of theatre letters among her autograph material. And once in St. Martin's Lane, it is not so very far, if walking towards the British Library, to the most memorable theatre bookshop anywhere—Andrew Block's in Barter Street (London WC1A 2AH). The indestructible Mr. Block has probably sold more theatre books, prints, and ephemera than any man alive, and he continues to have much more still available.

Europe. Two Continental theatre book specialists are the Librairie Garnier-Arnoul (39 rue de Seine, 75006 Paris, France) and G. N. Landré (Rozengracht 8, 8861 XZ Harlingen, The Netherlands). The former issues very handsome catalogues and ranges widely over the performing arts, with an emphasis on the French stage. The latter is primarily a specialist in music books, but their catalogues usually include sections on theatre, cinema, music hall, film, and dance. Both firms' holdings of British and American books are understandably limited, and their prices for these items are seldom competitive.

Booksellers with Strong Performing Arts Holdings

United States. A number of booksellers who make no claim of specializing in the theatre nevertheless have substantial numbers of theatre items and may even produce the occasional catalogue in the performing arts. William H. Allen Co. (2031 Walnut St., Philadelphia, PA 19103) almost always conclude their literature catalogues with an array of theatre and drama books that include uncommon 18th and 19th-century titles, and at prices so reasonable that one can overlook their tendency to rebind anything shabby in sturdy library buckram. Both The Scholar Gypsy, Ltd. (8 South 3rd St., Geneva, IL 60134) and Willis Monie Books (R.D. 1, Box 335, Cooperstown, NY 13326) offer a number of good theatre books in their lists. Cragsmoor Books (P.O. Box 66, Cragsmoor, NY 12420), although with no pretensions beyond offering general out-of-print American titles, almost always manages to have something that interests me. John Wm. Martin (49 North Stone Ave., La Grange, IL 60525) specializes in the Renaissance in England and can be counted on for interesting material on Shakespeare and his contemporaries. Once again a specialist in music (if the one catalogue seen is representative) deserves mention; Dorothy Elsberg (Box 178, West Stockbridge, MA 01266) listed some vocal scores of 19th-century English operas and musicals unknown to Nicoll and to Loewenberg.

Britain. Blackwell's (Broad Street, Oxford OX1 3BQ) and W. Heffer & Sons Ltd. (20 Trinity St., Cambridge CB2 3NG) should head the list of British booksellers who can be counted on for an occasional performing arts catalogue as well as a substantial number of theatre holdings (both new and out-of-print) in stock. Blackwell's antiquarian department has recently been rusticated, so to speak, and is now to be found at Fyfield Manor, Fyfield nr. Abingdon, Oxon. OX13 5LR, under the title "Blackwell's Rare Books." Their excellent music shop, at 38 Holywell Street, Oxford OX1 3SW (almost next door to the King's Arms, a pub with one of the finest selections of real ales in England), publishes catalogues of both new and second-hand books and scores. A Cambridge dealer who cannot lay claim to Heffer's longevity, but who produces handsome catalogues with some choice theatre items, is Siddeley & Hammond Ltd. (19 Clarendon St., Cambridge CB1 1JU). Eric & Joan Stevens (74 Fortune Green Rd., London NW6 1DS) occasionally issue a theatre catalogue and always have material of interest to collectors of late 19th and early 20th-century theatre books among their stock of general literature, biography, and criticism. Why booksellers specializing in the Royal Family should also issue occasional catalogues on "Entertainment" is a subject not to be questioned here, but it is indeed true of Gaby Goldschieder (29 Temple Rd., Windsor, Berks.) and Leslie & Patricia Parris (The Corner House, Hillcrest Ave., Llandrindod Wells, Powys, Wales). C. C. Kohler (12 Horsham Rd., Dorking, Surrey RH4 2JL) has issued, in recent years, among his general antiquarian catalogues, two devoted exclusively to collections of acting editions of 19th-century (and a few 18th-century) plays. A collection of 2,224 plays was sold for £5,000, and another of 725 plays for £2,900. Kohler makes a claim for rarity that is both true and untrue. The plays are probably not in fact scarce, but they are so seldom dignified with a place in a bookseller's catalogue or on his shelves that they might as well be termed scarce. One hates to contemplate the number of these flimsily wrapped items that have been consigned to the trash bins by booksellers who could not be bothered. Anyone interested in the aesthetic and artistic aspects of the late 19th and early 20th-century theatre simply must acquire at least the catalogues (if he cannot afford the contents) of Warrack & Perkins (Rectory Farm House, Church Enstone, Oxon. OX7 4NL), whose specialities are the Pre-Raphaelites, art nouveau, and some later movements, both British and Continental. Their handsomely illustrated catalogues of books, prints, and original works of art are works of art in themselves; their Claud Lovat Fraser catalogue seemed virtually a catalogue raisonné.

Antiquarian Booksellers with Some Theatre Items

United States. Three American antiquarian booksellers who can be counted on for a desirable theatre book or two in virtually every catalogue, and all at very reasonable prices, are Carnegie Book Shop Inc. (140 East 59th St., New York, NY 10022), Ken Leach (P.O. Box 78, Brattleboro, VT 05301), and Roger Butterfield Inc. (White House, Hartwick, NY 13348). Carnegie also issues catalogues of autograph material, again almost invariably with theatre items.

Britain. Dozens of British antiquarian booksellers have provided me, over the years, with theatre items that might have been slightly more expensive if acquired from a theatre book specialist. The Tyrrell Bookshop & Gallery (94

Christchurch Rd., Ringwood, Hants. BH24 1DR)—formerly "Henry Bristow Ltd." of the same address but now being distinguished from Henry Bristow Ltd. at 105 Christchurch Rd. which continues to offer a good variety of autograph material—can provide a wide range of books on popular culture and entertainment, as well as ephemera, including theatre programs. Derrick Nightingale (32 Coombe Rd., Kingston-upon-Thames, Surrey KT2 7AG), formerly *David* Bristow Ltd. (just to confuse things further or to sort them out) is also strong in popular material, as well as British topography, including books describing London theatres and the theatre scene. Peter Murray Hill Ltd. (35 North Hill, Highgate, London N6) issues catalogues that are both entertaining and informative. Thomas Thorp (47 Holborn Viaduct, London EC1) offers general antiquarian books from its London shop and a vast array of out-of-print and remaindered books at its Surrey branch (170 High St., Guildford). Ian Hodgkins & Co. Ltd. (Mount Vernon, Butterow, Rodborough, Stroud, Glocs. GL5 2LP), E. M. Lawson & Co. (Kingsholm, East Hagbourne, Oxon. OX11 9LN), and Anthony W. Laywood (Knipton, Grantham, Lincs. NG32 1RF) almost never fail to tempt me with one title or another. Not far behind this trio comes a host of others: Aurora Books (The Bothy, Puckrup, Tewkesbury, Glocs.), R. & J. Balding (81 Great King St., Edinburgh EH3 6RN), David Bickersteth (38 Fulbrooke Rd., Cambridge CB3 9EE), Andrew Boyle Ltd. (21 Friar St., Worcester WR1 2NA), Bridge Conachar (St. David's Bridge, Cranbrook, Kent TN17 3HJ), Charles Cox (Colemans, Cheritan Fitzpaine, Crediton, Devon EX17 4HW), Wm. Dawson & Sons Ltd. (Cannon House, Folkestone, Kent CT19 5EE), Deighton, Bell & Co./Frank Hammond (13 Trinity St., Cambridge CB2 1TD), Alex Fotheringham (Stone Bridge, Chawleigh, Chumleigh, Devon), George's (89, 81, & 52 Park St., Bristol BS1 5PW), T. & L. Hannas (33 Farnaby Rd., Bromley, Kent BR1 4BL), A. R. Heath (15 Badminton Rd., Downend, Bristol), Stanley Noble (24 Gladwell Rd., London N8), Sanders of Oxford (104 the High, Oxford OX1 4BW), J. Shotton (89 Elvet Bridge, Durham City, Durham DH1 3AQ), and Robin Waterfield Ltd. (36 Park End St., Oxford OX1 1HJ). Two specialists in Irish books, including all the figures associated with the Abbey Theatre, are Emerald Isle Books (539 Antrim Rd., Belfast BT15 3BU) and P. & B. Rowan (Carlton House, 92 Malone Rd., Belfast BT9 5HP), both in Northern Ireland. A specialist in Scottish subjects is James Thin Ltd. (53-59 South Bridge, Edinburgh EH1 1YS).

Dealers Specializing in Modern First Editions, etc.

United States. Dealers who concentrate on modern first editions and fine press books in some instances tend to be more expensive than general or antiquarian dealers, and their stock is often limited to figures with major literary or artistic reputations, such as Wilde, Shaw, Yeats, Synge, Craig,

O'Neill, Pinter, and Beckett. Within their specialities, however, their stock may have items virtually unobtainable elsewhere. George S. MacManus Co. (1317 Irving St., Philadelphia, PA 19107) deals primarily in American authors and is not particularly expensive, given the fine quality of their stock. The Jenkins Co. (Box 2085, Austin, TX) has a good selection of modern first editions. George Robert Minkoff (RFD #3, Box 147, Great Barrington, MA 01230) occasionally has some early theatre material but at decidedly high prices. Two dealers with more modest holdings, and prices to match, are Gramercy Book Shop (22 East 17th St., New York, NY 10003) and North Shore Books Ltd. (8 Green St., Huntington, NY 11743).

Britain. No one could list British booksellers of modern first editions without including Bertram Rota Ltd. (4, 5, & 6 Savile Row, London W1X 2LN), although I have somehow lost touch with them in recent years. Taking their place in recent years have been Dalian Books (14 Remington St., Islington, London N1 8DH), Deval & Muir (Takely, Bishop's Stortford, Herts. CM22 6NA), and Sevin Seydi (80 Marquis Rd., London NW1 9UB). The latter two have excellent holdings in fine printing and the graphic arts, as well as modern firsts. Theatre items are also to be found in the stock of Ian McKelvie (45 Hertford Rd., London N2 9BX), Robert Temple (The King's Cross Bookshop, 18 York Way, London N1 9AA), and I. D. Edrich (17 Selsdon Rd., London E11 2QF). Edrich has a large stock of literary periodicals, both runs and individual numbers.

General Out-of-Print Booksellers

I have been so well served by a few United States booksellers whose stock is general out-of-print material and whose prices are extremely reasonable that I feel an obligation to conclude this survey by mentioning them. They are Biblo & Tannen (63 Fourth Ave., New York, NY 10003),* R. Dunaway (6138 Delmar Blvd., Saint Louis, MO 63112), Robert L. Merriam (Newhall Rd., Conway, MA 01341), Robert Shuhi-Books (P.O. Box 268, Morris, CT 06763), and the Strand Book Store, Inc. (828 Broadway, New York, NY 10003).

I am grateful to New York dealer Richard Stoddard for the following list of "Antiquarian Booksellers *Specializing in Theatre*," some of whom have been mentioned.

Arena Books (V. J. Packwood), Shelsley Beauchamp, Worcester WR6 6RH, England
Backstage Books (Howard L. Ramey), P.O. Box 3676, Eugene, OR 97403
Geoffrey Clifton's Theatre Bookshop, Piccadilly Plaza, York St., Manchester M1 4AF, England
A. E. Cox, 21 Cecil Rd., Itchen, Southampton SO2 7HX, England
Drama Books, 511 Geary St., San Francisco, CA 94102

---

* Biblo & Tannen went out of business in July 1979 after fifty-one years of partnership. Cf. "Last Chapter in Biblo & Tannen Story," *The New York Times*, July 27, 1979.—Editor's Note.

Librairie Garnier Arnoul, 39, rue de Seine, 75006 Paris, France

Marina Henderson, Langton Gallery, 3 Langton St., London, S.W. 10, England (original stage designs)

Carolyn Kaplan, P.O. Box 201, Laguna Beach, CA 92652

J. W. McKenzie, 12 Stoneleigh Park Rd., Ewell, Epsom, Surrey, KT19 0QT, England

Motley Books, Ltd., Mottisfont Abbey, Romsey, Hampshire SO5 0LP, England

Pleasures of Past Times, 11 Cecil Court, Charing Cross Rd., London W.C.2, England

R. L. Shep, 163 Garfield St., Seattle, WA 98109

Anna Sosenko, 76 W. 82nd St., New York, NY 10024 (autographs and memorabilia)

Charles Spencer Theatre Gallery, Flat 11, 44 Grove End Rd., London, N.W.8 9NE, England (original stage designs)

Richard Stoddard, Performing Arts Books, 90 E. 10th St., New York, NY 10003 (books, ephemera, original stage designs)

Theatrebooks, 1576 Broadway, New York, NY 10036, (new and antiquarian)

Theatricana, Box 4244, Campus Sta., Athens, GA 30602

John S. Vinden, 15 Velindre, Three Cocks, Brecon Powys, LD3 0SY, England (new and antiquarian)

Peter Wood, 20 Stonehill Rd., Great Shelford, Cambridge, CB2 5JL, England

Although there are no antiquarian booksellers in Canada *specializing* in theatre materials, Heather McCallum, Head of the Theatre Department in the Metropolitan Toronto Library, reports four general antiquarian dealers who offer materials in the performing arts: Hugh Anson-Cartwright, 229 College Street, Toronto, Ontario M5T 1R4; Dora Hood's Bookroom Ltd., 34 Ross Street, Toronto, Ontario M5T 1Z9; David Mason Books, 638 Church Street, Toronto, Ontario M4Y 2G3; and William Nelson Books (Nelson Ball), 686 Richmond Street West, Toronto, Ontario M6J 1C3 (Canadian only).

PERFORMING ARTS RESOURCES—
A DIRECTORY

Significant performing arts collections and holdings—both large and small—are to be found in the following select listing of libraries, museums, and institutions. The arrangement is alphabetical by state or province, and then alphabetically by city.

ALABAMA
Mobile Public Library, Special Collections Division, 701 Government Street, *Mobile* 36602
Alabama Department of Archives and History, Manuscripts Division, *Montgomery* 36130

ALASKA
University of Alaska at Fairbanks, *Fairbanks* 99701

ARIZONA
Tucson Public Library, Fine Arts Room, 200 South Sixth Avenue, *Tucson* 85726
University of Arizona, *Tucson* 85721

ARKANSAS
University of Arkansas, *Fayetteville* 72701

CALIFORNIA
University of California, Special Collections, *Berkeley* 94720
Claremont College, Honnold Library, 900 North College Avenue, *Claremont* 91711
University of California, Davis, Shields Library, Department of Special Collections, *Davis* 95616
Academy of Motion Picture Arts and Sciences, 9038 Melrose Avenue, *Hollywood* 90069
University of California, Special Collections, *Irvine* 92713
California State University, Special Collections, 1250 Bellflower Boulevard, *Long Beach* 90840
Institute of the American Musical, 840 North Larrabee Street, *Los Angeles* 90069
Los Angeles Public Library, 630 West Fifth Street, *Los Angeles* 90071
Music Center Operating Company Archives, 135 North Grand Avenue, *Los Angeles* 90012
Natural History Museum of Los Angeles County, 900 Exposition Boulevard, *Los Angeles* 90007
University of California, Los Angeles, Theatre Arts Library, *Los Angeles* 90024
University of Southern California, Special Collections Department, University Park, *Los Angeles* 90007
Pasadena Public Library, Fine Arts Division, 285 East Walnut Street, *Pasadena* 91101
University of California, Riverside, University Library, 4045 Canyon Crest Drive, P.O. Box 5900, *Riverside* 92507
San Diego Public Library, 820 E Street, *San Diego* 92101
San Diego State University, 5300 Campanile Drive, *San Diego* 92182
California Historical Society, 2099 Pacific Avenue (mailing address: 2090 Jackson Street) *San Francisco* 94109
University of San Francisco, Richard A. Gleeson Library, Golden Gate and Parker Avenue, *San Francisco* 94117
Huntington Library, Art Gallery and Botanical Gardens, 1151 Oxford Road, *San Marino* 91108
University of California, Santa Barbara, Special Collections, *Santa Barbara* 93106
University of Santa Clara, Michael Orradre Library, *Santa Clara* 95053

University of California, Santa Cruz, McHenry Library, *Santa Cruz* 95064
Stanford University, *Stanford* 94305
University of the Pacific, Irving Martin Library, *Stockton* 95211
California Institute of the Arts, 24700 McBean Parkway, *Valencia* 91355

COLORADO
University of Colorado, Boulder, Norlin Library, *Boulder* 80309
Colorado Historical Society, 1300 Broadway, *Denver* 80203
Denver Public Library, 1357 Broadway, *Denver* 80203
University of Denver, Penrose Library, 2150 East Evans, *Denver* 80208

CONNECTICUT
Connecticut Historical Society, One Elizabeth Street, *Hartford* 06105
Connecticut State Library, 231 Capitol Avenue, *Hartford* 06115
Wesleyan University, Olin Memorial Library, *Middletown* 06457
Yale University, Crawford Theatre Collection, *New Haven* 06520
Yale University, Drama Library, Box 1903A, Yale Station, *New Haven* 06520
Yale University, Manuscripts and Archives, Box 1603A, Yale Station, *New Haven* 06520
Yale University, Yale Collection of Historical Sound Recordings, 120 High Street, *New Haven* 06520
University of Connecticut Library, *Storrs* 06268
Eugene O'Neill Theater Center, 305 Great Neck Road, *Waterford* 06385

DELAWARE
Historical Society of Delaware, 505 Market Street, *Wilmington* 19801

DISTRICT OF COLUMBIA
Folger Shakespeare Library, 201 East Capitol Street, *Washington*, D.C. 20003
Georgetown University, Joseph Mark Lauinger Library, 37th & O Streets., N.W., *Washington*, D.C. 20057
Howard University, Founders Library, 500 Howard Place, N.W., *Washington*, D.C. 20059
John F. Kennedy Center for the Performing Arts, Library of Congress Performing Arts Library, *Washington*, D.C. 20506
Library of Congress, Manuscript Division, *Washington*, D.C. 20540
Library of Congress, Rare Book and Special Collections, *Washington*, D.C. 20540
National Theatre Library/Archives, 1321 E Street, N.W., *Washington*, D.C. 20004

FLORIDA
University of Florida, Belknap Collection for the Performing Arts, 210 Library West, *Gainesville* 32611
Ringling Museum of Art, Art Research Library, P.O. Box 1838, *Sarasota* 33578
Charles MacArthur Center for American Theatre, Florida State University, *Tallahassee* 32304
University of South Florida, 4202 Fowler Avenue, *Tampa* 33620
University of Tampa, Merl Kelce Library, 401 West Kennedy Boulevard, *Tampa* 33606

GEORGIA
University of Georgia, *Athens* 30602
Emory University, General Libraries, *Atlanta* 30322
Georgia Southern College, Landrum Box 8074, *Statesboro* 30458
Rollins College, Mills Memorial Library, *Winter Park* 32789

HAWAII
University of Hawaii, 2550 The Mall, *Honolulu* 96822
Mariska Aldrich Memorial Foundation, Inc., Library of Music, 2512 Komo Mai Drive, *Pearl City* 96782

ILLINOIS
Southern Illinois University, Delyte W. Morris Library, *Carbondale* 62901

Chicago Historical Society, Clark Street & West North Avenue, *Chicago* 60614
Chicago Public Library, Special Collections, 425 North Michigan Avenue, *Chicago* 60611
Newberry Library, 60 West Walton Street, *Chicago* 60610
University of Chicago, Special Collections, Joseph Regenstein Library, 1100 East 57th Street, *Chicago* 60637
University of Illinois at Chicago Circle, 801 South Morgan Street, P.O. Box 8198, *Chicago* 60680
Northern Illinois University, Founders Memorial Library, *DeKalb* 60115
Southern Illinois University at Edwardsville, Elijah P. Lovejoy Library, *Edwardsville* 62025
Northwestern University Library, Special Collections Department, 1935 Sheridan Road, *Evanston* 60201
Lake Forest College, Donnelley Library, Sheridan and College Roads, *Lake Forest* 60045
Illinois State University, Milner Library, *Normal* 61761
University of Illinois, Urbana/Champaign, Music Library, *Urbana* 61801

INDIANA
Indiana University, Bloomington, Lilly Library, 10th Street & Jordan Avenue, *Bloomington* 47401
Indiana University, South Bend, 1700 Mishawaka Avenue, *South Bend* 46615
Purdue University Libraries and Audio-Visual Center, Stewart Center, *West Lafayette* 47907
Purdue University, North Central Campus Library, 1401 South U.S. Highway 421, *Westville* 46391

IOWA
Iowa State University, *Ames* 50011
University of Iowa, *Iowa City* 52242
Museum of Repertoire Americana, Midwest Old Threshers, *Mt. Pleasant* 52641

KANSAS
Independence Community Junior College, College Avenue and Brookside Drive (mailing address: Box 708) *Independence* 67301
University of Kansas, Watson Memorial Library, *Lawrence* 66045

KENTUCKY
Hopkinsville Community College, North Drive, *Hopkinsville* 42240
Louisville Free Public Library, Fourth and York Streets, *Louisville* 40203
University of Louisville, 2301 South 3rd Street, *Louisville* 40208

LOUISIANA
Louisiana State University, *Baton Rouge* 70803
New Orleans Public Library, Art and Music Division, 219 Loyola Avenue, *New Orleans* 70140
Tulane University, Howard-Tilton Memorial Library, Special Collections, 7001 Freret, *New Orleans* 70118

MAINE
Boothbay Theatre Museum, Corey Lane, *Boothbay* 04537
University of Maine, Special Collections, Raymond H. Fogler Library, *Orono* 04469

MARYLAND
Enoch Pratt Free Library, 400 Cathedral Street, *Baltimore* 21201
Johns Hopkins University Libraries, Milton E. Eisenhower Library, *Baltimore* 21218
Maryland Historical Society, 201 West Monument Street, *Baltimore* 21201
Goucher College, Julia Rogers Library, Dulaney Valley Road, *Towson* 21204

MASSACHUSETTS
Amherst College, *Amherst* 01002
Boston Public Library, Copley Square, *Boston* 02117
Boston University, Mugar Memorial Library, 771 Commonwealth Avenue, *Boston* 02215
Bostonian Society, Old State House, 206 Washington Street, *Boston* 02109

Emerson College, Abbot Memorial Library, 303 Berkeley Street, *Boston* 02116
Harvard University, Houghton Library, *Cambridge* 02138
Radcliffe College, Schlesinger Library, 3 James Street, *Cambridge* 02138
Tufts University, Cohen Arts Center, *Medford* 02155
Smith College, Werner Josten Library for the Performing Arts, *Northampton* 01063
Mount Holyoke College, Williston Memorial Library, *South Hadley* 01075
American Jewish Historical Society, 2 Thornton Road, *Waltham* 02154
Brandeis University, *Waltham* 02154
American Antiquarian Society, 185 Salisbury Street, *Worcester* 01609

MICHIGAN
University of Michigan, Department of Rare Books and Special Collections, *Ann Arbor* 48109
Detroit Institute of Arts, Research Library, 5200 Woodward Avenue, *Detroit* 48202
Detroit Public Library, Music and Performing Arts Department, 5201 Woodward Avenue, *Detroit* 48202
Wayne State University, General Library, *Detroit* 48202
Michigan State University, Special Collections Division, *East Lansing* 48824
Flint Public Library, Art, Music & Drama Department, 1026 East Kearsley Street, *Flint* 48502
American Museum of Magic, 107 East Michigan Avenue, *Marshall* 49068

MINNESOTA
Guthrie Theatre Foundation, 725 Vinaland Place, *Minneapolis* 55403
Minneapolis College of Art and Design, 200 East 25th Street, *Minneapolis* 55404
Minneapolis Public Library and Information Center, Literature and Language Department, 300 Nicollet Mall, *Minneapolis* 55401
Minnesota Historical Society, Cedar Street and Central Avenue, *St. Paul* 55101
St. Paul Public Library, 90 West 4th Street, *St. Paul* 55102

MISSISSIPPI
Mississippi Department of Archives and History, *Jackson* 39217

MISSOURI
Missouri Historical Society, *Columbia* 65201
University of Missouri, *Columbia* 65201
University of Missouri, Kansas City, Room 300 Playhouse, *Kansas City* 64110
Washington University, *St. Louis* 63130

NEBRASKA
Dana College, C. A. Dana Life Library, College Drive, *Blair* 68008
Nebraska State Historical Society, 1500 R Street, *Lincoln* 68508
University of Nebraska at Lincoln, *Lincoln* 68508

NEVADA
University of Nevada, *Reno* 89507

NEW HAMPSHIRE
University of New Hampshire, *Durham* 03824
Dartmouth College, Baker Library, *Hanover* 03755

NEW JERSEY
Rutgers University, *New Brunswick* 08903
Princeton University, William Seymour Theatre Collection, *Princeton* 08540
Monmouth College, Murry and Leonie Guggenheim Memorial Library, *West Long Branch* 07764

NEW MEXICO
Las Cruces Public Library, 200 East Picacho Avenue, *Las Cruces* 88001

NEW YORK
State University of New York, Binghamton, Glenn G. Bartle Library, *Binghamton* 13901
State University of New York, Brockport, Drake Memorial Library, *Brockport* 14420
Brooklyn College, *Brooklyn* 11210
Brooklyn Public Library, Grand Army Plaza, *Brooklyn* 11238
Hamilton College, *Clinton* 13323
Corning Community College, Arthur A. Houghton, Jr. Library, *Corning* 14830
Queens College, 65-30 Kissena Boulevard, *Flushing* 11367
Queens Historical Society, 143-35 37th Avenue, *Flushing* 11354
Hofstra University, *Hempstead* 11550
Cornell University, *Ithaca* 14853
Queensborough Public Library, Art and Music Division, 89-11 Merrick Boulevard, *Jamaica* 11432
New Rochelle Public Library, Fine Arts Department, 662 Main Street, *New Rochelle* 10805
American Academy of Arts and Letters, 633 West 155th Street, *New York* 10032
American Academy of Dramatic Arts, 120 Madison Avenue, *New York* 10016
American Museum of Natural History, 79th Street and Central Park West, *New York* 10024
American Place Theatre, 111 West 46th Street, *New York* 10036
Armstead-Johnson Foundation for Theatre Research, Hotel Chelsea, 222 West 23d Street, *New York* 10011
Columbia University, Special Collections, 525 Broadway, *New York* 10027
Cooper-Hewitt Museum of Decorative Arts and Design, Fifth Avenue at 90th Street, *New York* 10028
Fashion Institute of Technology, 227 West 27th Street, *New York* 10001
Hatch-Billops Archives, 491 Broadway, *New York* 10012
Hispanic Society of America, 613 West 155th Street, *New York* 10032
International Theatre Institute of the United States, Inc., 1860 Broadway, *New York* 10023
Juilliard School, Lila Acheson Wallace Library, Lincoln Center, *New York* 10023
Metropolitan Museum of Art, Irene Lewisohn Costume Reference Library, Fifth Avenue at 82d Street, *New York* 10028
Municipal Archives and Record Center, 23 Park Row, *New York* 10007
Museum of Broadcasting, 1 East 53d Street, *New York* 10022
Museum of the City of New York, Fifth Avenue at 103d Street, *New York* 10029
Nananne Porcher Osprey Designs, 49 West 96th Street, *New York* 10025
Neighborhood Playhouse School of the Theatre, Irene Lewisohn Library, 340 East 54th Street, *New York* 10022
New-York Historical Society, 170 Central Park West, *New York* 10024
New York Public Library, Performing Arts Research Center, 111 Amsterdam Avenue, *New York* 10023
New York University Library, Special Collections, 70 Washington Square South, *New York* 10012
Radio City Music Hall Library/Archives, 1260 Avenue of the Americas, *New York* 10020
Paul Robeson Archives, 157 West 57th Street, Suite 403, *New York* 10018
Shubert Archive, 234 West 44th Street, *New York* 10036
Theatre of Latin America, 1860 Broadway, *New York* 10023
Traphagen School of Fashion, 257 Park Avenue South, *New York* 10010
Walter Hampden-Edwin Booth Theatre Collection and Library, 16 Gramercy Park, *New York* 10003
YIVO Institute for Jewish Research, 1048 Fifth Avenue, *New York* 10028
Mount Pleasant Public Library, 350 Bedford Road, *Pleasantville* 10570
State University of New York, College at Purchase, Lincoln Avenue, *Purchase* 10580
University of Rochester, Department of Rare Books, Manuscripts and Archives, *Rochester* 14627
State Museum, Division of Historical Services, University of the State of New York, *Schenectady* 12306
State University of New York, Stony Brook, Special Collections, *Stony Brook* 11794
Syracuse University, *Syracuse* 13210
Chautauqua County Historical Society, East Main Street, Village Park, P.O. Box 173, *Westfield* 14787
American Museum of Comedy, William Treadwell Library, *Yonkers*

NORTH CAROLINA
Institute of Outdoor Drama, University of North Carolina, 202 Graham Memorial 052-A, *Chapel Hill* 27514
University of North Carolina, Chapel Hill, Wilson Library, *Chapel Hill* 27514
Duke University, William R. Perkins Library, *Durham* 27706
North Carolina School of the Arts, Semens Library, 200 Waughtown Street, *Winston-Salem* 27107

OHIO
Bowling Green State University, *Bowling Green* 43402
Cincinnati Historical Society, Eden Park, *Cincinnati* 45202
Hebrew Union College, Jewish Institute of Religion, Klau Library, 3101 Clifton Avenue, *Cincinnati* 45220
Public Library of Cincinnati and Hamilton County, Art and Music Department, 800 Vine Street, *Cincinnati* 45202
Cleveland Public Library, 325 Superior Avenue, *Cleveland* 44114
Ohio State University, Theatre Research Institute, 1712 Neil Avenue, *Columbus* 43210
Rutherford B. Hayes Library, 1337 Hayes Avenue, *Fremont* 43420
Kent State University, Department of Special Collections, *Kent* 44242
Miami University, Edgar W. King Library, *Oxford* 45056

OKLAHOMA
University of Oklahoma, Drama Library, 550 Parrington Oval, *Norman* 73019

OREGON
Oregon State University, *Corvallis* 97331
University of Oregon, *Eugene* 97403

PENNSYLVANIA
Bryn Mawr College, *Bryn Mawr* 19010
Haverford College, *Haverford* 19041
Franklin and Marshall College, *Lancaster* 17604
Drexel University Libraries, 32 & Chestnut Street, *Philadelphia* 19104
Free Library of Philadelphia, Logan Square, *Philadelphia* 19103
Historical Society of Pennsylvania, 1300 Locust Street, *Philadelphia* 19107
Temple University, Special Collections Department, *Philadelphia* 19122
University of Pennsylvania, Furness Library, 3420 Walnut Street, *Philadelphia* 19104
Carnegie Library of Pittsburgh, Art Division, 4400 Forbes Avenue, *Pittsburgh* 15213
University of Pittsburgh, Special Collections Department, 363 Hilman Library, *Pittsburgh* 15260
Pennsylvania State University, Fred Lewis Pattee Library, *University Park* 16801
Historical Society of York County, *York* 17405

RHODE ISLAND
Brown University, John Hay Library, 20 Prospect Street, *Providence* 02912
Rhode Island Historical Society, John Brown House, 52 Power Street, *Providence* 02906
Rhode Island School of Design, 2 College Street, *Providence* 02903

SOUTH CAROLINA
South Carolina Historical Society, Fireproof Building, *Charleston* 29401

TENNESSEE
Chattanooga Public Library, *Chattanooga* 37402
University of Tennessee, Knoxville, Special Collections, *Knoxville* 37916
Public Library of Nashville and Davidson County, Eighth Avenue, N. and Union, *Nashville* 37203

TEXAS
University of Texas, Austin, Hoblitzelle Theatre Arts Library, *Austin* 78712
Dallas Public Library, Central Research Library, 1954 Commerce Street, *Dallas* 75201

Dallas Public Library, Fine Arts Division, 1954 Commerce Street, *Dallas* 75201
Southern Methodist University, McCord Theatre Collection, *Dallas* 75275
Fort Worth Public Library, Arts Division, *Fort Worth* 76102
Texas Christian University, Mary Couts Burnett Library, Drawer E, Texas Christian University Station, *Fort Worth* 76129
Rice University, *Houston* 77001
University of Houston, M. D. Anderson Memorial Library, 4800 Calhoun Boulevard, *Houston* 77004
San Antonio Public Library, *San Antonio* 78205
Trinity University, 715 Stadium Drive, *San Antonio* 78212

UTAH
Brigham Young University, Clark Library, *Provo* 84601
University of Utah, *Salt Lake City* 84112

VERMONT
University of Vermont, Bailey Library, *Burlington* 05405

VIRGINIA
University of Virginia, Alderman Library, *Charlottesville* 22901
Research Center for the Federal Theatre Project, George Mason University, 4400 University Drive, *Fairfax* 22030
Virginia Historical Society, *Richmond* 23219
College of William and Mary, *Williamsburg* 23185

WASHINGTON
Washington State University, Manuscripts, Archives and Special Collections, *Pullman* 99164
University of Washington Libraries, Drama Library BH-20, *Seattle* 98195
The Crosby Library, Gonzaga University, East 502 Boone Avenue, *Spokane* 99258

WISCONSIN
University of Wisconsin, Madison, Memorial Library, 728 State Street, *Madison* 53706
Wisconsin Center for Film and Theatre Research, 1166 Van Hise Hall, 1220 Linden Drive, *Madison* 53706
Marquette University, 1415 West Wisconsin Avenue, *Milwaukee* 53233
Milwaukee Public Library, 814 West Wisconsin Avenue, *Milwaukee* 53233
University of Wisconsin-Milwaukee, 2311 East Hartford Avenue, P.O. Box 604, *Milwaukee* 53201
University of Wisconsin, Forrest R. Polk Library, 800 Algoma Boulevard, *Oshkosh* 54901

WYOMING
University of Wyoming, William Robertson Coe Library, *Laramie* 82070

CANADA

ALBERTA
University of Calgary, 2920 24th Avenue, N.W., *Calgary* T2N 1N4
University of Alberta, Cameron Library, *Edmonton* T6G 2J8

BRITISH COLUMBIA
Vancouver Public Library, Language and Literature Division, 750 Burrard Street, *Vancouver* V6Z 1X5

NEW BRUNSWICK
Mount Allison University, Ralph Pickard Bell Library, *Sackville* E0A 3C0

ONTARIO
McMaster University, Mills Memorial Library, Division of Archives and Research Collections, *Hamilton* L8S 4L6

Queens University at Kingston, Douglas Library, *Kingston* K7L 5C4
University of Western Ontario, 1151 Richmond Street, N., *London* N6A 3K7
Houdini Magical Hall of Fame, 1019 Centre Street, *Niagara Falls*
National Library of Canada, 395 Wellington Street, *Ottawa* K1A 0N4
Public Archives of Canada Library, 395 Wellington Street, *Ottawa* K1A 0N3
Stratford Shakespearean Festival Foundation of Canada, Archives, P.O. Box 520, *Stratford* N5A
  6V2
Metropolitan Toronto Library, Theatre Department, 789 Yonge Street, *Toronto* M4W 2G8
University of Toronto, Thomas Fisher Rare Book Library, 120 St. George Street, *Toronto* M5S
  1A5

QUEBEC
McGill University Libraries, 3459 McTavish Street, *Montreal* H3A 1Y1

LIST OF CURRENT THEATRE
AND DRAMA AWARDS

ACTORS' FUND MEDAL
   To encourage outstanding services rendered to the theatre by individuals and/or organizations by assisting the Actors' Fund of America in the achievement of its goals. Gilded bronze medal with the classic Greek masques of Tragedy and Comedy sculpted in the bas-relief on the obverse and the muses of Comedy, Tragedy, and choral dance and song on the reverse. Awarded only when merited. Established 1958. Administered by the Fund (1501 Broadway, New York, NY 10036).

AMERICAN ACADEMY OF ARTS AND LETTERS AWARD OF MERIT
   For recognition of outstanding work in one of the following arts, in the order named: (1) painting, (2) sculpture, (3) the novel, (4) poetry, (5) drama. To an individual in America not a member of the National Institute of Arts and Letters. Medal and $1,000. Awarded annually. Established 1940. Administered by the Academy (633 West 155th Street, New York, NY 10032).

AMERICAN ACADEMY OF ARTS AND LETTERS MEDAL FOR GOOD
SPEECH ON THE STAGE
   For recognition of correct use of language on the stage and in radio and television broadcasting. To performers and announcers in stage, radio, and television. Gold medal. Awarded irregularly. Administered by the Academy.

AMERICAN COLLEGE THEATRE FESTIVAL NATIONAL AWARD
   For recognition of an outstanding, original full-length play or musical written by a student in an undergraduate or graduate program. Production of the winning play is held in Washington, D.C. as part of the ACTA National Festival. The playwright receives the following: (1) exposure of the play to reviewers, producers, directors, and other professionals; (2) $2,500 from the William Morris Agency and the offer of an agency management contract; (3) full membership in the Dramatists Guild. In addition, Samuel French, Inc. will publish and distribute the play for stock and amateur production on the basis of its standard professional royalties. The American Playwrights Theatre will offer to distribute the play among its members of over 200 colleges on the basis of its usual conditions and royalties. The University/College Theatre Association presents $1,000 to the Drama Department of the winner's college or university. Awarded annually. Administered by the Festival (John F. Kennedy Center for the Performing Arts, Washington, D.C. 20566),

AMERICAN NATIONAL THEATRE AND ACADEMY WEST AWARD
See: ANTA WEST AWARD

AMERICAN THEATRE ASSOCIATION AWARD OF MERIT
   For recognition of distinguished service to educational theatre. Plaque or scroll. Awarded annually. Established 1956. Administered by the ATA (1029 Vermont Avenue, N.W., Washington, D.C. 20005).

AMERICAN THEATRE ASSOCIATION CITATION FOR DISTINGUISHED
SERVICE TO THE THEATRE
   For recognition of outstanding contribution to the American theatre. Plaque or scroll. Awarded annually. Established 1963. Administered by the ATA.

AMERICAN THEATRE WING   *See*: TONY AWARDS

ANTA WEST AWARD
    For recognition of an outstanding, original full-length play or musical written by a student in an undergraduate or graduate program. The play is presented in Hollywood, California by professional actors in cooperation with the American National Theatre and Academy West. The playwright receives expenses and round-trip transportation to California to attend rehearsals and performances. Awarded annually. Established 1976. Administered by the American College Theatre Festival.

DELIA AUSTRIAN MEDAL FOR DISTINGUISHED PERFORMANCE
    For recognition of the most outstanding performance on the New York stage during the current season, exclusive of a one-man or one-woman show. To an actor or actress. Bronze medal. Awarded annually. Established 1934. Administered by the Drama League of New York, Inc. (1035 Fifth Avenue, New York, NY 10028).

ST. CLAIR BAYFIELD AWARD
    To honor an outstanding actor or actress appearing in a non-featured role in a Shakespearean production offered in metropolitan New York or Stratford, Connecticut, or their environs during the theatre season ending Labor Day. Winner selected by several New York drama critics. Awarded annually. Established in 1972 to honor the memory of St. Clair Bayfield, a Shakespearean actor, by his widow. Administered by the Actors' Equity Association (165 West 46th Street, New York, NY 10036).

APHRA BEHN AWARD
    For one original, unproduced, unpublished full-length play by a contemporary woman playwright. Open to women playwrights of all nations. Established 1980. The first recipient will receive a reading of her play during the Women's International Theatre Festival at Skidmore College in June, 1981; written introductions to play publishers; and honoria for festival attendance. Women's International Theatre Alliance (6025 Cromwell Drive, Washington, D.C. 20016).

SUSAN SMITH BLACKBURN PRIZE
    To a woman playwright for "a work of outstanding quality for the English-speaking theatre." Monetary award of $2,000. Awarded annually. Established in 1979 in memory of Susan Smith Blackburn, an American actress and writer. Administered by the Susan Smith Blackburn Prize, Inc. (3239 Avalon Place, Houston, TX 77019).

MARC BLITZSTEIN AWARD FOR THE MUSICAL THEATRE
    To encourage the creation of works of merit for the musical theatre. To a composer, lyricist, or librettist. Monetary award of $2,500. Established in 1965 by friends of Marc Blitzstein. Administered by the National Institute of Arts and Letters (633 West 155th Street, New York, NY 10032).

DANIEL BLUM THEATRE WORLD AWARD   *See*: THEATRE WORLD AWARD

BOOKS ABROAD/NEUSTADT INTERNATIONAL PRIZE FOR LITERATURE
    For distinguished and continuing achievement in the fields of poetry, drama, or fiction. Work must be available in either French or English translation. To an author of any nationality. Silver Eagle Feather. Certificate, $10,000, and one issue of *Books Abroad* devoted to the laureate. Administered by *Books Abroad* (University of Oklahoma, Norman, OK 73019).

EDWIN BOOTH MEMORIAL AWARD   *See*: WALTER HAMPDEN-EDWIN BOOTH MEMORIAL AWARD

BRANDEIS UNIVERSITY CREATIVE ARTS AWARDS
    For the recognition of outstanding artistic contributions by contemporary artists in the fields of fine arts, music, literature, and theatre arts. Medals awarded to established artists in recognition

of a lifetime of distinguished achievement. Citations to younger artists for the furtherance of their creative careers. A special award given to a person or group for notable achievement in the creative arts. Monetary prize of $1,000 in each category. Presented annually. Established 1957. Administered by the Creative Arts Awards Commission, Brandeis University (12 East 77th Street, New York, NY 10021).

CHARLOTTE CHORPENNING AWARD

For recognition of an outstanding author of plays for children. Citation. Trophy cup. Awarded annually. Established 1967. Administered by the Children's Theatre Association of America (1029 Vermont Avenue, N.W., Washington, D.C. 20005).

GEORGE M. COHAN AWARD

For outstanding dedication and service to the theatre. To an individual. Awarded annually along with a scholarship to a nondenominational needy school. Established 1970. Administered by the Catholic Actors Guild (227 West 45th Street, New York, NY 10036).

COMMUNITY THEATRE DRAMA FESTIVAL AWARD

For recognition of the best production of a one-act play or a scene or cutting from a three-act play. To community theatres in New England which hold group membership in the New England Theatre Conference organization. Rotating engraved trophy with permanent engraved plaque presented to winner. Awarded annually. Established in 1954 by the Little Theatre League of Massachusetts. Administered by the New England Theatre Conference (50 Exchange Street, Waltham, MA 02154).

LOLA D'ANNUNZIO AWARD

For recognition of outstanding contributions to off-Broadway theatre. To an individual who has been active in off-Broadway during the current year. Plaque and $500. Awarded annually. Administered by the Lola D'Annunzio Award, Inc. (Current address unknown).

DAVID LIBRARY OF THE AMERICAN REVOLUTION AWARDS

For recognition of an outstanding, original full-length play on the subject of American freedom by a student in an undergraduate or graduate program. First prize is $2,000 to the playwright and $1,000 to the college or university drama department presenting the play; second prize of $1,000 to the playwright and $500 to the drama department presenting the play. Awarded annually. Supported by the David Library, Washington Crossing, Pennsylvania. Administered by the American College Theatre Festival.

SUZANNE M. DAVIS MEMORIAL AWARD

To honor distinguished achievement or service to Southern theatre or to the Southeastern Theatre Conference. Recipient must reside in the Southeastern region of the United States and be a member or past member of the Conference. Bronze plaque. Awarded annually. Established in 1965 by Alvin Cohen. Administered by the Southeastern Theatre Conference, Inc. (1209 West Market Street, Greensboro, NC 27412).

CLARENCE DERWENT AWARDS

To recognize two actors for the best male and the best female performances in nonfeatured roles on and off-Broadway. Four awards are made each year (two in New York and two in London). Engraved crystal memento and $1,000 to each person. Established 1945 (British awards were not presented until 1948). Administered by the Clarence Derwent Award Trust (c/o Carl Schaeffer, 410 Park Avenue, New York, NY 10022).

PHOEBE EPHRON SCHOLARSHIP AWARD

To "the most promising woman playwright" as chosen by the Hunter College Drama Department. Monetary prize of $2,500. Awarded annually. Established in 1981 by playwright Henry Ephron. Administered by Hunter College of the City of New York (695 Park Avenue, New York, NY 10021).

GEORGE FREEDLEY MEMORIAL AWARD

For recognition of an outstanding work in the field of legitimate theatre published in the United States. Only books related to live performance, including vaudeville, puppetry, pantomime, and circus are considered. To the author. Citation, plaque, or certificate. Awarded annually. Established 1968. Administered by the Theatre Library Association (111 Amsterdam Avenue, New York, NY 10023).

JOHN GASSNER AWARD

For recognition of the most outstanding new playwright on Broadway or off-Broadway. Medallion. Awarded annually. Established 1971. Administered by the Outer Critics Circle (c/o Charles K. Freeman, 18 Overlook Road, Ossining, NY 10562).

JOHN GASSNER MEMORIAL PLAYWRIGHTING AWARD

For recognition and encouragement of new playwrights. To the author of an original, unproduced, and unpublished one-act play. Monetary prize. Awarded annually. Established 1963. Administered by the New England Theatre Conference (50 Exchange Street, Waltham, MA 02154).

GAY PLAYWRITING AWARDS

To locate and encourage the writing of new gay plays. Monetary prizes of $500 and $250. Awarded annually. Established 1980. Administered and co-sponsored by The Glines, a nonprofit organization for gay arts, and the Gay Theatre Alliance (Northeast Region, P.O. Box 294, New York, NY 10014).

ROSAMOND GILDER AWARD

For creative achievement in the theatre with primary emphasis on writing and direction. To artists in relatively early stages of their careers (those who have not yet achieved widespread recognition). Monetary prize to be announced. Awarded annually. Established 1978. Administered by the New Drama Forum Association, Inc. (c/o Library & Museum of the Performing Arts, Lincoln Center, 111 Amsterdam Avenue, New York, NY 10023).

JOHN SIMON GUGGENHEIM MEMORIAL FOUNDATION FELLOWSHIPS

In recognition of individuals, ages thirty to forty, who have demonstrated unusual productive ability in their respective fields. To citizens of Canada, the Philippines, the United States, the Latin American republics, and the British Caribbean areas. Two categories: (1) Drama and (2) Stage Design and Production. Awarded annually. Established 1928. Administered by the Foundation (90 Park Avenue, New York, NY 10016).

JAMES K. HACKETT AWARD

For outstanding achievement in oratory or drama. To alumni and students of the City University of New York. Medal. Awarded annually. Administered by the City College of the City University of New York (138th Street and Convent Avenue, New York, NY 10031).

WALTER HAMPDEN-EDWIN BOOTH MEMORIAL AWARD

For recognition of distinguished service to the New York theatre. To an individual, group, or organization. Awarded annually, Established 1978. Administered by The Walter Hampden-Edwin Booth Theatre Collection and Library at The Players (16 Gramercy Park, New York, NY 10003).

LORRAINE HANSBERRY PLAYWRIGHTING AWARD

For recognition of an outstanding, original play on the Black experience in America written by a student in an undergraduate or graduate program. Monetary prizes of $2,000 to the playwright and $500 to the drama department presenting the play. Awarded annually. Funded by McDonald's Corporation. Administered by the American College Theatre Festival (John F. Kennedy Center for the Performing Arts, Washington, D.C. 20566).

MOSS HART MEMORIAL AWARD FOR PLAYS OF THE FREE WORLD

To encourage production of plays which stress virtues of freedom and human dignity and accent the positive virtues of courage, faith, and hope. To any secondary school, college, community, or professional theatre in New England. Trophy and plaque. Awarded annually. Established 1962. Co-sponsored by the *Boston Herald American* and *Boston Sunday Advertiser*. Administered by the New England Theatre Conference (50 Exchange Street, Waltham, MA 02154)

HASTY PUDDING MAN OF THE YEAR
To recognize the actor who has made the most outstanding contribution to the acting profession during the past year. Citation. Awarded annually. Established 1967. Administered by the Hasty Pudding Theatricals (12 Holyoke Street, Cambridge, MA 02138).

HASTY PUDDING WOMAN OF THE YEAR
To a woman who has shown great artistic skill and feminine qualities. Citation. Awarded annually. Established 1951. Administered by the Hasty Pudding Theatricals (12 Holyoke Street, Cambridge, MA 02138).

JENNIE HEIDEN AWARD
For recognition of professional excellence in the field of children's theatre. Certificate and $100. Awarded annually. Established 1966. Administered by the American Theatre Association (1029 Vermont Avenue, N.W., Washington, D.C. 20005).

BARNARD HEWITT AWARD
For outstanding research in theatre history. Awarded annually to an individual United States scholar or group of scholars. Monetary award of $500. Established 1975. Administered by the University Theatre of the University of Illinois at Urbana (61801) and the American Theatre Association.

ELIZABETH HULL - KATE WARRINER AWARD
To recognize a playwright whose work deals with controversial subjects involving the fields of politics, religion, or social mores of the time. For a play produced within the year in a first-class production, or an off-Broadway production, in New York City. Scroll and approximately $7,500. Awarded annually. Established in 1970 by the last will and testament of Elizabeth Van Vechten Schaefer Hull. The Bank of New York serves as trustee. Administered by the Dramatists Guild, Inc. (234 West 44th Street, New York, NY 10036).

MARGO JONES AWARD
To encourage the production of new plays by new playwrights as well as established playwrights, as was the dedicated purpose of Margo Jones in the Dallas Theatre. To a working theatre whose policy it is to perform hitherto unproduced plays, rather than museum pieces and Broadway carbon copies. Bronze medal with head of Miss Jones and $500. Awarded annually. Established in 1961 by Jerome Lawrence and Robert E. Lee. Administered by the Margo Jones Award, Inc. (c/o Jonas Silverstone, 230 Park Avenue, New York, NY 10017).

KANSAS CITY STAR - JOSEPH KAYE AWARD
For recognition of an outstanding young, promising Midwestern playwright. If no candidate exists in a given year, selection is made by the Outer Critics Circle of New York. Bronze Drake wreath medal. Awarded annually. Established 1975. Administered by the Kansas City Star Company (1729 Grand Avenue, Kansas City, MO 64108).

JOSEPH KAYE - KANSAS CITY STAR AWARD   *See*: KANSAS CITY STAR-JOSEPH KAYE AWARD

JOSEPH KESSELRING FUND AWARD
To give financial aid to playwrights. When author-actor-playwright Joseph Kesselring died in 1967, he left his estate in a trust and designated that a bequest be established as a fund for financial aid to playwrights upon the death of his beneficiary. This occurred in 1978. Monetary award of $5,000. Honorable Mention prize of $1,000. Awarded annually. Established 1980. Administered by the National Arts Club (15 Gramercy Park, New York, NY 10003).

NORMAN LEAR AWARD

For recognition of achievement in comedy playwriting by an undergraduate or graduate student. The winner receives a professional assignment to write a complete teleplay for one of the Norman Lear series. The playwright receives $2,500 for the completed teleplay and is installed as a member of the Writers Guild of America. Awarded annually. Sponsored by Norman Lear. Administered by the American College Theatre Festival (John F. Kennedy Center for the Performing Arts, Washington, D.C. 20566).

MAHARAM DESIGN AWARDS FOR BEST COSTUME AND SCENIC DESIGN

For recognition of outstanding costume and scenic design by individuals on the graduate school level in an American college or university. Monetary prize of $200 in each of the two categories. Awarded annually. Established in 1969 in cooperation with the Department of Theatre at Southern Illinois University. Administered by the Joseph Maharam Foundation, Inc. (21675 Juego Circle Villa 3A, Boca Raton, FL 33433).

MAHARAM THEATRICAL DESIGN AWARDS

For recognition of outstanding scenic and costume designs in Broadway and off-Broadway plays and musicals. To American stage and costume designers. A total of $1,000 for best scenic design: $500 for Broadway and $500 for off-Broadway; $500 for best costume design. Awarded annually at the Drama Desk - Sardi Luncheon. Established 1965. Sponsored by the American Theatre Wing. Administered by the Joseph Maharam Foundation.

MARGARET MAYORGA AWARD

For two original, unproduced, unpublished short plays by a contemporary woman playwright. Open to women playwrights of all nations. Established 1980. The first recipient will receive a reading of her play during the Women's International Theatre Festival at Skidmore College in June 1981; written introductions to play publishers; and honoria for festival attendance. Women's International Theatre Alliance (6205 Cromwell Drive, Washington, D.C. 20016).

GEORGE JEAN NATHAN AWARD FOR DRAMATIC CRITICISM

To encourage and assist in developing the art of drama criticism and the stimulation of intelligent playgoing. To an American drama critic. Silver medallion, engrossed certificate, and $5,000. Awarded annually. Established 1958. Award selection made jointly by heads of English Departments of Cornell, Princeton, and Yale Universities. Administered by the George Jean Nathan Trust—Manufacturers Hanover Trust Company (600 Fifth Avenue, New York, NY 10020).

NATIONAL INSTITUTE OF ARTS AND LETTERS GOLD MEDAL

For distinguished achievement in the following categories: architecture and poetry; drama and graphic art; belles lettres and criticism, and painting; biography and music; the novel and sculpture; the short story and history. Based on the entire work of the recipient who must be a United States citizen. Awarded annually in the categories in rotation by the Institute in the name of the American Academy of Arts and Letters (633 West 155th Street, New York, NY 10032).

NATIONAL THEATRE CONFERENCE CITATION

In recognition of distinguished service to the nonprofessional theatre. Inscribed walnut plaque. Awarded annually. Established 1968. Administered by the National Theatre Conference (c/o Paul Myers, Secretary, Theatre Collection, Library & Museum of the Performing Arts, Lincoln Center, 111 Amsterdam Avenue, New York, NY 10023).

NEW ENGLAND THEATRE CONFERENCE AWARD FOR OUTSTANDING CREATIVE ACHIEVEMENT IN THE AMERICAN THEATRE

To honor a theatre personality who has made outstanding creative achievement in the American theatre. To an actor, designer, playwright, or director. Engraved Paul Revere Bowl. Awarded annually. Established 1957. Administered by the NETC (50 Exchange Street, Waltham, MA 02154).

NEW ENGLAND THEATRE CONFERENCE REGIONAL CITATION

To honor a personality or organization in New England for special contributions in a particular theatre area and to focus public attention and offer needed recognition to creative theatre achievement. Engraved plaque. Awarded annually. Established 1957. Administered by the NETC.

NEW ENGLAND THEATRE CONFERENCE SPECIAL AWARD
For recognition and reward for innovations or advancements in the interest of theatre on a national level. To an individual or organization. Engraved plaque. Awarded annually. Established 1957. Administered by the NETC.

NEW YORK DRAMA CRITICS' CIRCLE AWARD
For recognition of the "Best Play of the Year" and to encourage good plays and improve the state of the theatre. To the author of a play presented for the first time in New York City on or off-Broadway. Scroll and $1,000. Awarded annually. Established 1935. Administered by the New York Drama Critics' Circle (c/o Dr. Joseph T. Shipley, 29 West 46th Street, New York, NY 10036).

NEW YORK DRAMA CRITICS' CIRCLE AWARD FOR AN AMERICAN PLAY
For recognition of the "Best American Play of the Year." To an American playwright. Scroll. Awarded when not covered by the previous award.

NEW YORK DRAMA CRITICS' CIRCLE MUSICAL AWARD
To honor the "Best Musical of the Year." Scroll. Awarded irregularly.

NEWSDAY PLAYWRITING AWARD   *See*: GEORGE OPPENHEIMER - NEWSDAY PLAYWRITING AWARD

"OBIE" AWARDS
For recognition of the best plays, actors, directors, and other artists in off-Broadway and off-off-Broadway productions, Categories and titles of categories change from year to year, and awards are not always made in each category every year. Certificate: monetary prize of $500 for "Best Play." Awarded annually. Established in 1956 by The Plumsoul Fund and *The Village Voice*. Administered by *The Village Voice* (80 University Place, New York, NY 10003).

OFF-BROADWAY AND OFF-OFF-BROADWAY AWARDS   *See*: "OBIE" AWARDS

EUGENE O'NEILL AWARD
For "enriching the universal understanding" of Eugene O'Neill. To an individual in the performing arts. Medal. Awarded annually. Established in 1980 to commemorate O'Neill's birth in 1888. The first recipient was Brooks Atkinson. Administered by the Theater Committee for Eugene O'Neill (1860 Broadway, New York, NY 10023).

GEORGE OPPENHEIMER - NEWSDAY PLAYWRITING AWARD
To a new American playwright whose work is produced in New York City or Long Island. Monetary prize of $1,000. Awarded annually. Established in 1979 by *Newsday* in memory of George Oppenheimer, *Newsday*'s drama critic. Administered by *Newsday* (550 Stewart Avenue, Garden City, NY 11530).

OUTER CRITICS CIRCLE PERFORMANCE AWARDS
To recognize the best play of the New York theatre season, outstanding performers of the season, and notable performances by young players. Special citations may be given to organizations for various contributions to the theatre arts. Presented annually at an awards dinner. Administered by the Outer Critics Circle (c/o Charles K. Freeman, 18 Overlook Road, Ossining, NY 10562).

ANTOINETTE PERRY AWARDS   *See*: "TONY" AWARDS

PLAYBILL AWARD
For playwriting excellence. Competition open to members of the New Dramatists, a profes-

sional resource program, founded in 1949 for young playwrights. Monetary prize of $5,000. Awarded annually. Established 1980. Administered by *Playbill Magazine* (151 East 50th Street, New York, NY 10022).

THE PLAYERS   *See*: WALTER HAMPDEN-EDWIN BOOTH
THEATRE MEMORIAL AWARD

PRIX VICTOR-MORIN
   For recognition of an outstanding professional actor or actress whose activities serve to strengthen French-Canadian culture. Monetary prize of $500. Awarded annually. Established 1962. Administered by the Société Saint Jean Baptiste de Montreal (82 ouest, Sherbrooke, Montreal, Quebec, Canada).

PULTIZER PRIZE
   For recognition of a distinguished play by an American author, preferably original in its source and dealing with American life. Monetary prize of $1,000. Established 1917. Awarded annually through the Graduate School of Journalism of Columbia University (304 Journalism Building, New York, NY 10027).

SIR WALTER RALEIGH CUP
   For recognition of outstanding works of fiction, including the novel, drama, short story, and poetry. To a resident of North Carolina. Statuette and cup. Awarded annually. Established in 1952 by the Historical Book Club of North Carolina. Administered by the North Carolina Literary and Historical Association (109 East Jones Street, Raleigh, NC 27611).

RELIGIOUS ARTS GUILD DRAMA AWARD
   For recognition of an outstanding, unpublished one-act play that calls for no more than five players and has a contemporary setting. Awarded annually. Announced at the General Assembly of the Unitarian Universalist Association. Administered by the Religious Arts Guild (25 Beacon Street, Boston, MA 02108).

RICHARD RODGERS PRODUCTION AWARD
   To finance a production by a nonprofit theatre in New York of a musical play by an artist not previously recognized in the field. Monetary award from income on a one million dollar endowment. Established by Richard Rodgers in 1978. First awarded in 1980. Administered by the American Academy and Institute of Arts and Letters (633 West 155th Street, New York, NY 10032).

ST. GENESIUS AWARD
   For special service to the Catholic Actors Guild, the Profession, and the Church. To an individual. Medal. Awarded annually. Established 1960. St. Genesius is the Patron Saint of Actors. Administered by the Catholic Actors Guild (227 West 45th Street, New York, NY 10036).

ST. GENESIUS GOLD MEDAL AWARD
   For outstanding dedication to the promotion of Christian principles in the acting profession. Instituted in 1965 to commemorate the restoration of the Patron Saint of the Theatre's shrine in the Church of Santa Susanna in Rome, Italy. Awarded irregularly. Administered by the Church of Santa Susanna which serves American Roman Catholics.

CHARLES H. SERGEL DRAMA PRIZE
   To encourage the writing of new American plays. To the playwright. Monetary prize of $1,500. Awarded biennially. Established by Anne Meyers Sergel and administered by the University of Chicago Theater (5706 South University Avenue, Chicago, IL 60637).

SHUBERT FOUNDATION AWARDS
   In recognition of the most outstanding individual contribution to the New York theatrical season. Awarded annually. Established in 1954 in memory of Sam S. Shubert. Administered by the Foundation (234 West 44th Street, New York, NY 10036).

SARAH SIDDONS AWARD

In recognition of an outstanding performance on the Chicago stage. To the actress chosen as "Chicago's Actress of the Year." The award's forerunner was the fictitious Sarah Siddons Award created by Joseph Mankiewicz in his Academy Award winning movie, *All About Eve* (1950). Established in 1953 by the Sarah Siddons Society of Chicago. Administered by the Society. (Current address unknown).

SOCIETY OF COLONIAL WARS ANNUAL AWARD

For recognition of contributions of outstanding excellence, produced during the previous calendar year, in the field of literature, drama, music, or art relative to Colonial Americana, 1607-1775. Bronze medallion and citation. Awarded annually. Established 1951. Administered by the Society (122 East 58th Street, New York, NY 10022).

SOCIETY OF STAGE DIRECTORS AND CHOREOGRAPHERS AWARD OF MERIT

In recognition of outstanding achievement in the performing arts. Bronze bust of awardee. Awarded infrequently. Established 1965. Administered by the Society (1501 Broadway, New York, NY 10036).

SOUTHEASTERN THEATRE CONFERENCE DISTINGUISHED CAREER AWARD

To honor distinguished service to the American theatre. Preference given to individuals born in the South. Plaque. Awarded at the annual convention. Established 1960. Administered by the Conference (1209 West Market Street, Greensboro, NC 27412).

SOUTHWEST THEATRE CONFERENCE NEW PLAY AWARD

For recognition of an outstanding new play written by a resident of Texas, Oklahoma, New Mexico, Arkansas, or Louisiana. The material must comprise a full evening of theatre: a series of one-act plays or a full-length play previously unproduced. To the author. Monetary prize of $1,000 and possible production by the Permian Playhouse of Odessa, Texas. Awarded annually. Established 1976. Administered by the Conference (Department of Speech and Drama, Southwest Texas State University, San Marcos, TX 78666).

STANLEY DRAMA AWARD

For recognition of an original full-length play or musical which has not been professionally produced or received trade-book publication. To the playwright. Monetary prize of $500 and possible production of the play. Awarded annually. Established in 1974 and funded by Robert Stanley and the Stanley-Timolat Foundation in memory of Mrs. Robert C. Stanley of Dongan Hills, Staten Island. Administered by Wagner College (Rymes Hill, Staten Island, 10301).

JACK STEIN MAKE-UP AWARDS

To encourage and reward excellence in theatrical make-up in a theatre production. Presented to one secondary school, one college, and one community theatre group in New England. Engraved drama plaques. Awarded annually. Established in 1976 by make-up artist Jack Stein of Boston. Administered by the New England Theatre Conference (50 Exchange Street, Waltham, MA 02154).

STRAW HAT AWARD

In recognition of excellence in the American summer theatre. For work done during the previous year in eight categories. Gold straw hat. Awarded annually. Established 1970. Administered by the Council of Stock Theatres (c/o Taplinger Associates, 415 Madison Avenue, New York, NY 10017).

"TEDDY" AWARDS

A parody of the "Tony" Awards. Established in 1979 by Ted Hook, New York restaurant entrepreneur of Backstage and On Stage. The "Teddy" is a Backstage Restaurant lamp. Administered by Ted Hook (318 West 45th Street, New York, NY 10036).

THEATRE LA SALLE AWARD

To promote the appreciation of outstanding dramatic achievement by recognizing distinguished service to the American theatre outside New York City. Inscribed plaque. Awarded periodically, not more than once a year. Established in 1970 by the Theatre La Salle. Administered by La Salle College (20th Street and Olney Avenue, Philadelphia, PA 19141).

THEATRE WORLD AWARDS

To recognize, reward, and encourage promising new talent in the theatre. To twelve outstanding actors and actresses for outstanding performances in a theatrical debut or a first appearance in an important role. Bronze Harry Marinsky sculpture. Awarded annually at the end of each theatre season. Established in 1944 by Daniel Blum. Administered by *Theatre World* (John Willis, Editor, 190 Riverside Drive, New York, NY 10024).

THETA ALPHA PHI MEDALLION OF HONOR

To honor long-term, outstanding, and distinguished service to the theatre on the national level. To an individual. Wooden shield-shaped plaque with theatre mask in raised gold-finish medal. Awarded annually. Established 1956. Administered by National Theta Alpha Phi (58 West College Avenue, Westerville, OH 43081).

"TONY" (ANTOINETTE PERRY) AWARDS

To signify outstanding achievement in the Broadway theatre. For legitimate theatrical productions opening in Broadway theatres during the year. For achievement in creative categories including the following: *Musical*: Best Actor; Best Actress; Best Musical; Best Supporting Actor; Best Supporting Actress; Best Director; Best Costume Design; and Best Choreography; *Drama*: Best Play; Best Actor; Best Actress; Best Supporting Actor; Best Supporting Actress; Best Director; Best Scenic Designer; and Special Awards. Silver medallion embossed with masks of comedy and tragedy. Awarded annually. Established in 1947 and awarded under the authorization of the American Theatre Wing. Administered by the League of New York Theatres and Producers, Inc. (226 West 47th Street, New York, NY 10036).

VILLAGE VOICE OFF AND OFF-OFF-BROADWAY AWARDS
See: "OBIE" AWARDS

KATE WARRINGER AWARD   *See*: ELIZABETH HULL -
KATE WARRINGER AWARD

JOHN F. WHARTON AWARD

In recognition of original contributions to the business practices of the theatre. To one or more stage professionals in either the commercial or nonprofit sector. Monetary prize of about $5,000. Awarded annually. Established in 1980 by the law firm of Paul Weiss, Rifkind, Wharton & Garrison. Administered by the Theatre Development Fund (1501 Broadway, New York, NY 10036).

AUDREY WOOD AWARD IN PLAYWRITING

For recognition of the best original unproduced script of any length. To the playwright. Production of the play and $500. Awarded annually. Established 1971. Administered by the American University Department of Performing Arts (Massachusetts and Nebraska Avenues, N.W., Washington, D.C. 20016).

WORLD THEATRE AWARD

For recognition of accomplishments of international renown in the performing arts. Scroll. Awarded annually. Established in 1967 by the International Theatre Institute and the American Theatre Association. Administered by the American Theatre Association (1029 Vermont Avenue, N.W., Washington, D.C. 20005).

ASSOCIATIONS AND INSTITUTIONS

(Each award listed under the following organizations appears in the preceding list of current theatre and drama awards.)

ACTORS' EQUITY ASSOCIATION
St. Clair Bayfield Award

AMERICAN ACADEMY OF ARTS AND
LETTERS
Award of Merit
Medal for Good Speech
Richard Rodgers Production Award

AMERICAN COLLEGE THEATRE
FESTIVAL
ANTA West Award
David Library of the American
Revolution Awards
Lorraine Hansberry Playwriting Award
Norman Lear Award
National Award

AMERICAN THEATRE ASSOCIATION
Award of Merit
Citation for Distinguished Service to the
Theatre
Jennie Heiden Award
Barnard Hewitt Award
World Theatre Award

AMERICAN UNIVERSITY
DEPARTMENT OF
PERFORMING ARTS
Audrey Wood Award in Playwriting

SUSAN SMITH BLACKBURN PRIZE,
INC.
Susan Smith Blackburn Prize

CATHOLIC ACTORS GUILD
George M. Cohan Award
St. Genesius Award

CHILDREN's THEATRE ASSOCIATION
OF AMERICA
Charlotte Chorpenning Award

CHURCH OF SANTA SUSANNA,
ROME, ITALY
St. Genesius Gold Medal Award

CITY COLLEGE OF THE CITY
UNIVERSITY OF NEW YORK
James K. Hackett Award

COLUMBIA UNIVERSITY GRADUATE
SCHOOL OF JOURNALISM
Pulitzer Prize

COUNCIL OF STOCK THEATRES
Straw Hat Award

CREATIVE ARTS AWARDS
COMMISSION
Brandeis University Creative Arts Awards

DRAMA LEAGUE OF NEW YORK, INC.
Delia Austrian Medal for Distinguished
Performance

DRAMATISTS GUILD, INC.
Elizabeth Hull - Kate Warriner Award

GAY THEATRE ALLIANCE
Gay Playwriting Awards

TED HOOK, RESTAURANT
ENTREPRENEUR
"Teddy" Awards

HUNTER COLLEGE OF THE CITY OF
NEW YORK
Phoebe Ephron Scholarship Award

LA SALLE COLLEGE
Theatre La Salle Award

NATIONAL INSTITUTE OF ARTS
AND LETTERS
Marc Blitzstein Award for the Musical
Theatre
Gold Medal

NATIONAL THETA ALPHA PHI
Theta Alpha Phi Medallion of Honor

NEW DRAMA FORUM ASSOCIATION,
INC.
Rosamond Gilder Award

NEW ENGLAND THEATRE
CONFERENCE
Community Theatre Drama Festival
Award
John Gassner Memorial Playwriting
Award
Moss Hart Memorial Award
Outstanding Creative Achievement in the
American Theatre Award
Regional Citation
Special Award
Jack Stein Make-up Award

NORTH CAROLINA LITERARY AND
HISTORICAL ASSOCIATION, INC.
Sir Walter Raleigh Cup

OUTER CRITICS CIRCLE
John Gassner Award
Performance Awards

PLAYBILL MAGAZINE
  Playbill Award

SOCIÉTÉ SAINT JEAN BAPTISTE
DE MONTREAL
  Prix Victor-Morin

SOUTHEASTERN THEATRE
CONFERENCE, INC.
  Suzanne M. Davis Memorial Award
  Distinguished Career Award
  New Play Award

THEATER COMMITTEE FOR
EUGENE O'NEILL
  Eugene O'Neill Award

THEATRE DEVELOPMENT FUND
  John F. Wharton Award

THEATRE LIBRARY ASSOCIATION
  George Freedley Memorial Award

UNIVERSITY OF CHICAGO THEATER
  Charles H. Sergel Drama Prize

UNIVERSITY OF ILLINOIS
AT URBANA
  Barnard Hewitt Award

WAGNER COLLEGE
  Stanley Drama Award

WOMEN'S INTERNATIONAL
THEATRE ALLIANCE
  Aphra Behn Award
  Margaret Mayorga Award

REVIEW NOTES OF INTEREST

These pages, compiled by the Guest Editor and the General Editor, will appear in each issue of Special Collections. *They will refer, first, to publications relative to the issue's subject; secondly, the General Editor will comment on publications in the following groupings: Guides to Collections and Resources; Indexes; Directories; Dictionaries, Encyclopedias, Atlases, and Other Reference Books (including subject histories); Bibliographies and Special Booksellers' Catalogues; Books About Books— Rare Books, Collecting, Essays, Biographies, etc.; Special Collection and Archival Administration. Citations, keyed to letters or numbers in the text, with names of publishers and prices, are listed following the notes.*

Librarians, publishers, booksellers, and others are requested to send copies of publications for consideration to the General Editor, Special Collections, *66 Humiston Drive, Bethany, CT 06525.*

RECENT MATERIALS FOR THEATRE COLLECTIONS

Compiled by the Guest Editor

Guides to Collections and Resources

Each volume of *Performing Arts Resources* (KK), published annually since 1974 by the Theatre Library Association, provides a collection of articles enabling librarians, archivists, and researchers to locate, identify, and classify information about theatre, film, broadcasting, and popular entertainment. The five volumes published thus far include guides to various archives and collections, analyses of individual collections, descriptions of regional holdings, studies in curatorship, bibliographies, indexes, and surveys of research materials. A new dimension was added with the appearance of the 1979 volume: the publication of a hitherto unpublished autobiography of the 19th-century English actor, O. Smith. As the editor, Mary Henderson, states, "if the publication is to live up to its name, 'resources' must also include reference matter that will augment library collections and give researchers access to rare material." It is a point well taken.

The seven annotated volumes, to date, of Gale Research Company's "Performing Arts Information Series" are recommended for all theatre collections regardless of size. Marion Whalon's *Performing Arts Research* (ZZ) covers the broad spectrum of information sources in the field including the audiovisual scene. The extremely useful *Stage Scenery, Machinery, and Lighting* (QQ), by Richard Stoddard, is the first book-length bibliography on the subject published since 1928, while his indispensable *Theatre and Cinema Architecture* (RR) is the first of its kind ever. Another updated "practical, utilitarian listing," with special attention to publications since 1957, is Jackson Kesler's *Theatrical Costume* (BB). Don Wilmeth's *American and English Popular Entertainment* (AA) is a successful pioneering attempt to assemble in one volume sources relating to various forms of "popular entertainment" such as the circus, fairs, pleasure gardens, dime museums, medicine shows, burlesque, and vaudeville. Users will find his *The American Stage to World War I* (BBB) a substantial and well-organized reference work as well. Although somewhat limited in scope, the specialized *Guide to Dance in Film* (JJ), by David L. Parker and Esther Siegel, is essential—especially to film and dance collections.

The *Bibliographic Guide to Theatre Arts: 1979* (F) is the latest supplement to the *Catalog of the Theatre and Drama Collections, The Research Libraries of The New York Public Library* (G. K. Hall, 1967). This standard reference has been published annually since 1975 with revisions each year reflecting current trends in the literature of the performing arts. Entries for all types of materials (fugitive as well as books and serials) are arranged in alphabetical sequence. Items are listed by subject, title, personal name, corporate name, conference or meeting title, and series. The 1979 volume includes over 11,000 references cataloged between September 1, 1978 and August 31, 1979 with extensive *see* and *see also* cross references.

The two-volume *Women's History Sources* (CCC), edited by Andrea Hinding, is a general guide to manuscript collections and archives in America, but theatre librarians will find it worth the price. A number of theatrical holdings are to be found among the 18,000 collections described in over 1,500 repositories—many of which were not reported for inclusion in the 5th edition of Ash's *Subject Collections*. A representative sampling of subject entries are Drama, Dramatic Critics, Dramatists Alliance, Theatre Audiences, Theatre Management, Theatre and Society, Theatrical Agencies, as well as hundreds of individual names in the performing arts. Volume II comprises the index to the geographical listing of collections by city and state cited in Volume I. The Western Historical Collections of the University of Colorado Libraries at Boulder has published its own *Guide to Manuscript Collections* (YY), compiled by Ellen Arguimbau and edited by Curator John A. Brennan. Theatre librarians and researchers are advised to make its acquaintance for theatrical subjects indigenous to the West, such as the Central City Opera House Association, the Denver Theatre from 1887 through the 1970s, and programs of touring performances at the Tabor Grand Opera House in Leadville.

Indexes

Two primary reference tools serving similar functions, but with somewhat different perspectives, are J. P. Wearing's *American and British Theatrical Biography* (WW) and Dennis La Beau's *Theatre, Film and Television Biographies Master Index* (TT). In indexing over 200 volumes, Wearing has produced a directory to biographical information on approximately 50,000 American, British, and foreign stage personalities (when the source surveyed made mention of their contribution to the English-speaking stage). Each entry includes name (with cross references to stage names and pseudonyms), dates of birth and death, nationality, theatrical occupation, and a code to sources containing more complete biographical information. The *Theatre, Film and Television Biographies Master Index* provides more than 100,000 citations to biographical sketches appearing in over forty biographical dictionaries and directories devoted to the stage, screen, opera, popular music, radio, and television. Each citation gives the person's name followed by the years of birth and date. Codes for the books indexed follow the dates.

One of the most ambitious singular undertakings within recent years is William P. Halstead's 12-volume *Shakespeare as Spoken* (V). Sponsored by the American Theatre Association, this work provides a collation of all known Shakespearean acting editions and promptbooks in the United Kingdom and North America. Covering the years 1594 to 1975, the volumes furnish a line-by-line collation for scholars who are attempting to reconstruct past performances, make comparisons, and trace influences in methods of production and direction. Halstead's efforts will surely be appreciated by those studying the work of actor-producers such as Garrick, Kemble, Macready, Phelps, Irving, Booth, Ben Iden Payne, Margaret Webster, Tyrone Guthrie, and others, as revealed by their annotations, cuts and alterations, and stage business. Another comprehensive computer-produced catalog-index is *Theatre at Stratford-upon-Avon* (SS), compiled and edited by Michael Mullin with Karen Morris Muriello. This two-volume work lists each production of the Shakespeare Memorial/Royal Shakespeare Theatre for the years 1879-1978 by play title, with date of first performance, playwright, director, lighting designer, actors and their respective roles, and a list of reviews and reviewers. A chronology of year-by-year performances enables researchers to trace theatrical developments, while the introduction provides a concise history of theatre at Stratford during the past century. The work will be most helpful to the student who does not have access to the actual archives. A specialized work of interest and value to advanced researchers is *An Index of*

Characters in English Printed Drama to the Restoration (E), by Thomas L. Berger and William C. Bradford, Jr. If so inclined, one can locate a character by surname, given name, nationality, occupation, religious proclivity, and/or psychological state.

The revised and expanded edition of Dean Keller's *Index to Plays in Periodicals* (AA) is most welcome. The first edition (1971) identified more than 5,000 plays in 103 indexed periodicals. The 1973 supplement indexed an additional 2,334 plays in sixteen periodicals included in the original list plus an additional thirty-seven. This new edition indexes 267 periodicals through 1976 with a total of 9,562 entries. The format remains the same. Intended for locational purposes, the title index refers to the main (author) section's numbered entries with numerous cross references. In spite of deficiencies and inconsistencies in the Chicorel index series over the years, reference libraries will find *Chicorel Theatre Index to Plays in Anthologies and Collections: 1970-1976* (P) serviceable. The work covers 556 volumes of dramatic literature of all types including one-act plays, children's plays, and radio and film plays. The entries for anthology titles, play titles, and dramatists are interfiled. There is a separate index of "subject indicators" to anthologies, but unfortunately, not to plays. Additional indexes provide access to editors, compilers, adapters, and translators.

Particularly helpful to the layman, as well as the professional, is the new *Rodgers and Hammerstein Fact Book* (NN), edited by Stanley Green. It is a "show-by-show chronicle" of Rodgers and Hammerstein contributions spanning sixty-five years, including production statistics, synopses, musical numbers, reviews, revivals, and British and film versions. A bibliography of books and articles, as well as a complete discography and categorical listings of songs enhance the volume.

Directories

The information on each of the 165 alphabetical listings of nonprofit professional regional theatre groups surveyed in the expanded and improved *Theatre Profiles 4* (UU) is current as of Summer 1979. First published in 1973, the directory continues to be a handy and reliable guide to the constituents of the Theatre Communications Group, the national service organization for nonprofit professional theatre. At a glance one can find names of artistic and administrative directors, founding date, season dates, schedule, facilities, finances, audience attendance, touring contact, booked-in events, programs and services, production lists, artistic statements, and types of Actors' Equity Association contracts. New features in the fourth edition include a quick reference guide to touring theatres and a chronology of the resident theatre movement. Another directory in this field, now in its third edition, is the *National Directory for the Performing Arts and Civic Centers* (HH) under the editorship of Beatrice Handel. Its objective is "to chronicle the magnitude and diversity of the performing arts in America by recording permanent performing arts organizations, their staffs, purpose, supportive boards, source of income, season, and information about performance facilities." Although it is a more comprehensive directory than *Theatre Profiles* (in that it covers dance and music, both vocal and instrumental), its theatre listings are not always as complete or as informative. A companion volume, *The National Directory for the Performing Arts/Educational* (II), gives basic information on major schools and institutions that offer courses and training in the performing arts. Entries in both volumes are arranged by state, city, and category. Alphabetical indexes are also provided.

Some, if not all, answers to an increasing number of inquiries concerning foreign performing arts festivals can be found in the *International Directory of Theatre, Dance and Folklore Festivals* (FF) where "a festival is a festival, a fair, a feast, a fiesta, a carnival, a ceremony, a celebration, an encounter, a ritual, a review." In this initial survey by the International Theatre Institute of the United States, more than 850 festivals in fifty-six countries have been documented. Through no fault of compilers Jennifer Merin and Elizabeth B. Burdick, some nations are not represented, and the coverage of others is incomplete, only because the respective requests for information met with no response. But what we have is gratifying. The directory is organized alphabetically by country, then by city or town where the festival occurs, and by festival title in English, with exceptions as explained in the introduction. A festival calendar, a bibliography, and an index of festivals are added.

The coming of age of American regional and repertory theatre is reflected, in part, in *The Shakespeare Complex: a Guide to Summer Festivals and Year-round Repertory in North America* (DD), by Glenn Loney and Patricia Mac-Kay. Handsomely illustrated with black-and-white photographs, the authors preface their discussions on the various festivals, organizations, and celebrations with a discourse on the "Shakespeare Complex" which they believe is "a collection of theatre organizations, some repertory companies, and summer festivals, as well as a number of colleges and universities that are devoting all, or part, of their production work to the plays of William Shakespeare," as well as a philosophical "state of mind." With the publication of the *American Theatre Annual 1978-79* (X), Catharine Hughes has expanded her coverage of American theatre while continuing to provide easy reference to the casts, credits, plots, and reviews of Broadway, off-Broadway, and off-off-Broadway. Originally titled *New York Theatre Annual*, the work now offers an extensive report on available touring companies and photo-and-text reports on selected major resident companies throughout the country. This broader amplification is to be encouraged.

An essential item for all general, as well as specialized reference collections, is the one and only directory of its kind thus far, *Contemporary American Thea-*

ter Critics (Q), compiled by M. E. Comtois and Lynn F. Miller. Of the 291 alphabetical listings giving biographical data and sample reviews, it is the lesser known who cover the nation's developing regional theatre scene who are emphasized. The volume is enhanced by a "Selected Bibliography of Books and Articles on American Theater Criticism, 1900-1976," and geographical, publisher/broadcaster, and play/musical title indexes. Despite limitations and omissions, the *National Playwrights Directory (Z)*, edited by Phyllis Johnson Kaye, offers information on current plays and playwrights not obtainable elsewhere. Sponsored by the O'Neill Theater Center in collaboration with the Theatre Development Fund, the alphabetical roster includes the dramatist's address, photograph, agent, titles of plays written (published, unpublished, availability, and productions), and synopses when accessible.

Although not written as a reference book, mention must be made of Dinah Luise Leavitt's *Feminist Theatre Groups* (CC), the first book published on Feminist Theatre, if only for her "List of American Feminist Theater Groups," chapter notes, bibliography, and list of plays. Edward Mapp's *Directory of Blacks in the Performing Arts* (EE) lists 850 black performers—living and dead—who appeared in films, television, night clubs, opera, ballet, jazz and classical concert, and the stage. It is an excellent source on early black performers who are not to be found in the standard bibliographical tools. Each entry includes personal data followed by performance information with appropriate cross references. A "Directory of Organizations" and a bibliography are included. Not to be overlooked is the remarkable *Gay Theatre Alliance Directory of Gay Plays* (17) researched by Terry Helbing, which is described in the General Editor's "Notes on Other Publications," following this section.

Two comprehensive directories of special interest to theatre librarians, counselors, and educators are *A Directory of Canadian Theatre Schools* (N), edited by Don Rubin and Alison Cranmer-Byng, and the revised edition of *Canadian Theatre Checklist* (M), edited by Rubin and Mimi Mekler. The *Directory*—the intensive record of its kind in Canada—provides documentation on eighty university and community college undergraduate and graduate programs, private schools, schools associated with theatre companies, and mime schools. Expanded to cover Canada's more than 170 professional theatre companies, the *Checklist* provides address, telephone number, names of key personnel, theatre type, seating capacity, year of founding, union status, and an overview of the theatre's philosophy and program.

Dictionaries, Encyclopedias, and Other Reference Works

Volumes 5 and 6 (published simultaneously) of the monumental *Biographical Dictionary of Actors, Actresses, Musicians, Dancers, Managers & Other Stage Personnel in London, 1660-1800* (G) are the latest in this multi-volume undertaking (a proposed twelve in all) to appear. No major reference library can afford to ignore these works in which authors Philip H. Highfill, Jr., Kalman A. Burnim, and Edward A. Langhans continue their census of London theatrical persons of all ranks, from the Restoration to the Regency—clowns and carpenters, scene painters and strolling players, dancers and dwarfs, managers and monologists. Theirs is the fruit of a search of many years through sixty-five libraries. The entries are illuminated by over 200 portraits and illustrations gleaned from public galleries and private collections all over the world. The set is a reference work of the first order.

The initial three volumes in the estimated 50-volume set of *Records of Early English Drama* (REED, for short) (LL, MM) have just been published. REED's aim is to make available in an accurate and usable edition all surviving documentary evidence of drama, minstrelsy, and ceremonial in Great Britain from the first record in any given location to the closing of the theatres in 1642. The two volumes covering the city of York present a fascinating picture of the social and economic life of this provincial town. The hiring, firing, censuring, suspending, and occasional restoring of individual musicians makes intriguing study, as does the civic pageantry surrounding the royal visits of the Plantagenet and Tudor monarchs. The Chester volume includes a discussion on the Midsummer Show and one zealous mayor's suppression of the entertainment because of the "Butchers' devil in his feathers, the naked boys, and the giants," only to have the show revived by subsequent mayors.

The publication of the *Papers and Proceedings of the Conference on the History of American Popular Entertainment* (A) constitutes a creative history. As editor Myron Matlaw states, "through the scholarly inquiries by academicians and through performances and reminiscences by members of the entertainment profession, it helps to re-create our cultural heritage by presenting an overview of popular entertainment and by sorting out the individual forms of the genre." The book is enhanced with Don B. Wilmeth's excellent "Historical Perspective Bibliography," which first appeared in the October 1977 issue of *Choice*. The conference, the first of its kind in the United States, was held at Lincoln Center in New York in November 1977.

The Encyclopedia of World Theatre (S), edited by Martin Esslin, is a translation of the revised and updated edition of the *Friedrichs Theater-lexikon*. Unlike many other encyclopedias of the theatre, this work is both a ready reference and a browsing tool. The entries are compact, but detailed, and cross references are used to indicate related themes or ideas. There is also a profusion of illustrations. Edwin Bronner's revised *Encyclopedia of the American Theatre*, 1900-1975 (J) is full of theatrical trivia and useful facts in its capsule evaluations and plot summaries of nearly every major theatrical presentation—and some less than memorable—on and off Broadway. A previous edition covered American drama through 1925.

The definitive work to date on the American musical is Gerald Bordman's *The American Musical Theatre* (I). For its range and wealth of material it has no rival, in spite of minor errors. The volume chronicles the Broadway musical, season by season, from the abortive opening night of *The Disappointment* (1767) to *Beatlemania* (1978), and designates trends and fashions in the theatre from early underrated foreign influences to the current search for new directions. Three comprehensive indexes—Shows and Sources, Songs, and People—make for easy reference. Arthur Jackson's *The Best Musicals—from "Show Boat" to "A Chorus Line"* (Y) surveys the great stage musicals of the 19th and 20th centuries with some attention to Hollywood adaptations and to key figures of the genre such as Busby Berkeley. Added attractions are the who's who of composers, filmographies, discographies, and listing of major show tunes and sources—not to mention the excellent illustrations.

For an hour or more of fun, browse through Roy Busby's *British Music Hall: an Illustrated Who's Who from 1850 to the Present Day* (K). Busby combed the newspapers and theatrical journals of the day for information and assembled a distinctive collection of signed photographs and other music hall ephemera. There are some 500 entries, over half are illustrated, covering most of the great and major performers, and many of the "wines and spirits" (supporting acts whose names appeared low on the bill of program and often in smaller type than the bar prices). There are cross references but no index. *On Singing Onstage* (R), by David Craig, is also a witty and articulate handbook for anyone aspiring to follow in the footsteps of Dennis King or Alfred Drake. It is a detailed study of the texts and structures of songs, defining moods and attitudes, and showing how diction, phrasing, gesture, and posture are all necessary to fusing the performer and the song into a self-revealing artistic unity.

Designed for the lay reader and the student of drama, Jack A. Vaughn's *Drama A to Z: a Handbook* (VV), is an alphabetical listing of dramatic terms with a detailed definition for each entry. It is clearly written, and many excellent examples are used in the definitions. An annotated chronology of dramatic theory and criticism is a helpful feature. Albert F. C. Wehlburg has collected a goodly number of theatre lighting terms and defined each in a concise manner in his *Theatre Lighting: an Illustrated Glossary* (XX). Many of the definitions are accompanied by first rate line drawings.

Canada on Stage: Canadian Theatre Review Yearbook 1978 (L), edited by Don Rubin, is the fifth volume in a series documenting the artistic life of Canada. With 350 photographs, this lively visual record contains complete credits and opening and closing dates for every professional production in the country. Highlights of the year are discussed in seven regional essays, as well as a special essay on children's theatre—all written for this yearbook. Theatre collections as well as Women's Studies programs will surely want the second volume in the Canadian Theatre Review's critically acclaimed series, *Canada's*

Lost Plays. Entitled *Women Pioneers* (O) and edited by Anton Wagner, the work presents the texts of six major plays by Canadian women written between 1840 and 1955, as well as an enlightening article which provides the literary and historical background for the sudden post-1967 emergence of Canadian women dramatists. For the record, Volume 1 of this series was entitled *The Nineteenth Century* and presented five comedies and one verse play from 1856 to 1895 dealing with the issues of Canadian political, economic, cultural, and social life.

Bibliographies

Continuing interest in black drama as a vital creative force has produced a number of much needed bibliographies of black American playwrights. *Black Ameican Playwrights, 1800 to the Present* (B), by Esther Spring Arata and Nicholas John Rotoli, was one of the first to be acclaimed as an authoritative source. Although the entries in Arata's *More Black American Playwrights* (C) span the years from 1970 to 1978, the information published in her 1976 volume is not duplicated here; a symbol placed near a playwright's name indicates that additional material is available in the first work. The book is in three sections: an alphabetical listing of dramatists and their works, together with criticisms, reviews, and awards; a general bibliography; and an index of play titles. *Black Playwrights, 1823-1977: an Annotated Bibliography of Plays* (W), compiled and edited by James V. Hatch and OMANii Abdullah, covers many of the same listings as the Arata volumes, but also features plot summaries, dates of composition or copyright, genre, cast, length, production data, publication data, library source, and information on permissions. Although it does not indicate sources of reviews and criticisms, there are lists of anthologies, dissertations and theses, taped interviews, awards, and addresses of playwrights, agents, and agencies. Another useful survey of bibliographical and critical material is the two-volume *Black American Writers: Bibliographic Essays* (H). Both volumes identify and assess manuscript sources, bibliographies, editions, letters, autobiographies and biographies, and special collections, and provide hundreds of summaries of critical articles.

Bibliographies on magic tend to be styled for the bibliophile rather than for the student of magic or even the prestidigitator. With the appearance of Robert Gill's *Magic as a Performing Art: a Bibliography of Conjuring* (U), the scene has changed. This is the first basic annotated bibliography of performing magic literature evaluating more than 1,000 books and pamphlets on conjuring published since 1935. Each entry is annotated with an assessment of value to performer as well as to standard bibliographic citations. There are subject, name, and title indexes; listings of magical societies, organizations, publishers, and booksellers; and a section on the availability of magic materials. What a further joy it is to touch, examine, and peruse the handsomely designed and illustrated *Descriptive and Bibliographic Catalog of the Circus & Related Arts Collection at Illinois State University* (PP), written and compiled by Special Collections Librarian Robert Sokan. If interested in acquiring it, the time to act is now, because only 400 copies were printed.

Bibliographies and guides to children's theatre are few and far between. At the moment there is nothing on the market comparable to Rachel Fordyce's *Children's Theatre and Creative Dramatics: an Anotated Bibliography of Critical Works* (T). The book's three main divisions deal with works of a critical, instructional, and evaluative nature only. Ninety percent of the 2,269 source materials are briefly annotated. *American Actors, 1861-1910: an Annotated Bibliography of Books Published in the United States in English from 1861 through 1976* (GG), by Ronald L. Moyer, is an alphabetical bibliographical listing of 363 books on American actors and actresses active between the Civil War and World War I. Although Moyer's entries are greater in number than those found in Wilmeth's *The American Stage to World War I* (BBB), they are uncritical. Wilmeth's is the more helpful guide for researchers.

Although authoritative and comprehensive guides to Canadian theatre history have yet to be compiled and published, we can appreciate the labors and the results of Dorothy Sedgwick's *Bibliography of English-Language Theatre and Drama in Canada 1800-1914* (OO) and John Ball and Richard Plant's *A Bibliography of Canadian Theatre History: 1583-1975* (B) and their newly published 1975-1976 supplement. Sedgwick's work is broken down into divisions on theatre history, dramatists, theatres, stage-tours and visits, and reference and bibliography, as well as a listing of the source materials used in compiling the bibliography. Ball and Plant's initial bibliography provides 2,015 listings classified within thirteen categories: general surveys; history to 1900; 20th century English-Canadian theatre; 20th century French-Canadian theatre; the little theatre movement; the Dominion Drama Festival; the Stratford Festival; Theatre Education; theatre architecture, facilities, stage design and lighting; biography and criticism; actors, actresses, and playwrights; theses; periodicals; and bibliography of theatre bibliographies. The supplement adds 1,040 entries, listing items published in 1976 and rectifying omissions. A fourteenth category, books on stagecraft, is added.

Louis A. Rachow

A   *American Popular Entertainment: Papers and Proceedings of the Conference on the History of American Popular Entertainment.* Ed. by Myron Matlaw. (Contributions in Drama and Theatre Studies, 1). 338pp. Westport, CN: Greenwood Press, 1979. $25.

B   Arata, Esther Spring; & Rotoli, Nicholas John. *Black American Playwrights, 1800 to the Present: a Bibliography.* 295pp. Metuchen, NJ: Scarecrow Press, 1976. $12.

C   Arata, Esther Spring. *More Black American Playwrights: a Bibliography.* 321pp. Metuchen, NJ: Scarecrow Press, 1978. $13.50.

D   Ball, John; & Plant, Richard. *A Bibliography of Canadian Theatre History: 1583-1975.* Toronto: Playwrights Co-op, 1976; *The Bibliography of Canadian Theatre History Supplement, 1975-1976.* Toronto: Playwrights Co-op, 1979. No price.

E   Berger, Thomas L.; & Bradford, William C., Jr. *An Index of Characters in English Printed Drama to the Restoration.* 222pp. Englewood, CO: Microcard Editions Books, 1975. $19.95

F   *Bibliographic Guide to Theatre Arts: 1979.* 310pp. Boston: G. K. Hall, 1979. $70

G   *A Biographical Dictionary of Actors, Actresses, Musicians, Dancers, Managers & Other Stage Personnel in London, 1660-1800,* by Philip H. Highfill, Jr., Kalman A. Burnim and Edward A. Langhans. Illus. 6 vols. Carbondale, IL: Southern Illinois University Press, 1973-78. $25 each.

H   *Black American Writers: Bibliographic Essays.* Ed. by Thomas M. Inge & others. 2 vols. New York: St. Martin's Press, 1978. $29.90

I   Bordman, Gerald. *The American Musical Theatre: a Chronicle.* 736pp. New York: Oxford University Press, 1978. $35.

J   Bronner, Edwin. *The Encyclopedia of the American Theatre, 1900-1975.* Rev. Edn. Illus. New York: A. S. Barnes, 1979. $30.

K   Busby, Roy. *British Music Hall: an Illustrated Who's Who from 1850 to the Present Day.* 191pp. Salem, NH: Paul Elek, 1977. $19.95

L   *Canada on Stage: Canadian Theatre Review Yearbook, 1978.* Ed. by Don Rubin. Illus. 448pp. Downsview, Ontario: Canadian Theatre Review Publications, 1979. $18.95

M   *Canadian Theatre Checklist.* Ed. by Don Rubin & Mimi Mekler. 48pp. Downsview, Ontario: Canadian Theatre Review Publications, 1979. Paper, $2.50

N   *Canadian Theatre Schools, A Directory of.* Ed. by Don Rubin. 52pp. Downsview, Ontario: Canadian Theatre Review Publications, 1979. Paper, $2.50

O   *Canada's Lost Plays: Women Pioneers.* Ed. by Anton Wagner. Illus. 224pp. Downsview, Ontario: Canadian Theatre Review Publications, 1978, $13.95

P   *Chicorel Theater Index to Plays in Anthologies and Collections: 1970-1976.* Ed. by Marietta Chicorel. 479pp. New York: Chicorel, 1977. $60.

Q   Comtois, M. E. ; & Miller, Lynn F., comps. *Contemporary American Theater Critics: a Directory and Anthology of their Works.* 979pp. Metuchen, NJ: Scarecrow Press, 1977. $35.

R   Craig, David. *On Singing Onstage.* 288pp. New York: Macmillan, 1978. $12.95. Paper, $5.95

S   Esslin, Martin, ed. *The Encyclopedia of World Theater.* Profusely Illus. 319pp. New York: Scribner's, 1977. $25.

T   Fordyce, Rachel. *Children's Theatre and Creative Dramatics: an Annotated Bibliography of Critical Works.* 275pp. Boston: G. K. Hall, 1975. $21.

U   Gill, Robert. *Magic as a Performing Art: a Bibliography of Conjuring.* 252pp. New York: Bowker, 1977. $18.

V   Halstead, William P. *Shakespeare as Spoken: a Collation of 5000 Acting Editions and Promptbooks of Shakespeare.* 12 vols. Published for the American Theatre Association. Ann Arbor, MI: University Microfilms International, 1977-79. Price range: $27.50 to $38 per vol.

W   Hatch, James V.; & OMANii Abdullah, comps. *Black Playwrights, 1823-1977: an Annotated Bibliography of Plays.* 319pp. New York: Bowker, 1977. $18.50

X   Hughes, Catharine, ed. *American Theatre Annual 1978-79: Covering Regional Theatre and National Touring Companies and Incorporating the New York Theatre Annual.* Illus. 280pp. Detroit: Gale Research Company, 1980. $32.

Y   Jackson, Arthur. *The Best Musicals—from "Show Boat" to "A Chorus Line": Broadway, Off-Broadway, London.* Illus. 208pp. New York: Crown, 1977. $15.95.

Z   Kaye, Phyllis Johnson, ed. *National Playwrights Directory.* Illus. 384pp. Published in association with the O'Neill Theater Center and the Theatre Development Fund. New York: Drama Book Specialists (Publishers), 1977. $15. Paper, $10.

AA   Keller, Dean H. *Index to Plays in Periodicals.* Rev. & expanded Edn. 824pp. Metuchen, NJ: Scarecrow Press, 1979. $35.

BB   Kesler, Jackson. *Theatrical Costume: a Guide to Information Sources.* (Performing Arts Information Guide Series, 6). 308pp. Detroit: Gale Research Company, 1979. $28.

CC   Leavitt, Dinah Luise. *Feminist Theatre Groups.* 153pp. Jefferson, NC: McFarland & Co. 1980. $10.95.

DD   Loney, Glenn; & MacKay, Patricia. *The Shakespeare Complex: a Guide to Summer Festivals and Year-round Repertory in North America.* Illus. 182pp. New York: Drama Book Specialists (Publishers), 1976. $12.50. Paper, $7.95

EE   Mapp, Edward. *Directory of Blacks in the Performing Arts*. 428pp. Metuchen, NJ: Scarecrow Press, 1978. $17.50

FF   Merin, Jennifer with Burdick, Elizabeth B. *International Directory of Theatre, Dance, and Folklore Festivals*. 480pp. Westport, CN: Greenwood Press, 1979. $19.95. Paper, $10.

GG   Moyer, Ronald L. *American Actors, 1861-1910: an Annotated Bibliography of Books Published in the United States in English from 1861 through 1976*. 268pp. Troy, NY: Whitston, 1979. $18.

HH   *The National Directory for the Performing Arts and Civic Centers*. 3d Edn. Ed. by Beatrice Handel. 1049pp. New York: John Wiley, 1978. $50.

II   *The National Directory for the Performing Arts/Educational*. 3d Edn. Ed. by Beatrice Handel. 669pp. New York: John Wiley, 1978. $45.

JJ   Parker, David L.; & Siegel, Esther. *Guide to Dance in Film: a Catalog of U. S. Productions including Dance Sequences, with Names of Dancers, Choreographers, Directors, and Other Details*. (Performing Arts Information Guide Series, 3). 220pp. Detroit: Gale Research Company, 1978. $28.

KK   *Performing Arts Resources*. Vols. 1-3, ed. by Ted Perry; Vols. 4-5, ed. by Mary C. Henderson. New York: Theatre Library Association, 1975-79. Price upon request.

LL   *Records of Early English Drama: Chester*. Ed. by Lawrence M. Clopper. 591pp. Toronto: University of Toronto Press, 1979. $40.

MM   *Records of Early English Drama: York*. Ed. by Alexandra F. Johnston and Margaret Rogerson. 2 vols. Toronto: University of Toronto Press, 1979. $69.95

NN   *Rodgers and Hammerstein Fact Book: a Record of their Works Together and with Other Collaborators*. Ed. by Stanley Green. 792pp. New York: Drama Book Specialists (Publishers), 1980. Paper, $17.95

OO   Sedgwick, Dorothy. *A Bibliography of English-Language Theatre and Drama in Canada 1800-1914*. (Occasional Publications, 1). 48pp. Edmonton: Alberta: Nineteenth Century Theatre Research, 1976. Paper, $2.50

PP   Sokan, Robert. *A Descriptive and Bibliographic Catalog of the Circus & Related Arts Collection at Illinois State University, Normal, Illinois*. Illus. 173pp. Bloomington, IL: Scarlet Ibis Press, 1976. $30.

QQ   Stoddard, Richard. *Stage Scenery, Machinery, and Lighting: a Guide to Information Sources*. (Performing Arts Information Guide Series, 2). 274pp. Detroit: Gale Research Company, 1977. $28.

RR   Stoddard, Richard. *Theatre and Cinema Architecture: a Guide to Information Sources*. (Performing Arts Information Guide Series, 5). 368pp. Detroit: Gale Research Company, 1978. $28.

SS   *Theatre at Stratford-upon-Avon: a Catalogue-Index to Productions of the Shakespeare Memorial/Royal Shakespeare Theatre, 1879-1978*. Comp. & ed. by Michael Mullin with Karen Morris Muriello. 2 vols. Westport, CN: Greenwood Press, 1980. $60.

TT   *Theatre, Film and Television Biographies Master Index: a Consolidated Guide to Over 100,000 Biographical Sketches of Persons Living and Dead, as they appear in Over 40 of the Principal Biographical Dictionaries devoted to the Theatre, Film and Television*. Ed. by Dennis La Beau. (Biographical Index Series, 5) 477pp. Detroit: Gale Research Company, 1979. $35.

UU   *Theatre Profiles 4: a Resource Book of Nonprofit Professional Theatres in the United States*. Introd. by John Houseman. Illus. 276pp. New York: Theatre Communications Group, 1979. Paper, $12.95

VV   Vaughn, Jack A. *Drama A to Z: a Handbook*. 224pp. New York: Frederick Ungar, 1979. $9.95. Paper, $3.95

WW   Wearing, J.P. *American and British Theatrical Biography: a Directory*. 1007pp. Metuchen, NJ: Scarecrow Press, 1979. $37.50

XX   Wehlburg, Albert F. C. *Theatre Lighting: an Illustrated Glossary*. 62pp. New York: Drama Book Specialists (Publishers), 1976. Paper, $7.95

YY   (Western Historical Collections). Arguimbau, Ellen, comp. *A Guide to Manuscript Collections*. Ed. by John A. Brennan, Curator. (Western Historical Collections, University of Colorado at Boulder). 112pp. 1977. $5.

ZZ   Whalon, Marion K. *Performing Arts Research: a Guide to Information Sources*. (Performing Arts Information Guide Series, 1). 280pp. Detroit: Gale Research Company, 1976. $28.

AAA   Wilmeth, Don B. *American and English Popular Entertainment: a Guide to Information Sources.* (Performing Arts Information Guide Series, 7). 465pp. Detroit: Gale Research Company, 1980. $28.

BBB   Wilmeth, Don B. *The American Stage to World War I: a Guide to Information Sources.* (Performing Arts Information Guide Series, 4). 269pp. Detroit: Gale Research Company, 1978. $28.

CCC   *Women's History Sources: a Guide to Archives and Manuscript Collections in the United States.* Ed. by Andrea Hinding. 2 vols. New York: Bowker, 1979. $175.

NOTES ON OTHER PUBLICATIONS

Compiled by the General Editor

Guides to Collections and Resources

A very full and remarkably interesting volume published for the Southeastern Library Association is *Special Collections in Libraries of the Southeast* (20), edited by J. B. Howell. Over 2,000 subject collections are described in libraries from Alabama to Virginia and West Virginia. Many collections are of local interest and have not been reported to the larger national guides, but hundreds—also not previously reported—include important resources in unexpected places. Arranged by state, city, and library, there are full geographical, corporate, and general subject indexes. Including library addresses and zip codes, this is a fine work that could serve as a model for other regional, state, and local guides. The New Jersey Historical Society has issued its *Guide to the Manuscript Collections* in its care (30), compiled by Don C. Skemer and Robert C. Morris. There are 1,057 entries describing each manuscript group, including revised entries of the Society's 1957 *Guide*, but the new *Guide* very sensibly retains the group reference numbers of the previous inventory. Manuscript groups are reviewed in sufficient detail to suggest many avenues of use to researchers. The index contains about 3,000 citations to this remarkably rich historical collection.

Three publications of the Gale Research Company in Detroit serve as examples of the prolific "Guide to Information Resources" series issued by that company: Vladimir Wertsman's *The Romanians in America and Canada* (35) is a review of ethnic resources of considerable immediate interest in various parts of both countries. The entries are revelatory of the surprisingly numerous contributions these Central Europeans have made here; secondly, *Medical Education in the United States* (26), by Francis Cordasco with David N. Alloway, ranges widely and includes a large section on the history of medicine and an appendix (among others) of American and Canadian biomedical journals with addresses; last to be noted is Ann-Marie Cutul's *Twentieth-Century European Painting* (31), a very competent annotated review of the literature that, in addition, includes fine sections on periodicals, museums, art organizations, libraries and documentation centers, major publishers and distributors of art books, etc., all indexed by author, title, and subject.

Indexes

Some of the foremost prose writers and poets made interesting contributions, now first identified through a very useful *Index to The London Magazine* (24), compiled by Frank P. Riga and Claude A. Prance and covering the years 1820-23, when the magazine was a major challenge to the famed *Blackwood's*. Lamb, DeQuincey, John Clare, Hazlitt, and Hood all set up high standards for *London Magazine's* content. The compilers have made an issue by issue list of contents, identifying many contributions difficult to place. They have thoroughly indexed authors and contributors, detected the names of authors of initialed and pseudonymous contributions, listed book reviews (by author and by title), prepared a large bibliography, and noted the plates in each volume that contained any. The book is indispensable to literary researchers working in the period. Hours of work will be saved for students and researchers by Daniel A. Wells' *Literary Index to American Magazines, 1815-1865* (2), which analyzes twenty-five of the most important literary periodicals of the period under some 400 major headings including writers and artists. Listed under authors' names are general comments on their lives and careers, an alphabetical list of all cited works, and lists of their articles, poems, reviews, and stories from all departments of each of the magazines. Pieces of special significance are underlined. The Index serves as a comprehensive guide to references, helping to determine the writings and reception in this country of American, British, and Continental writers including many minor authors. A wonderful work by a professor of English at the University of South Florida to whom we are all greatly indebted.

Mention should be made of *A Cumulative Index to [Evan I.] Farber's "Periodicals for College Libraries" [Appearing] in "Choice", September 1974-October 1978* (33), compiled by Anna Bruce Neal and others. This is a tool that refers one quickly to the excellently annotated entries that Farber has contributed to the reviews of new publications in monthly issues of *Choice*. It would be careless of the General Editor to omit reference to the second edition of his own publication, *Serial Publications Containing Medical Classics: an Index to Citations in Garrison/Morton (3d Edition, 1970)*, compiled in collaboration with Michael A. Murray (27). This edition, with about 1,000 more entries than in the 1961 publication, indexes, by title of periodical, some 6,000 of the classics of medicine that have appeared in serial publications. The book is meant for collectors, librarians, and antiquarian booksellers, to help them recognize and identify contributions important to the history of medicine and related sciences.

Directories

Anyone connected with a special collection can cull from the Book Publishers Directory (10) numerous new ideas (and perhaps materials) for collections relevant to special interests. Annie M. Brewer and Elizabeth A. Geiser, editors, have provided an astonishing guide to new and established, private and special interest, avant-garde and alternative, organization and association, government and institution presses. For more than 3,400 entries they give address, telephone, founding date, ISBN number, and, in most instances, information about affiliates, names of officers and managers, number of titles, subjects covered, selected titles, and other important facts. Arranged alphabetically, there are also indexes of publishers, *subjects*, and geographical locations by state and city. Not too far removed in subject interest is *The Directory of British Alternative Periodicals 1965-1974* (33A), edited by John Noyce (who also edits *Librarians for Social Change*). This is the most substantial listing of the underground and alternative press in Britain, 1965-1974, with some 1975 coverage. Since many of the 1,253 titles listed sold fewer than 500 copies (some were printed in editions of only 50!), Noyce's research was enormous, a task in which he persevered to give all possible information about each title—its name, dates of issue, frequency, place of publication, description of character and contents (including names of some contributors), quantity printed, format, indexes, availability in microform, library holdings, references, and a full index. This is a fine record of an era of amateur journalistic endeavor, and Noyce has met the challenge of recording much of it with rigorous and careful scholarship.

Terry Helbing has done a fine job of researching the *Gay Theatre Alliance Directory of Gay Plays* (17), a volume of comprehensive information on plays with major gay characters or predominantly gay themes. Strict—and very interesting—definitions exclude several types of plays with good reasoning. Dozens of plays, however, are presented alphabetically by title, and listings contain information on author, type of play (drama, comedy, etc.), number of acts, number of characters (male or female), number of interior and exterior sets, plot synopsis, location and date of first production (if produced), book title-date-publisher, amateur royalties, name and address of playwright's agent, and, if a musical, in what form the score is available. There are two unusual appendixes: "Lost" Plays (about which complete information could not be obtained) and a list of Gay Theatre Companies (with addresses); there is an index of playwrights, etc. A directory that is not quite so good is Roger & Judith Sheppard's *Literary Societies for Bookmen* (23A), an uneven collection of names, addresses, and descriptions (of some) societies, clubs, and periodicals in England and America relating to literature and the arts. Unfortunately much of the information is obsolete; there are notable omissions and quite a lot of inaccurate information. The idea is a good one, and the book could be useful. Eventually it will be, one supposes, for this is the kind of directory that improves with successive editions, witness the Sheppards' well-known *International Directory of Book Collectors*, the 1981-83 edition of which has been compiled for publication scheduled early in 1981.

Dictionaries, Encyclopedias, Atlases, and Other Reference Works

This is a broad category in which we will note miscellaneous books that come our way that ought to be useful in conjunction with special collections in libraries. First we draw attention to the handsome *ALA World Encyclopedia of Library and Information Services* (21), which was published this past spring. While not specifically for the use of subject specialists, one would expect the book to become a familiar companion to any librarian concerned with the history, development, and present condition of the profession worldwide. All but the smallest libraries should be able to make good use of it in the reference department. Of particular interest to any specialist librarian, however, is the ever-increasingly helpful *American Reference Books Annual* (3), now in its 1980 edition and, this spring, to be followed by 1981. Anyone doing any kind of reference work should be familiar with this *effectively critical* tool and its signed evaluative descriptions of each title, all written by specialist reviewers. Now in its second decade of publication, *"ARBA"* is helpful retrospectively both for acquisition and for weeding collections. Any library would find a standing order worthwhile. Arranged within 42 major categories, there is a complete index.

Names are often of interest to special collections, and two books should be cited for our readers, *Twentieth-Century American Nicknames* (28) and the 3d edition of *Nicknames and Sobriquets of U.S. Cities, States, and Counties* (29), both of which can provide answers to frequent questions and waste hours of time in fun-searching by anyone who handles them. Similarly, G. A. Wilkes' *A Dictionary of Australian Colloquialisms* (7) will pass some happy hours with profit for language searchers and enjoyment for others who fall upon such colorful entries as "cobber" or "poddy-dodger," and phrases like "knock back." Who among you readers knew—before now—about the "improvised bush delicacy, 'Phar Lap,' wild dog with the hair burnt off, trussed, and cooked in ashes"? While writing about language books, we would be remiss if we failed to mention that pleasant way to study German through the recently published 4th edition of Doring's *Colloquial German* (17A). Nonetheless, I still hesitate to believe that even in "The German Alphabet: . . . W, veh, X, iks, Y, üpsilon, Z, tset!" We have received a *Concise Dictionary of Physics and Related Subjects* (34), 2d edition, by J. Thewlis, which will be of tremendous use in any collection related to the sciences. The scope of the work includes such related subjects as Astronomy, Astrophysics, Aerodynamics, Biophysics, Crystallography, Geophysics, Hydraulics, Mathematics, Medical Physics, Meteorology, Metrology, Photography, Physical Chemistry, Physical Metallurgy, and so on. Surely libraries with subject emphasis in any of these fields will require this up-to-date dictionary with its carefully exact definitions.

Although not written as a reference book, *Recreating the Past: British History and the Victorian Painter* (30A), by Roy Strong, which is fully illustrated (including color plates), will appeal to the historically and artistically minded reference person interested in the influence of literary tradition on the visual interpretation of historic incidents. Reference to books and folklore used and learned by the artists can help to understand their pictures—rather like reading Lowes' *The Road to Xanadu*. British history comes alive also in another visual medium through G. S. P. Freeman-Grenville's *Atlas of British History* (5), with fine and not oversimplified cartography by Lorraine Kessel. The maps represent the principal themes and events in the British Isles from prehistoric times until 1978, relating political, social, and economic history to its physical setting. The legends and type sizes are clear and intelligently related to the maps which are good to use with any reading about British history. This small volume is a helpful companion to Michael Hardwick's *A Literary Atlas & Gazeteer of the British Isles* (1973). Also with regard to the world's geography, it is a pleasure to see Dover's excellent reprint of Lloyd A. Brown's *The Story of Maps* (25), originally published in 1949 and quite expensive in the antiquarian book market. This is certainly the very best and most readable book ever written on maps and cartography for use by the intelligent layman. References to the historical literature abound throughout the text and provide the collector and special collections librarian with a guide that is not otherwise easily available.

Geography of outerspace is approached in another Dover reprint in the well-illustrated book, *The History of the Telescope* (36), by Henry C. King, first issued in 1955. The historical and bibliographical aspects of this basic volume (though it is not easy reading) cover the literature with great thoroughness. Back to earth, we must mention the excellence—as a model—of the handsomely illustrated 32d edition of *The Milepost: Mile-by-Mile Logs of the Alaska Highway, All Highways in Alaska, and the Major Travel Routes Through Western Canada* (1). The maps alone make this a basic reference volume about the area covered, while the text entries and profusion of advertisement provide information found in no other books. Would that all states and nations had such a good guide—well edited, accurate, and attractively crowded with nearly current information. Finally, among general reference books, we must point out *A Concise History of Japanese Art* (19), an urgent acquisition for any library—even the most general collection—by Peter C. Swann. This is a completely revised edition of the book "first published as *An Introduction to the Arts of Japan* by Bruno Cassirer [sic], Oxford, England (1958)." The nine chapters treat of all of the arts in the chronological order of historic Japanese periods. Excellent black-and-white illustrations and frankly critical writing enhance the depth of analysis of this authoritative standard work.

Bibliographies and Special Booksellers' Catalogues

Among this lot, the first book at hand will be of greatest interest to special collection libraries. It is the 2d edition of *Fine Arts: a Bibliographic Guide to Basic Reference Works, Histories, and Handbooks* (15), by Donald L. Ehresmann. Expanded, updated, and revised, the second edition supersedes the much older Chamberlin (within the scope of the volume) and brings coverage forward to 1978; it includes annotated entries numbering over 1,670 titles—books and periodicals published after 1830. Western European art is emphasized, but the New World and other areas are not overlooked. Generally, coverage stops at the level of national and period works, with specific exceptions, such as works dealing with the art of some provinces themselves important centers of European art. General histories and handbooks listed are those published since 1875. Bibliographical citations are complete and expert, and the descriptive annotations are excellent, critical where necessary. The index contains authors, editors, main entry and series titles, with a greatly expanded subject index. This is a volume necessary to any fine arts collection. Bruce Stevenson's ample *Reader's Guide to Great Britain* (18) is "for the general reader who requires a comprehensive bibliography of the language, literature, life, customs, and institutions of the British people." It includes under some sixty sections about 300 subheads as subject groupings, with references to every aspect of British life and history. The majority of the titles referred to are in print in Britain (and available in the United States), and, indeed, for many needs the volume can almost serve as a partial British BIP for modern works of good quality. To this end, and since the book was published by the National Book League in association with the British Council, it might be considered for subsequent editions to include a list of publishers of titles listed and their addresses. A few sections are weak (for example Medicine, Finance & Banking, Parliament, etc.), but on the whole the lists are of real quality and well selected.

Contrary to the practicality of the two previous titles, it is very difficult to understand the reason for publishing Karl J. R. Arndt's *The Annotated and Enlarged Edition of Ernst Steiger's Precentennial Bibliography "The Periodical Literature of the United States of America"* (32). For all of the excellence of its physical appearance, its size, and impressively high cost, it is improbable that many researchers will ever make use of it except to provide a footnote. Not being a periodicals or newspaper librarian, I could be mistaken, but it seems to me that there is little in the book that is not readily found elsewhere. Arndt's fine and important biographical essay on Steiger would have been better served if it were more compact and had been published in a periodical devoted to bibliography or library history; similarly, for his interesting second part, "The International Press and Ernst Steiger's Exhibition of Periodical Literature at the 1873 Vienna Exposition." I can find some small antiquarian enthusiasm for the subject index, but the paucity of references is not likely to supply any substantive information, especially since most of the periodicals cited contained only secondary or superficial articles.

Of more universal or, at least, broader interest is the University of Kansas Publication, Number 44 in its Library Series, *Anglo-Scottish Tracts, 1701-1714*

(4), a project that required years of effort to compile and for which we must be grateful to W. R. & V. B. McLeod for their patience with a list for which they have included only those 535 works and editions they were able to examine personally. The intriguing titles, many by or attributed to such persons as DeFoe, John Hamilton, George MacKenzie, Steele, and Swift, along with other political activists of Queen Anne's reign between the years 1701 and 1714, refer to the debate between England and Scotland concerning union and some peripheral matters. Bibliographical citations are title transcriptions with collations and full imprint, author attributions, and copy locations (12 English and Scottish libraries, 12 American, all well distributed geographically). Most of the entries are followed by scholarly explanations of the intent of the tract and details about the author or about the historical setting of the incident treated. Nearly a third of the book is given over to biographical studies of just over half of the authors whose works are cited in the Checklist. This compilation will be helpful to scholars for many years.

There is good fun to be had in Los Angeles antiquarian bookseller Peggy Christian's catalogue called *Collations and Potations: Old, Curious, and Standard Books, Pamphlets, Menus, etc., on Food, Drink, and Related Subjects* (16). This is a very handsome (itself collectible) piece designed by Grant Dahlstrom and printed at The Castle Press, Pasadena. There are 379 items listed for sale, each presented by a careful bibliographical description and frequently with the addition of notes. Many of the items came from the distinguished cookery collection of Carlotta Marjorie Freeman, and one hopes that most will go to people who will enjoy them as she did. Some highlights are editions of Hannah Glasse's *The Art of Cookery, Made Plain and Easy* (1755 and 1788), Husmann's *Grape Culture and Wine-Making in California* (1888), *Los Angeles Cookery* (1881), the first edition in English of *A Perfect School of Instructions for the Officers of the Mouth* (1682), and Hannah Wolley's *The Accomplish'd Lady's Delight . . .* (1677). These listings, along with many other "comfortable" books, put this charming catalogue in a place by itself for reference and reading about food and drink.

We wonder how many bookpersons have an opportunity to enjoy the great semiannual auction catalogues of "F. Dörling, Buch- und Kunstantiquariat" (5A), catalogues that deserve permanent retention for their reference value and descriptions of books, manuscripts, autographs, old and modern art, of all kinds, and decorative graphics. The most recent catalogue, classed, with nearly 6,000 lots sold in June 1980, has fine representations in each of these fields. About half of the catalogue's entries are annotated with pertinent notes. Gallery estimates, in DM, are shown for each lot. Appended to the catalogue is a list of important mapmakers and their dates, a long bibliography of authorities cited, and a fine 5-page list of German abbreviations spelled out in German, English, and French; there is also a 22-page, double-columned index.

California specialists will revel in *John Howell - Books' Catalogue 50* [in five parts] (12), issued over the past two years. This was the collection of the late Jennie Crocker Henderson (1887-1974) and the last of the great collections of Californiana to come on the market. It is a magnificent catalogue and will long serve as an important annotated reference tool. Its various Parts are exciting reading and great to savor, even if the gems are beyond the reach of most of us: I, Spanish Exploration to Statehood; II, 1850 to the Twentieth Century, A-L; III, M-Z; IV, Literature; V, Fine Printing & Limited Editions; Addenda & Index. While the index is helpful, it is exasperating since it "does not include authors' names listed in the [five] alphabetical sequences, except for those who appear as subjects in other works or in multiple listings." Nevertheless, this is an essential catalogue of Americana to read and study.

It would be difficult to fail to mention Oak Knoll Books' six-part (and index) sale catalogue of the *Alida Roochvarg Collection of Books About Books* (10B), which may still be available to persons who did not subscribe to it. The prices listed are fair and can set a modern-day standard except for the vagaries of inflation. The most unusual feature of the collection was the superb lot of editions of Richard de Bury's *The Philobiblon*, from the first printing (Oxford, 1599) through one of 1976, 38 lots in all, to be sold as a unit. The next item can be classified for this review section or the next; it is another publication by Oak Knoll Books, *Bookman's Quintet* (10A), a cumulated reprint of five of the very important sales catalogues issued by the house of Leona Rostenberg (and Madeleine Stern) from 1946 to 1967, all about bibliography, printing history, booksellers, libraries, presses, and collectors. Two of the catalogues dealt separately (and exclusively) with extensive selections from the Aldine Press and the House of Elzevier. The wonderfully informative notes make for fine reading (so do the old prices!), and there is a good index to the entire volume. Just as I completed copy for this column came *The English Experience: Books Printed in England Before 1640, a Descriptive Catalogue of Nine Hundred and Sixty-Four Facsimile Editions Now Available* (14A) from Walter J. Johnson. This completes the listings that the reprint publisher has been offering (in groups of about 70 titles) in 14 groups since 1964 and is cumulative for all previous lists. The new catalogue is introduced by a subject index, and the alphabetically arranged main entries which follow include *STC* and other bibliographical citations along with explanatory notes about the books.

Books About Books, Rare Books, Collecting, Essays, Biographies, etc.

The top title for bookpersons' appreciation and months of fun is Morton N. Cohen's two-volume set of *The Letters of Lewis Carroll* (14), which of itself will take any reader right down the rabbit's hole to Wonderland. We know that Carroll wrote over a 100,000 letters (he logged them all, coming and going!). Having selected two-volumes' worth, this great collection, *filled with reference to persons and events*, makes unbelievably good reading for those of us who love Carroll, Alice, English literature of the 19th century, and those who peopled the period. Extensively indexed for keying into almost anyone. Also a 19th century specialist, *Michael Sadleir, 1888-1951*, by Roy Stokes (9), makes this legendary man come alive as one of the truly important persons who influenced bibliography and book collecting in modern times. The story of Sadleir's investigations into the social, economic, and literary life of England, of Trollope, and of all aspects of the book demonstrates those qualities that make "the complete bookman." This is for all younger enthusiasts of the book, and a lovely reminiscence for all of us who may be somewhat older. I wonder how many readers know the delights of his modest 1940 novel, *Fanny by Gaslight?*

More miscellaneous is the small collection of chapters called *The Oldest Library Motto, and Other Library Essays*, by Cora E. Lutz (11), mostly stemming from Miss Lutz' unusual researches as she spent her many years as Yale University's cataloguer of pre-1600 manuscripts. There is good variety and enjoyable reading here, each essay short enough to read with the evening cocktail, as I did. Judaica scholars will be pleased to see the extensive "Catalogue of Catalogues: Bibliographical Survey of a Century of Temporary Exhibitions of Jewish Art," which appeared in the *Journal of Jewish Art*, Vol. VI, (19A). The first exhibition, a century ago, was part of the Universal Exhibition of 1878 in Paris. The bibliography describes 339 catalogues and includes location and subject indexes; there is also a list of founding dates of the major Jewish museums: 1897 in Vienna to 1978 in Bucharest and Tel Aviv. This handsome publication, which I had not seen before, has many other articles that refer to the arts, manuscripts, bibliography. I wish to mention, very briefly, the happy occurrence of Dover's reprinting of the now famous catalogue, *2000 Years of Calligraphy* (13), that remarkably exciting 1965 joint exhibition organized by the Baltimore Museum of Art, Peabody Institute Library, and the Walters Art Gallery.

Special Collections Administration

Two significant volumes to appear this year reached us in late summer. Both of them are required reading for every reader of *Special Collections*; indeed, they should be required reading for anyone involved with the care of books, manuscripts, or archives, and I must endorse them with considerable emphasis on their importance. First is Susan G. Swartzburg's *Preserving Library Materials: a Manual* (23), which is an authoritative statement, based on experience and understanding of the rapidly changing movement for materials preservation in libraries. While acknowledging these continuing changes, the author teaches the reader the essential problems that arise and the basic approaches to the care of all types of materials. *Preventive care* is the key approach that anyone can learn from this important book, and I beg anyone who wonders about the devastation of deterioration or the terrors of physical disaster in libraries to read it carefully. I find myself greatly annoyed by some of the petty disputatious criticism of slight errors in this fine contribution.

Second, Ellsworth Mason's *Mason On Library Buildings* (22) joins the texts by Joseph Wheeler, Ralph Ellsworth, and Keyes Metcalf as one of the four most important books ever written on library building, planning, and architecture. Based on his years of experience as a consultant planning academic (and some other) libraries, Mason describes library building problems, analyzes six major constructions in the United States and Canada, comments on one hundred-five buildings, and provides a "Demonstration Model Program for a New Library." Supported by photographs and plans, Mason comments on all of this in some strong terms and brings his critical acumen to point accusingly to errors that thoughtful planning and analysis might have avoided. More constructively, he shows how to think about building and design so that similar mistakes might not be made. Strangely (for library literature) both of these books are easy reading, and, in fact, Mason's caustic comments on some people's idiocy and his good humor peppered into the text are amusing factors that support his arguments throughout.

Lee Ash

1. (*Alaska*). *The Milepost: Mile-by-Mile Logs of the Alaska Highway, All Highways in Alaska, and Major Travel Routes Through Western Canada*. Profusely Illus. and with a Large Fold-Out Color Map of Alaska and Western Canada. 32d Edn. 498pp. Edmonds, WA: Alaska Northwest Publishing Co. [130 Second Ave., South, Zip 98020], 1980. $7.95.

2. *American Magazines, The Literary Index to, 1815-1865*, by Daniel A. Wells. 218pp. Metuchen, NJ: Scarecrow Press, 1980. $12.00.

3. *American Reference Books Annual, 1980*, Vol. 11, Bohdan S. Wynar, ed. xxviii, 765pp. Littleton, CO: Libraries Unlimited, 1980. $37.50.

4. *Anglo-Scottish Tracts, 1701-1714*: a Descriptive Checklist, Comp. by W. R. and V. B. McLeod. (University of Kansas Publications Library Series, 44). xvii, 211 pp. Lawrence: University of Kansas Libraries, 1979. Paper, $12.00.

5. *Atlas of British History*, by G. S. P. Freeman-Grenville. Cartography by Lorraine Kessel. Map Illus. London: Rex Collings [distr: Rowman & Littlefield, 81 Adams Drive, Totowa, NJ 07512], 1979. $16.50; $8.95.

5A. (*Auction Catalogue*). F. Dörling, Buch- und Kunstantiquariat. 100. Auktion, 12-14 Juni 1980. [5798 lots]. 647pp. Hamburg: F. Dörling (Neuer Wall 40-42, 2000 Hamburg 36), 1980. DM 20.

6. (*Australia*). Clark, C. M. H. *A History of Australia*. I, Earliest Times to the Age of Macquarie; II, New South Wales and Van Diemen's Land, 1822-1838; III, Beginning of an Australian Civilization, 1824-1851; IV, The Earth Abideth For Ever, 1851-1888. 4 vols. Illus. Melbourne: Melbourne University Press [distr: ISBS, Inc., P.O. Box 555, Forest Grove, OR 97116], V.d. Price: Inquire.

7. *Australian Colloquialisms, A Dictionary of*, by G. A. Wilkes. 370 double-columned pp. Sydney: Sydney University Press [distr: ISBS, Inc., P.O. Box 555, Forest Grove, OR 97116], 1978. $19.95.

8. (*Autobiography*). Rhodes, Carolyn H., ed. *First Person Female American*; a Selected and Annotated Bibliography of the Autobiographies of American Women Living After 1950.

(*American Notes & Queries*, Supplement, Vol. II), xlix, 404pp. Troy, NY: Whitson Publishing Co. [P.O. Box 958, Zip 12181], 1980. $28.50.

9. (*Bibliographer*). Stokes, Roy. *Michael Sadleir, 1888-1957*. (The Great Bibliographers Series, No. 5). 154pp. Metuchen, NJ: Scarecrow Press, 1980. $8.50.

10. *Book Publishers Directory*: a Guide to New and Established Private and Special Interest, Avant-Garde and Alternative, Organization and Association, Government and Institution Presses. 2d Edn. Annie M. Brewer & Elizabeth A. Geiser, eds. 668 double-columned pp. Detroit: Gale Research Co., 1979. $110.00

10A. *Bookman's Quintet*: Five Catalogues About Books, by Leona Rostenberg and Madeleine B. Stern. Illus. 283pp. Newakr, DE: Oak Knoll Books [414 Delaware St., Zip 19720], 1980. $25.00.

10B. *Books About Books, The Alida Roochvarg Collection of* [in six parts and index; 2690 lots]. New Castle, DE: Oak Knoll Books [414 Delaware St., Zip 19720], 1979-80. Unbound, $15.00; bound, $35.00.

11. (*Books About Books*). Lutz, Cora E. *The Oldest Library Motto, and Other Library Essays*. Illus. 176pp. Hamden, CT: Shoe String Press, 1979. $15.00.

12. *California, Catalogue 50*. [in 5 parts]. Illus. San Francisco: John Howell - Books [434 Post St., Zip 94102], 1979-80. $25.00.

13. *Calligraphy, 2000 Years of*: a Three-Part Exhibition Organized by The Baltimore Museum of Art, Peabody Institute Library, Walters Art Gallery - A Comprehensive Catalog (1965). Illus. 201pp. New York: Taplinger Publishing Co., 1980. Paper, $9.95.

14. *Carroll, Lewis, The Letters of*, Ed. by Morton N. Cohen, With the Assistance of Roger Lancelyn Green. Illus. 2 vols. New York: Oxford University Press, 1979. $60.00.

14A. (*English Books*). The English Experience: Books Printed in England Before 1640. A Descriptive Catalogue of Nine Hundred and Sixty-Four Facsimile Editions Now Available . . . 257pp. Norwood, NJ: Walter J. Johnson [355 Chestnut St., Zip 07648], 1980. Request.

15. *Fine Arts*; a Bibliographic Guide to Basic Reference Works, Histories, and Handbooks, 2d Edn, by Donald L. Ehresmann. 349pp. Littleton, CO: Libraries Unlimited, 1979. $19.50.

16. (*Food & Drink*). Collations and Potations; Old, Curious, and Standard Books, Pamphlets, Meus, etc., on Food, Drink, and Related Subjects, [379 items] Offered for Sale . . . [Designed by Grant Dahlstrom and Printed at The Castle Press, Pasadena]. Illus. 63pp. Los Angeles: Peggy Christian [110 South LaBrea Ave., Zip 90036], 1980. $3.50.

17. *Gay Theatre Alliance. Directory of Gay Plays*. Comp. & Ed., With an Introd. by Terry Helbing. 133pp. New York: J H Press [distr: Gay Theatre Alliance, Room 300, 51 West 4th St., Zip 10012], 1980. $5.95.

17A. *German, Colloquial*, by P. F. Doring. 4th Rev. Edn by Inge Hubmann-Uhlich. 149pp. Boston: Routledge & Kegan Paul, 1980. $6.50.

18. *Great Britain, Reader's Guide to*; a Bibliography, Comp. by Bruce Stevenson. 558pp. London: National Book League [distr: R. R. Bowker, 1180 Avenue of the Americas, New York NY 10036], 1977. $28.50.

19. *Japanese Art, A Concise History of*, by Peter C. Swann. [orig. pub. as *An Introduction to the Arts of Japan*, by Bruno Cassirer, Oxford, 1958]. Illus. 332pp. New York: Kodansha International Ltd., 1979. $14.95.

19A. *Journal of Jewish Art*, Vol. VI. Illus., incl. Color Plates. 168pp. Jerusalem: Centre for Jewish Art of the Hebrew University [distr: Abner Schram, 36 Park St., Montclair, NJ 07042]. $15.00.

20. (Libraries), Howell, J. B., ed. *Special Collections in Libraries of the Southeast*. Published for the Southeastern Library Association, 423pp. Jackson, MS: Howick House [distr: Southeastern Library Association, P.O. Box 987, Tucker, GA 30084], 1978.

21. *Library and Information Services, ALA World Encyclopedia*. Ed. by Robert Wedgeworth & others. Illus. xxii, 601 double-column pp. Chicago: American Library Association, 1980. $85.00.

22. *Library Buildings, Mason on*, by Ellsworth Mason. Illus. 333pp. Metuchen, NJ: Scarecrow Press, 1980. $25.00.

23. *Library Materials, Preserving*: a Manual, by Susan G. Swartzburg. Illus. 282pp. Metuchen, NJ: Scarecrow Press, 1980. $12.50.

23A. *Literary Societies for Bookmen*, Comp. by Roger & Judith Sheppard. Illus. 80pp. Beckenham, Kent: Trigon Press [distr: Abner Schram, 36 Park St., Montclair, NJ 07042], 1979. $15.00.

24. *London Magazine, The, Index to*, by Frank P. Riga & Claude A. Prance. xlvii, 324pp. New York: Garland Publishing, 1978. $35.00.

25. *Maps, The Story of*, by Lloyd A. Brown, (1949), 86 Illus. 397pp. New York: Dover Publications, 1979. $6.00.

26. *Medical Education in the United States*: a Guide to Information Sources, by Francesco Cordasco and David N. Alloway (Education Information Guide Series, Vol. 8). 393pp. Detroit: Gale Research Co., 1980.

27. (*Medical History*). Ash, Lee. *Serial Publications Containing Medical Classics*: an Index to Citations in Garrison/Morton (3d Edition, 1970). 2d Edn, Rev. & Enl. Foreword by Gertrude L. Annan. X, 169pp. Bethany, CT: The Antiquarium [66 Humiston Drive, Zip 06525], 1979. $22.50.

28. *Nicknames, Twentieth-Century American*. Ed. by Laurence Urdang. comp. by Walter C. Kidney & George C. Kohn. 398pp. New York: H. W. Wilson, 1979. $18.00.

29. *Nicknames and Sobriquets of U.S. Cities, States, and Counties*. 3d Edn, by Joseph Nathan Kane & Gerard L. Alexander. xvi, 429pp. Metuchen, NJ: Scarecrow Press, 1979. $17.50.

30. (*New Jersey*). Skemer, Don C. & Robert C. Morris. *Guide to the Manuscript Collections of the New Jersey Historical Society*. Illus. 245pp. Newark: The Society [230 Broadway, Zip 07104], 1979. $21.00.

30A. (*Painting*). Strong, Roy. *Recreating the Past*: British History and the Victorian Painter. 186 Illus., 13 in Color. Published with The Pierpont Morgan Library. New York: Thames & Hudson, [c1978]. $16.95.

31. *Painting, Twentieth-Century European*: a Guide to Information Sources, by Ann-Marie Cutul. (Art and Architecture Information Guide Series, Vol. 9). 520pp. Detroit: Gale Research Co., 1980. $28.00.

32. (*Periodicals*). Arndt, Karl J. R. *The Annotated and Enlarged Edition of Ernst Steiger's Precentennial Bibliography*, "*The Periodical Literature of the United States of America*." (1878). Port. & Facs. 228 double-columned pp. Millwood, NY: Kraus International Publications, 1979. $55.00.

33. (*Periodicals*). Neal, Anna Bruce, et al., eds. A Cumulative Index to Farber's "Periodicals for College Libraries" in *Choice*, September 1974 - October 1978. 43pp. [Nashville: Dept of Library Science, Box 501, George Peabody College for Teachers of Vanderbilt University], 1979. $2.50, checks to Vanderbilt University.

33A. (*Periodicals*). Noyce, John, ed. *The Directory of British Alternative Periodicals, 1965-1974*. 359pp. Sussex: The Harvester Press; Atlantic Highlands, NJ: Humanities Press [Zip 07716], 1979. $50.00.

34. *Physics, Concise Dictionary of, and Related Subjects*, 2d Edn, Rev. & Enl., by J. Thewlis. Fold. Tables. 366 double-columned pp. New York: Pergamon Press, 1979. $52.00.

35. *Romanians, The, in America and Canada*: a Guide to Information Sources, by Vladimir Wertsman. (Ethic Studies Information Guide Series, Vol. 5). xvi, 164pp. Detroit: Gale Research Co., 1980.

36. *Telescope, The History of the*, by Henry C. King (1955). Illus. 456pp. New York: Dover Publications, 1979.